T

ME

LIES AND MISDIRECTION(BOOK 4)

K. J. MCGILLICK

TRUST ME
Copyright © 2018 by Kathleen McGillick

Interior Design & Formatting by: Champagne Book Design
www.champagnebookdesign.com

Proofreading: Judy Zweifel Judy's Proofreading
www.judysproofreading.com

ALL RIGHTS RESERVED. This book contains material protected under International and Federal Copyright Laws and Treaties. In accordance with the U.S. Copyright Act of 1976, the scanning, uploading, and electronic sharing of any part of this book without the permission of the author/publisher is unlawful piracy and theft of the author's intellectual property. No part of this text may be reproduced, transmitted, downloaded, decompiled, reverse engineered, or stored in or introduced into any information storage and retrieval system, in any form or by any means, whether electronic or mechanical, now known or hereinafter invented, without the express written permission of the author-publisher.

The author acknowledges the trademark status and trademark ownership of all trademarks, service marks, and word marks mentioned in this book. All possibly trademarked names are honored by italics and no infringement is intended. No part of this publication may be reproduced or transmitted in any form or by any means, electronic or mechanical, including photography, recording, or any information storage and retrieval system without the permission of the author, nor be otherwise circulated in any form of binding or cover other than that in which it is originally published. This book is a work of fiction. Names, characters, places, and incidents are the product of the author's imagination or are used fictitiously. Any references to historical or actual events, locales, business establishments, places or persons, living or dead, is coincidental.

DEDICATION

In memory of my grandparents Florence and William
My Grandmother, my partner in crime, who always had my
back and whom I credit I am today because of her.

Dedicated to my son Mark-Michael and grandchildren Rinoa
and Jude.

TRUST ME

CHAPTER ONE

Poppy

I SAT IN A GUNMETAL-GRAY ROOM AS LARGE AS A HIGH SCHOOL cafeteria. Disgusting paint chips, the size of dinner plates, barely clung to the walls. Old beat-up linoleum floors were a trip-and-fall lawsuit waiting to happen. The tables were crammed with disheveled men of all ages and races clad in orange jail jumpsuits; none cared how they appeared for court. Across from me sat my assigned client, Marquis Dawson, a repeat offender, with a badly shaved head, tattoos not of the professional variety on his hands and arms, and such rancid breath I had to hold my own when he spoke. *Welcome to my hell.*

"Look, bitch, you go out there and get me off on some technicality. This is bullshit, and I didn't hire you to tell me to take some damn plea deal. You hear me?" He slammed his big hand with dirt-caked nails on the table.

I jumped back. If truth be told, Marquis could reach across the table with one of his large meaty hands and choke me to death, before a guard could make his way through the room to help.

"First of all, you didn't hire me; the judge appointed me to your case. Furthermore, if you want to take this to trial,

1

where you will certainly be found guilty, a new attorney will take my place. So lucky you, our time is limited. Second, and might I point out the most important issue at hand, the police caught you on tape robbing that store. No face mask, and no gloves, so you left plenty of fingerprints for them. They have you breaking and entering, then robbing the place. Also, let's not skip over the fact you couldn't even bother to try to hide the stuff. Oh no, you took your loot and walked three doors down to a pawn shop which also had a camera. So, making it even easier for them to make a case against you, you helpfully gave the pawn shop owner your ID. In legalese, Marquis, you are screwed," I told my latest genius client.

I'm sure he could hear the frustration laced with obvious disdain in my voice. I no longer tried to hide my feelings from my clients. They didn't deserve the effort it took to do so. He was just one in a line of clients I would represent at an arraignment today, all guilty and all who wanted to walk free. If found guilty, they told me most assuredly it would be my fault. Some even warned there would be consequences.

Jackass. Hopefully, someone gives you some soap on a rope for where you're going.

I had to admit; I was a desperate woman. I felt boxed in with no means of escape. No hope of a better life than the black hole I had dug myself into.

Law school may have provided the theory of our legal system. However, it did not show me how to practice law, nor the business end of being a lawyer. It didn't prepare me for the real judicial system. Grit and hard knocks taught me how to navigate the halls of justice. Well, if you could call them such, with a straight face. The practice of law came down to which lawyer was a better actor, whose clients lied with more finesse, and who could put out the fires the quickest when your case exploded in real time.

Last year I graduated in a class of one hundred fifty students from one of three law schools in Colorado. My tenure at the school was nothing exceptional. I didn't graduate in the top ten percent, nor did I earn a place on law review. I missed more classes than I should have. My home from four to midnight was in an upscale restaurant working as a waitress to supplement the stipend paid from my one-hundred-eighty-thousand-dollar law school debt. My work ethic, drive, and ambition were all I thought I'd need to rely on to propel me to the top of the heap. That should have been all I needed to land a plum job in a law firm which could help me pay down the burden of debt under which I struggled. Apparently not.

Legal job offers were at a premium. Reality soon hit that if I wanted to work as an attorney, I would have to hang out my shingle and chase after cases to survive. What was that term? You eat what you kill. I wasn't killing much, and I was almost homeless. How humiliating.

My fantasy I clung to throughout law school was to be a constitutional lawyer, a force to be reckoned with, a legal powerhouse. However, the closest I would ever get into the practice of constitutional law was explaining the fourth, fifth, and sixth amendment of the constitution to the clients I picked up from the indigent defense committee. These were people who doled out leftovers from the overflow of the public defender's office. The cases they assigned were at a premium, and at times, I found myself begging for a case. The clients appointed to me to represent could not afford a private lawyer and had been through the revolving door of a system that promised them adequate representation. Not surprisingly, some of my clients knew their rights better than me.

Man, things were pretty bleak. I held onto my waitress job at night for dear life as I tried to build up my law practice during the day. Since passing the bar, I had graduated from being appointed misdemeanors to felonies, and with that opportunity, came some scary characters.

Truth be told, most, if not all, were guilty of the crime accused, yet demanded their day in court. The state paid me sixty-five dollars an hour with a cap of three hundred to give these stellar citizens their right to a trial. I had yet to win an acquittal.

As I became more confident in my legal skills, I branched out and offered simple wills as part of estate planning. I soon realized people called for the free consultation I provided just so they could pick my brain. They completed the form they had downloaded from the internet, and voila, the will was complete. Once I started charging for a consultation, the calls dried up.

Of course, it would be ideal to diversify. But to offer bankruptcy services, I would have to invest thousands of dollars I didn't have in specialized software. Forget networking contacts, and I couldn't afford malpractice insurance to offer real estate closings. So what was left? The dreaded family law, clients no one wanted.

The people labeled family law clients were the most challenging of all that crossed my path. These were people whose life had reached a crisis point. A good family lawyer was a financial advisor, a social worker, and a psychologist. My life experience had not prepared me to offer any of these skills to a client. However, I was driven to succeed, so I dipped my toe in the shallow end of the vast pool of emotionally wrecked people. The Domestic Violence Center offered a steady stream of clients for which they paid a flat fee of seventy-five dollars per client. I agreed to assist women to obtain protective orders against the men they accused of violence. By doing so, I helped them navigate the government maze to secure low-income housing, food stamps, and temporary aid. If any of these women wanted a divorce, the center would pay an additional small flat fee for me to help them get one.

What started as a valiant crusade to champion oppressed women soon turned into a crash-and-burn scenario for me personally. After all the emotional investment in assuring these women were safe, most dismissed the temporary orders before they even reached a final protective order stage. Shortly after that, they reunited with "their man" and tried to convince themselves and me it would not happen again. It did. The divorces filed in haste when emotions ran high were dismissed just as quickly. I morphed into a lawyer, social worker, and therapist for these women who called me long after their cases had ended. Eventually, I ran out of steam trying to keep these people afloat.

After one year in the trenches of the practice of law, I was ready to throw in the towel. I had become a road warrior chasing client leads in my fifteen-year-old Honda. A real office to see clients was financially out of my reach, and I couldn't afford a secretary. Even office-sharing schemes proved too expensive. If it weren't for my waitress job, I'd be living in a box under a bridge. So, when a letter reached my mailbox offering me the opportunity to interview for an associate position at a startup law firm where a salary was guaranteed, I was ecstatic. All I had to do was forward my resume to the office manager and show up on Thursday, November 8. There was no time listed, nor specifics of how an interview would proceed, and it sounded like a bit of an open-audition scenario. I was desperate. I was eager to sell myself and prove I was the best fit. That job had to be mine.

I was prepared to fight and fight dirty to get the job. The one suit I had for court appearances hung on my door pressed and ready. My shirt was crisp, water spots wiped off my fake black leather shoes, and my hose was hole free. If only I could afford a health plan that allowed me mental health visits, I would have availed myself of it and stored upon a supply of antianxiety drugs. I had to land this job.

To scope out the building, I set out an hour early before most offices opened. Parking can be a bitch in downtown and arriving early would show I meant business. The office, a mid-sized building amongst the high-rises, sported a lovely landscaped front. Wow, this place was high-end. An inviting place where people not economically challenged would feel comfortable. Maybe this wasn't such a great idea. How would I feel when I entered a room filled with dozens of people competing for the job? My self-esteem was low enough, did I need it battered anymore? My gut said turn around, now. Yet, my feet kept moving forward. With a knot in my stomach and on the verge of puking, I entered the elevator and rode it to my destination. I decided I could just wait until the doors open and then hit the down button and escape without being noticed. Yes, that was my plan. I patiently waited for the doors to slide open. At the last minute, instead of hitting the down button, I stepped out. The glass wall in front of me heralded I had reached my destination. Oddly, there was only one person in the waiting area. Had I missed the initial call?

I stepped inside and took a seat next to a man that looked to be at least sixty years old. Was he here for the associate attorney job as well? No, can't be. His hair had more gray than blond, and his face had the weathered look of someone with some miles on him. I didn't like his lips; they were rubbery and smashed together in a scowl. He had the look of a banker impeccably dressed in a charcoal-gray three-piece wool suit. My eyes glanced to his feet. Black Oxford shoes planted tightly together in front of him, buffed to perfection. How long had he been sitting there checking his pocket watch like the white rabbit in *Alice in Wonderland*? It seemed bad-mannered.

"So, are you here about the associate job?" I leaned forward and whispered.

At first, I didn't think he heard me. He placed the watch back in his pocket and looked straight ahead at the wall. *Old and deaf. Great.*

"Why else would I be sitting here?" He said it with a haughty disdain as if I must be stupid.

Okay, that was rude. What a jackass!

Before I could respond to him, a woman swung open the door to the waiting area. She stood there a minute studying us. It threw me back in time to elementary school when I waited to enter a room where punishment was doled out. Her piercing gaze caused me to straighten my back and place my feet flat on the floor.

"Mr. Martin and Ms. Pacheco, I'm Mary Cormier. Please call me Mary. I will conduct your interview today. Follow me," she said and opened the door for us to pass.

Were we the only job applicants? Was this good or bad? I stood to follow her when she stopped short.

She suddenly turned, and with her face mere inches from mine, asked: "Is your name really Poppy Pacheco?"

The old guy said nothing, but I could see his eyes slide

toward me.

Yes, I got that a lot. It wasn't worth it to try to explain that when I was born, my mother had been off her bipolar medication and my father too scared to challenge her choice. I just shrugged and nodded.

"Interesting," she replied. She tilted her head for us to follow her and motioned to a conference room on the right. Mr. Martin waited for me to enter the room. As I passed him, I had the feeling he judged me even more. *Well, screw him.*

"Have a seat," Mary offered as she placed two folders in front of her.

She looked somewhat familiar. Short in stature, puffy white hair, black owl glasses, way past seventy years old and what I would call a no-nonsense face. She had a buzz of energy about her, almost electrifying. Who did she remind me of? Maybe someone on TV? It would come to me.

"Evans, West, and Grey is a start-up firm and looking for people unafraid of hard work," she said as she slapped the table with her palm. "We are a somewhat boutique law firm. By that I mean we choose our clients with great discrimination. I'm your first line of defense against the public, and no one gets past me to become a client that I deem undesirable. We offer criminal defense, but only to people we feel are innocent clients. We also have an estate planning division and civil litigation division that includes matrimonial law. We fight hard for our clients, but we aren't street brawlers, nor do we chase ambulances. Questions?"

I raised my hand slightly which garnered a look of condescension from Mr. Martin.

"Yes, Poppy?"

"How many lawyers are in the firm?" I asked. I thought it

was a practical question.

"We have three practicing lawyers in this office, and two other lawyers that run a security firm who interact with us," she replied. "Dalia Grey oversees the criminal division, Eloise Evans handles all the estate matters, and Tallulah West manages the various civil and domestic cases. Neither of you appears to have extensive legal experience, which means you've not picked up bad habits or shortcuts. That's always a plus. Poppy, you indicated on your resume that you have experience working with the criminal indigent defense bar. Do you have enough trial experience to feel comfortable conducting complex cases?"

"Yes, I have bench trial experience, but not jury trials. To be honest, the felonies were not capital crimes, but more like aggravated assault, battery, and theft, nothing more serious."

I wanted to sell myself to get the job, but I also didn't want to bite off more than I could chew. There was no way I'd be prepared to try a more serious case by myself.

I watched Mary make a note, and then it hit me. She looked exactly like the old mother on the *Golden Girls* TV series. I hope she wasn't as surly or sarcastic as that character.

"Samuel—" Mary started.

"Mr. Martin. I prefer Mr. Martin or Attorney Martin in the workplace," he said as he straightened his back.

What a jerk.

Mary acted as if she hadn't heard him and didn't address his remark.

"Mr. Martin. I see you are a recent law school graduate and that your life experience has been long-term within the insurance industry. You started in claims and over your lifetime worked your way through various departments in a management position. You retired, returned to school, and here you are. I also see you picked up an MBA along the way and have a good handle on taxation."

"Yes," he replied with an air of superiority.

Mary closed the file and placed my file on top of his and tapped them on the table to adjust any loose papers.

"I'll cut to the chase. We are offering you each a position starting at ninety thousand dollars a year with health benefits. Poppy, you'll work with Dalia in our criminal defense department and do some crossover into family law from time to time with Tallulah. Mr. Martin, you'll be working with Eloise in our estate planning and insurance fraud division. The job is yours if you want it, and I need an answer within twenty-four hours," Mary stated.

I didn't have to think about it at all, and I felt the pressing need to lock it in. "I want it."

Mary smiled, nodded, and patted my hand. "Good decision."

"I have some questions," Mr. Martin replied and cleared his throat.

Seriously? Ninety thousand dollars and health benefits, what questions could he have? This man was obviously trouble.

"Go ahead," Mary encouraged as we watched him remove a Mont Blanc pen from his pocket along with a small moleskin notebook. He carefully removed the cap and placed it on the opposite end.

"Will you require me to take criminal or matrimonial cases?" he asked, poised to record a response.

Mary sat back and appeared to give her answer some thought.

"Matrimonial, no. I don't think that would be a good fit for you. Criminal defense? Possibly the white-collar crimes that cross our desks. I'd say something like embezzlement, cyber-crime, money laundering, identity theft, and forgery would be some areas you'd see some action. Alternatively, there may be some elements of a crime in the insurance fraud cases we could use your expertise."

"*Hmm.* I want to be clear. My interest lies in transactional law, and I have no interest in trial work. That would be a deal breaker," he said, placing his pen on the conference table next to his notepad.

"Yes, Mr. Martin, I agree. You would not be a courtroom star. Not to worry, you won't be trying cases," Mary said.

Score one for Mary.

He placed his cap back on his pen and nodded. I thought he might be insulted and turn down the offer out of hand, but he replied, "Acceptable."

"We'd like you to start on Monday," she said. "If you have commitments, cases you need to close out or any you must bring over you still are involved in, we can accommodate those and work with you."

I raised my hand again.

"Don't the attorneys want to interview us?" I asked.

"Poppy, I run this organization from top to bottom and if I say you are hired, take it to the bank. Now for the mundane. We reimburse mileage and checks issue biweekly. Health insurance starts on Monday, and the 401K is noncontributory. Anything else?"

I shook my head. I was just ecstatic to have a job that prom-ised a steady paycheck.

Mr. Martin placed his hands with his palms down on the table and leaned forward.

"Do you cover our malpractice insurance?" he asked.

11

"Yes."

"Do you demand or expect more than a forty-hour work week?" he inquired, tapping his index finger on the table.

"Ordinarily not. But there might be a time or two when that is required. You will be compensated with time off if you wish. I failed to mention we pay you for holidays and there is a three-week vacation package," Mary added.

"I see. Thank you for the offer," Mr. Martin said as he stood. "I will respond within the twenty-four-hour period."

Is he crazy? What was there to think about? What a great offer. Regular paychecks, health insurance, paid vacation and the thought of not begging for work.

"Is there an employment contract I can review?" he asked.

Mary smiled and produced a brown envelope for each of us with our names on the front. "Sign it and return it on Monday if you decide to accept the offer."

I desperately wanted to sign it right now just to make sure she would not realize she made a mistake and retracted the offer.

"If there is nothing more, I can show you out," she said.

As Mr. Martin and I waited for the elevator in silence, I wondered if it would embarrass him if I did a happy dance on the way down?

CHAPTER TWO

Poppy

RIDAYS. I DREADED FRIDAYS. IN THE HALLS OF JUSTICE, FRIDAY WAS the meet 'em and greet 'em day. Today was the day I normally traveled from courtroom to courtroom waiting for the assignment of a newly incarcerated client. It would be my job to help him or her determine if they should accept a plea deal and move right away toward an arraignment, or waive the arraignment and opt for a trial. Guilty or not guilty? Sure, in the end, it was the client's decision.

Nevertheless, most would plead not guilty, against my advice. Even though the evidence against them was clear. Today for the first time in a year I would not be attending the meet and greet cattle call of attorneys. I would be free from the shackles of that game.

Seated at my small kitchen table, I removed the employment contract from the envelope. I didn't even have to read it to know I would sign it. A quick perusal, everything appeared in order. Why wait until Monday to return it? I needed the security of knowing the job was mine. I signed it, finished my coffee, and decided to stake my claim and drop it off. Today was the start of my new life.

Standing in front of my open closet, I eyed my choices. Since I was just dropping off papers, I could throw on some jeans, a cute pullover sweater, and my cashmere blazer. I imagine I could dress the outfit up with my one pair of knee-high brown leather boots. I slowly pushed a few pieces of clothing around that hung on cheap wire hangers but found nothing acceptable. No, everything felt wrong. The least I could do was try to convince them I had some type of decent wardrobe although that was a sham. Even the slim pickings I had from the consignment stores couldn't impress the people at that firm. Clearly, the first order of business when I received my initial check was to up my game and buy new clothes. Something that said I had arrived, and my law degree had some meaning.

As I alighted from the elevator, I noticed the office was a hive of activity. Three people were moving about in the waiting area, and Mary seemed to be directing traffic. My eyes met hers as I got closer and a broad smile broke out across her face as I waved the brown envelope above my head.

I walked into the reception space, and she asked, "Ready to start early?"

Taken aback by her offer, but nonetheless ready to do anything to make sure I had my foot firmly planted in the door, I smiled and nodded.

"Yes, but I'm embarrassed to say I'm not dressed for business."

Today, although I wore what I considered my best pants, they would not pass for anything more than business casual. My work wardrobe consisted of a dress, two skirts, three blouses, and two jackets—all from consignment stores.

She held out her hand to take the brown envelope and motioned me to follow her.

Mary led me to a nicely decorated office where a woman sat behind a desk trolling the internet while the printer on the side credenza spewed paper.

"Dalia, this is Poppy, and she's ready to start today if you need her," Mary said.

A quick handshake over the desk and Dalia directed me to sit in a wingback chair across from her. Mary chose the other. Plaques from the schools she attended covered the left wall, along with some photos of politicians I recognized. The right wall showcased two lovely pieces of contemporary art I'd kill to own. I had to hand it to her; the woman had excellent taste.

"Welcome aboard. I've been slammed this morning, so how do you feel about hitting the deck running? I've reviewed your resume, and Mary provided me with examples of your court filings. It's clear you're a quick learner," she stated with a grin.

From my research on the firm, I knew her background was that of a prosecuting attorney for the New York district attorney's office. According to her website profile, she had completed a degree in cybersecurity. Her conviction rate at the D.A.'s office spoke for itself, *res ipsa loquitur*, and it was a damn good record. She was a superstar in the legal arena. Recently, a popular news show extensively interviewed Dalia for her role in a murder and theft case that made national headlines. That's the kind of excitement I could sink my teeth into.

"I'm all yours," I replied.

Dalia slid a yellow pad and a pen across the desk toward me. She swiveled in her seat and retrieved the printed material waiting for her on the printer bed. Tapping the papers on her desk to line them up, she positioned them in front of her.

"We have the opportunity to evaluate a new case and

decide if we want to take it. I am very picky about the criminal defense cases to which I commit myself. Upfront I will tell you, I don't represent people accused of child molestation, child pornography, or rapists. That's my hard line.

"Many attorneys profess everyone is innocent until proven guilty and entitled to a defense. That's the cornerstone of the legal system. We all come to the practice of law with individual life experiences and rely on our gut. Granted, it's the prosecutor's job to prove every element of a crime they accuse the defendant of, and not the defendant's obligation to demonstrate they are innocent. Still, if my instinct says the potential client is lying, then I feel no obligation to go with him or her to defend their lie. My gut must feel comfortable along with my mind. I have worked enough cases to know that at times people take shortcuts during an investigation and defendants are wrongly accused. I can usually ferret out problems from sloppy work.

"Moreover, I'm enough of a realist to know sometimes investigators try to fit the facts to make their theory work. Having worked in the D.A.'s office gives me an edge evaluating a criminal defense case. Now that I've crossed the aisle to the defense bar, the obligation to check that the police have not abused their power, and the prosecution has a tight case, falls on me."

I nodded. I could understand that too. If the police work up a case and present it to a prosecutor to indict a person accused of a crime, the prosecutor is obligated to make sure he crosses the t's , and dots the i's. If the prosecutor was slipshod and left things hanging, then the defense had the right, no, the obligation to hold them to account.

"I received a call this morning from an attorney. The police questioned her husband, a physician, regarding the murder of a nurse at the hospital where he is an attending. The husband and wife are highly visible people and active in the community. They attend all the right social functions and are comfortable in the most expensive country clubs."

Dalia handed me the news articles of the husband and the wife which she had retrieved from the printer.

I studied the reports with fascination. Something about the husband's posture struck me as arrogant and cocky, and the wife's as a bit self-conscious. He appeared to be about forty, and she looked older, around fifty. That was just a guess. The man had a face that Leonardo DaVinci would call symmetrical and balanced, clearly someone who enjoyed being captured by the photographer. I would label him not only well built, a man who knew his way around a gym, but he also had an exotic mystery about him. I wanted to know more about this man.

"Why him? I mean, why question him?" I asked them.

"From the few discrete inquiries we made, we found Dr. Blackwell has a reputation as a serial philanderer. He's been in and out of trouble with the hospital, and until this point, they have kept things under wraps," Dalia responded.

"What sort of trouble?"

Was I a bad person because I wanted juicy details?

Dalia appeared to be crafting a thoughtful response and Mary jumped in.

"Two problems this year alone," Mary interjected leaning forward in her chair. "The first happened in March when the hospital administration discovered him having sex with a nurse at night in the O.R. suite. Neither knew the hospital had recently placed cameras there because of a theft problem. In reviewing the tapes, the administrator discovered them using the O.R. table for their liaisons. Moreover, it was happening with such frequency that the chief of surgery had to address the issue. To make the problem disappear, Dr. Blackwell offered the hospital a twenty-thousand-dollar donation; the nurse wasn't so fortunate. The director of nursing disciplined the nurse for leaving her station, and then the hospital administrator fired her for cause. Somebody leaked the tape, and it found its way into circulation. Not onto the internet or YouTube, but it's public nonetheless."

Well, that's awkward.

"And the other problem?"

As if that wasn't enough.

"An eighteen-year-old granddaughter of one of his patients accused him of sexually harassing her which escalated to stalking," Mary added. Her tone was judgmental, and I suppose with good cause.

"Dr. Blackwell describes himself as a sex addict that has sought treatment. However, it appears he claims this only in response to problems arising from litigation and when a discrete monetary offer couldn't settle the issue. Two of his office personnel left under a cloud of having an affair with him, and an office manager from another practice made it public they were carrying on as well," Dalia interjected.

Judgmental. That's what I was, judgmental. Not only did I judge the doctor, but also the lawyer wife who put up with this aberrant behavior. I realized that thought would have to be compartmentalized.

"So how can I help?" I asked.

"He is being brought in for the second round of questioning by the police tomorrow. I scheduled us to meet with him later this morning to talk to him and decide if we want to take the case," Dalia said. "I'd like you to sit in on the interview and

Mary will give you her file to review so you can get up to speed. It's an ugly case, and it certainly will be high profile if the police make him a target. Take a look at the incident report," she said.

Mary moved a few papers on Dalia's desk and retrieved what looked like a preliminary police report and handed it to me. I skimmed it for the vital information, and my stomach turned.

The police found a young woman, thought to be in her middle twenties beaten and left for dead in her car. Her face was crushed by some object that displaced her nose to the right, knocked out her front teeth, and she also sustained a gaping wound across her forehead. Her roommate reported her missing, and forty-eight hours after the last shift, the police found her in an abandoned lot. The victim was dressed in a nurse's uniform with a name pin identifying her as the missing woman. The cause of death appeared to be blunt force trauma. Her pocketbook and telephone were missing, and from the blood spatter pattern, the phone and purse might have been covered with the victim's blood and possibly the assailants. The police hadn't determined yet if there was a sexual assault.

"Now read the news clips," Mary said.

Of course, the news sensationalized the story based more on gossip and innuendo than fact. It described Marsha Anderson as a young woman who was a registered nurse that worked in the hospital's cardio-thoracic intensive care unit. From all accounts, she had just come off the evening shift when someone may have overpowered her and driven her to an abandoned area. Once there she was beaten beyond recognition, and damage to the body continued postmortem. Although not confirmed, it likely involved two assailants. The article laid out information about education and job history, and concluded she was a well-liked nurse whose life had been tragically cut short.

"So, what leads the police to Dr. Blackwell?" I asked.

"Hospital scuttlebutt is that he and Ms. Anderson were personally involved. Apparently, it was a turbulent relationship that had taken a turn for the worse. The police printed her car, and Dr. Blackwell's prints were in there, but not fresh prints in the blood. No surprise to find them if they were romantically involved," Dalia said.

"And?"

"The problem is he can't, or won't, account for his time when this occurred. The hospital cameras place him inside the parking deck within five minutes of Marsha Anderson leaving and then he's gone," she said.

"Are they charging him?" I asked.

"There has been no arrest yet, but it doesn't look good that they want to bring him in for a second interview so quickly. I could use another set of ears and eyes evaluating his demeanor during the interview we have scheduled to take place shortly. Are you ready to put your skills to work?" Dalia asked, leaning toward me.

"Of course," I stated with a bounce of excitement.

"I want to emphasize that I don't take cases unless I'm comfortable that my client is telling the truth. I'm not about pimping my service to help some scumbag find a technicality to flee justice. I'll hold the state to their duty to prove a crime was committed. That's the bedrock of our system. However, when I get an acquittal, I want it to be because the jury believes my client is innocent. Not simply that the state for whatever reason didn't present a good case," Dalia preached.

It sounded idealistic, but she had put her time in, and she deserved to take the cases she wanted.

Me? My right and left shoulder devil battled it out. If this case walked into a law firm I owned, one part of me would take the case, no questions asked, I know the retainer would be enormous. I could live off that money for three years. However, the other part said this was trouble and where there's smoke there's fire. In my mind, he was guilty and would have to prove his innocence to me—quite the conundrum. Either way, I wanted a front-row seat to this train wreck of a case.

CHAPTER THREE

Poppy

A T PRECISELY ELEVEN O'CLOCK, TWO SMARTLY DRESSED PEOPLE sauntered into the waiting area, and their energy was palpable. Almost electric. The lithe woman with close-cropped blond hair whom I recognized from the news article was Ms. Sandra Blake, attorney at law. The man was most definitely Dr. Gabriel Blackwell.

Dalia introduced each member of the firm. I sensed Dr. Blackwell's eyes linger on me just a little too long. I also felt the chill of a hand quickly withdrawn from mine by his wife when she noticed her husband staring at me.

Mary and Dalia escorted the power couple to the conference room, and once seated, offered refreshments. I perceived that Ms. Blake tried her best to block her husband's view of me. But Dalia decided early on that I needed to sit where I could study Dr. Blackwell's expressions and body language. Thus, I moved to a corner seat with a pad, well within eye view of Dr. Blackwell. I understood my role. We were now ready to begin, all systems engaged.

"Dr. Blackwell and Ms. Blake, welcome to our firm. Although you haven't retained the firm yet, nor have we decided to take the case, everything discussed is confidential. Dr. Blackwell, as your wife has probably told you if she remains in here during the meeting, spousal immunity covers the communication in this room. That means the prosecution cannot call her to testify. It is my preference that only the client is part of the legal discussions so as not to hamper the flow of honest and open communication. Therefore, I would invite Ms. Blake to wait in the waiting area while we interview Dr. Blackwell," Dalia said. She looked from Ms. Blake to her husband and back to Ms. Blake again.

"Absolutely not! Until now I have been his counsel, and I want to remain in the loop on the defense strategy," Ms. Blake said, sitting forward, placing her palms on the table.

"Well, that doesn't work for me," Dalia said as she stood. "You are not a member of our firm nor would I consider adding you as a counsel of record in this case. If that's a hard line for you, then I thank you for coming in, but respectfully decline any further involvement."

The silence in the room was such that I could hear my heartbeat pulsating in my ears. A bold move on Dalia's part. *Who would blink first?*

"There is a multitude of other firms that would be thrilled to have me help with the defense of my husband," Ms. Blake said remaining seated.

"You are welcome to explore that opportunity with them, but I don't conduct business that way," Dalia replied. Her voice was calm, her tone level and facial expression unaffected by the knowledge that a large retainer would soon walk out the door.

"I'd like to hear what Ms. Grey has to say," Dr. Blackwell interrupted waving Dalia down to sit. "So, Sandy, why don't you retire to the waiting area and we can discuss this after the meeting. If Ms. Grey and I decide to move forward, then we can determine your role."

It was as if all the air was suddenly sucked from the room and only a suffocating vacuum remained. No one moved, no one even appeared to breathe waiting on a response. Would Sandra Blake erupt and storm out and demand he follow her? Or would she try to recapture control of the situation by insisting she stay? If so, I was sure a battle of wills would ensue between her and Dalia. Surprisingly, Ms. Blake abruptly pushed back from the table and without a further scene left the room.

Wow, that was unexpected. I was almost looking forward to a verbal catfight. God, what did that say about me?

"I'm sorry for Sandy's behavior," Dr. Blackwell offered, turning toward me. "Young, beautiful women threaten her, and that causes her to act out inappropriately."

Mary's eyebrows shot up quickly, nearly reaching her scalp. She appeared poised to make what promised to be a cutting response. But was shut down by a glance from Dalia.

"Shall we refocus on the case?" Dalia asked as she sat back down and rolled her chair closer to the table.

"Ask me whatever you want, I'm an open book." Dr. Blackwell smiled and extended his arms outward. "And please, call me Gabriel."

"Fine, Gabriel. Tell us why you think the police have decided to make you a person of interest," Dalia asked.

He bit his lower lip and relaxed back into the chair with both hands casually resting on the armrests. Dalia was right. The man would be cagey in his answers, and from his posture, intended to give measured information. After what was only probably a minute, but seemed more like ten, he replied.

"I don't know." He shrugged.

Dalia eyed him skeptically.

"How did you know the victim?"

"From the hospital. Ms. Anderson was one of the nurses on the evening shift assigned to my patients in the cardio-thoracic intensive care unit," Gabriel responded with a slight nod.

Did he intend to make her drag everything out of him? This tactic could, though, be a positive sign, if he was as stingy with the details when questioned by the police.

"Did you come in contact with her regularly?" Dalia inquired.

"Define regular," he asked of her.

"At least once a day, maybe more."

"Yes."

"Had you formulated an opinion about her?" Dalia followed up.

Tapping his finger on the armrest, he appeared lost in thought. "In what way?"

"Professionally? Personally?" she responded.

"Yes."

"And that was…"

"She was a warm, caring person whose wonderful sense of humor perked her patients up," he offered, nodding his head affirmatively twice.

Now we were getting somewhere. Dr. Blackwell used the words warm, caring, and a wonderful sense of humor instead of highly competent or professional. It was personal.

"And you voiced exactly that to the police?" Dalia asked.

"Well, their questions were more circumspect. I believe I may have told them that I found that Ms. Anderson was a very professional nurse whom I felt had a firm handle on what type of care my patients needed," he said, shifting forward in his seat.

He gave the impression of being guarded. Yes, he knew how to play the game. This interview would take forever if Dalia had to tease every piece of information from him.

Suddenly Mary carelessly tossed her pad on the table and leaned forward to engage him. That startled him. We all turned our attention to her.

"Look, let's cut to the chase here. You have a reputation for chasing skirts. Was she a conquest of yours? Is that why you're in the frame?" she asked with a hint of irritation in her voice.

Gabriel stopped, twisted his body toward Mary, and appeared to need a second or two to tamp down his emotions. For that short interval, I saw a flash of anger spark in his eyes. It was there.

"And exactly who are you?" he threw back at her evading her question.

"Mary Cormier, the investigator in this firm. The person who wants to know what type of man we're dealing with here. If you're a man innocent of any part of her murder who can't keep it in your pants, that's one thing. However, if you're a man who murdered your most recent honey to keep a secret or over a dispute, that's another thing. Right now, the jury's out on what motive the police are cooking up which they can hang on you. Law enforcement already has a three-day lead on us. So, Dr. Blackwell, I'm ninety years old and time's ticking," she said tapping her watch.

He glanced at me, then back at Dalia and nodded his head.

"Fair enough. You've done your homework and have researched me sufficiently enough to know I have some peccadillos. Tell me what you know about my circumstance, and I'll fill in the blanks," Dr. Blackwell offered.

"That's not how it works," Dalia interjected. "I have an

orderly flow of information I want to elicit—"

It was as if Mary had not even heard Dalia speaking. She stood and walked toward the bank of windows, looked out, and then turned back to face him. Mary was in control of the room.

"We're not interested in where you attended undergraduate school or received your medical training. That, along with where you did your internship, residency, and fellowship are all a matter of public record. What we need to know is why your personal life is such a public mess. Also, I'm not going to mislead you and say we don't need details; that your private life is your own business. Because that's not true, we want all the salacious details so we can figure out what the police will assign as the means, motive, and opportunity. Because believe me, a jury will convict you just as easily on circumstantial evidence as direct," she said pointing her finger at him.

He looked over at me as if he could see right through my clothes. I returned the stare.

"Yes, my behavior can be bad. I tire of things quickly and am easily bored," Dr. Blackwell offered.

"So, are you stating that you have had, shall we say several extramarital relationships?" Dalia asked.

"Yes."

"Was Marsha Anderson one of the women we could add to that category?"

"Yes."

"Ongoing or over?" Dalia asked, waiting to record his response.

He looked at me, glanced down at my crossed legs and lingered there too long. If he was trying to throw me off my game, he had the wrong person. Many a morning I'd sit in the jail where a room full of men were meeting with their lawyers and had to deflect lascivious looks and catcalls.

"That is a question I can answer in the affirmative. It is *over*," Dr. Blackwell stated with an emphasis on the last word.

"Why are you so sure?" Dalia asked.

"Because she's dead," he said. He raised an eyebrow and shrugged.

Pretty damn cold and detached bastard. I can't imagine Dr. Blackwell would be much of a giving lover. Hmm. But he sure was good to look at.

"If she wasn't dead, would the affair have continued?" Dalia inquired with a note of irritation. I could tell she didn't appreciate the word games he was playing.

"The affair? Not Likely. I was ready to move on," he answered with a tone of boredom. "Now, ladies, to quote your investigator, let's cut to the chase. I didn't kill Marsha, and therefore I don't fear sitting through another police interview. Can they assassinate my character? Yes. Might it be relevant in a trial? I don't see how as I've had dozens of affairs and none wound up dead. So, what's my motive?" he asked engaging me with the question.

"I will say that I don't know enough to determine if you had a motive. Unfortunately, sometimes a jury will rely on a gut feeling to find a person guilty of a crime, even though logic dictates that there are no facts to support the decision—" Dalia started.

"Isn't that where a judge has the discretion to issue a directed verdict if at the end of the prosecution's case the state can't prove the elements of a crime?" he queried with a tone more challenging than inquisitive.

Not a surprising question. One which I'm sure Dr. Blackwell and his wife discussed.

"Yes. Still, a rare occurrence and not something you can rely on. No judge wants to take a verdict away from a jury."

"Well, we could spend all day here going on about my flaws, but this matter truly revolves around one issue, am I guilty? The answer is no. Give me a polygraph. I'll pass it. At this point I need your decision; the second interview is tomorrow. Do I have an attorney or not?" he asked, pulling his jacket together to button it at the middle.

I was confident we would turn him down. And there was a little piece of me which hoped we didn't. He had a psychopath vibe to him that made me feel conflicted yet captivated me. Did I want him to be innocent and remain a free man? Or because he was so arrogant, want him punished for a multitude of sins and trespasses that had nothing to do with the murder? This case promised to be quite the spectacle if the D.A. charged him with the woman's death. A part of me, I hated to admit, was looking forward to some drama and chaos.

"I've got a retainer agreement right here," Mary said and slid a document toward him. Apparently, she made the decision to accept him as a client. "Sign at the bottom, and we will need a retainer of ten thousand dollars, which will take you to the indictment phase, no further. Once you are at that point, the contract allows us to withdraw from the case, if we choose. If this goes to trial, then we will require another one hundred thousand to cover attorney fees, expert witnesses, and an investigator. Bail comes out of your pocket, not from this fee. We'll arrange for the police to interview you here Monday afternoon, not tomorrow."

He glanced over the document, signed it, and removed a check from his jacket and made it out to the firm.

"Now I need my wife to join us. She has put together my

alibi," he said to Mary as he lifted his chin toward the door.
Mary stood and stepped outside to talk to Ms. Blake.

"So, will you be my hand-holder?" he asked me with what
he probably thought was a roguish grin.

"No, that would be Mary," Dalia informed him. "She is the
person with whom you will have the most contact."

"Pity," he responded as he stared at me.

The way Dalia said that I could tell it gave her a slight satisfaction, knowing she had put a speed bump in the road to his
lascivious thoughts.

The door opened quickly, and Mary, followed by Ms. Blake,
stepped in, retaking their previous seats. Ms. Blake, not unexpectedly, took control of the room.

"As you may or may not be aware, I am a mergers and ac-
quisition attorney. Although my grasp of criminal law and criminal procedure is rusty, I know my way around a set of facts. I've
worked out a timeline from my husband's calendar and made
a list of character witnesses you may wish to speak to. I've also
put together relevant facts about Ms. Anderson," she added and
placed the inch-thick folder on the table. "Now, from here on
out, I want to be a working member of the case. I'll be at every
meeting. Gabriel and I will be partners in your strategy."

"Not going to happen," Dalia said, short and sweet.

"And why not?" she snapped.

"Because I still don't know who killed Ms. Anderson. Can
you prove to me you didn't kill her?" Dalia asked.

"I didn't even know the woman," she snapped right back.

Interesting, she didn't say no. Should I read anything into
that? Probably not. But still.

The power couple left, and in their wake, I felt their energy linger in the room. The tension that Ms. Blake emitted

was palpable. That woman was a bundle of raw energy. I didn't like either person, and I felt no pity for Ms. Blake.

"What are your thoughts, Poppy," Dalia asked.

"Well, not much really. I feel as if I know no more now than when they came in. We really didn't elicit considerable information," I shrugged.

Dalia picked up her pen and made a few notes as I waited. "What questions would you have asked?"

I gave it some thought and had a few questions I thought should have been asked, and answers explored.

"Well, for one, what he was doing at the time of the murder," I said.

"And what time frame was the murder?" she asked, rocking her pen between her thumb and index finger.

"I don't know."

"And why is that?" she asked as she leaned back.

The light bulb went off. "Because we don't have an autopsy report."

"Correct. Until we have a postmortem report, we won't know an approximate time of death or the weapon. Remember, even hands can be weapons. The medical examiner might be able to tell us the height of the assailant and if he or she is right or left-handed," she offered. "So next question. How are you going to protect the client in a police interview?"

I had to think. The downfall of most people was their need to offer irrelevant information. Alternatively, too much, which often gave the police that tiny morsel to grab onto they could blow up and possibly exploit.

"I'm embarrassed to say I've never accompanied a client into an interview. By the time I get them, they've already spoken to the police and buried themselves to the point of no return by

31

admitting to the crime. Or, have provided police with probable cause to believe they had committed the crime."

"Okay. This is how it will work. We don't know what Dr. Blackwell said in the first interview; but he had his wife there, and hopefully, she protected his interests adequately. Normally in a first interview, the police are spreading a wide net and trying to lock someone into their alibi so they can pick it apart later. It's the follow-up interview that is critical. Because at this point the police want to follow up on leads or try to elicit more information. Our job will be to listen carefully to a question, and either allow him to answer or instruct him not to. We always run the fine line of cooperation and protecting the client," she said.

"By now, the police probably have interviewed hospital and office staff, so they may have more information to come at Dr. Blackwell with," Mary offered.

"Why have they zeroed in on him?" I asked.

"We won't know for sure until I speak with them, but sex and money are always the top motives in a murder. Moreover, Dr. Blackwell's reputation as a philanderer hurts him. He admitted to the affair, so for now, that's enough. When I talk to the investigating officer, I may decide not to cooperate with another interview," Dalia said.

The ringing of Dalia's phone interrupted the meeting. "Give me a minute, it's Declan," she said.

She answered the call and left the room.

"So, what are your thoughts," Mary asked.

"I have no thoughts right now about his guilt, but personally I don't like the man. I have no idea if the victim had enemies or if she led a lifestyle that lent itself to violence. Was she the intended target? Was it a carjacking gone wrong? Was she in the wrong place at the wrong time? There are just too many variables," I replied.

"Very good. I made a good choice with you," Mary replied and patted my hand.

Dalia walked back in the room, her face was tight, and her motions a bit jerky.

"Declan?" Mary asked about the caller.

"He was calling to tell me he spoke with Ms. Blake and she referred him to call us. The police have issued a warrant for Gabriel's arrest, and we can surrender him by the end of the business day. So unless we can get the D.A. to agree to a consent bond, then he will have to remain in jail over the weekend. There's no bail hearing until Monday. *Perfect, just perfect.* I'll call Gabriel and meet with him to go over the procedure of the arrest," Dalia said.

"So, Declan's involved. Won't that be a conflict of interest?" Mary posed.

"Who's Declan?" I asked.

"My fiancé and a detective in Major Crimes. And no, it's not a conflict because he's filled out whatever paperwork he needs for full disclosure. Plus, he won't be the primary on it. If things get too heated, he can always pull out," she replied.

Dalia's right hand went to her forehead to rub it, and she tapped her foot as she thought.

"Poppy, I need an entry of appearance form to file with the D.A. and a motion for bond. We have a template and Mary can walk you through it. Mary, can you get me the A.D.A. on the case, I want to see if we can set a consent bond, so he is released right after they book him. Gabriel has ties to the community and isn't a flight risk. I'm thinking we ask for a bond on his own recognizance, they will ask for a million, and we can split the baby in their favor at seven hundred fifty thousand. Thoughts?" Dalia said.

"Sounds good," I replied. What did I know?

"Okay, let's get working, we're already behind the curve. Poppy, we have a medical examiner who we employ to review the final autopsy, which can take the ME six weeks to publish. In the meantime, I want you on top of the preliminary report and interacting with our medical examiner. Right now, I want you to focus on time and cause of death. That's information which is pivotal. Look for patterned abrasions; the lack of significant injuries can signify a slow death, which always adds years to a sentence. I'll be able to help you more when we get the prelim," Dalia told me.

Mary heard her email ding, downloaded it, and read the attached document. She then looked to Dalia.

"His arrest warrant is for first-degree murder and the unlawful termination of a pregnancy. Marsha Anderson was pregnant."

CHAPTER FOUR

Tallulah

WHEN I JOINED THE PARTNERSHIP OF EVANS, WEST, AND GREY, I recognized that family law clients would fall to me. I was the expert, no matter how much I despised high-asset cases. High asset meant high conflict, and high conflict meant a lot of contact and hand-holding.

Here it was first thing Monday morning and my day was already shot to hell. My head was throbbing, a beat that went from irritating to pounding. I should never have agreed to take this case. It was not as though I couldn't predict that my client Vanessa Abernathy would be anything but high-maintenance and drama-driven. She sat across the desk from me as I once again attempted to explain the facts to her in a way she could understand them.

"The firm uses an investigation team for just such issues, Vanessa. Both men are former FBI agents and have worked high-ticket theft cases before and are experts at tracking money. If you hold a legal interest in your husband's business, we may have a problem where you could be held complicit in what I would label tax evasion. In my opinion, you are digging your-self in deeper if you declare an interest in the property he alleges has been stolen. This whole theft smells more and more like insurance fraud," I told her.

Vanessa, my most challenging client, had hired me for her pending divorce. My definition of the term fair when discussing a split of assets involved an equitable division of property. Her interpretation was to gut the man and leave him bankrupt. Her husband knew her well and expected her moves. He apparently had preemptively disposed of the property before we officially filed the divorce. If he had moved them through a fraudulent third-party transfer, we could deal with that. He took a different route. Someone stole the art and rare book collection, and we were sure he had a hand in it.

"Tax fraud! Don't be silly. I know nothing about taxes. I left that all to Richard," she replied, waving me off.

Richard, her hedge-fund husband, played fast and loose with his money. After reviewing his returns, I sensed he felt it his duty to exploit every loophole that the tax code allowed. Which was fine until he decided to forge a few holes not legally sanctioned by the government. Voluntarily signing her name to a joint return made her complicit in his crime. What the hell was wrong with people?

"We've been over this before, anything you sign makes you just as liable as him. Your marriage was short-term. Additionally, you can't ask a judge to give you the property he owned before the marriage, where marital money did not enhance the value after you married him. Let me recap. Marital property is generally those items bought or received during the marriage. However, it doesn't include assets owned individually before marriage, or gifts, nor inheritance. In Colorado, marital property isn't automatically assumed to be owned by both parties like in California, a community property state. Instead, the court divides marital property in an *equitable* not *equal* manner. Sometimes that means the higher-earning spouse receives a bigger piece of the pie upon divorce," I once again explained.

It was like talking to a brick wall. Vanessa wanted him stripped bare of all his assets and left begging her to return. We had argued about this before, and I knew the argument would continue.

"It's unfair. No, unacceptable, and I won't have Richard left standing. I want him pushed to the point where he wants to kill himself," she responded as she moved a chunk of her thick auburn hair behind her ear.

Living with her I'm sure he thought of that often.

"Be that as it may, we have a long row to hoe. Richard, using his company, has opened several shell corporations to hide money offshore. He overvalued the art and rare books he collects which in turn were over-insured. As much as you want a piece of the art and books, he purchased them through his shell corporations. If things go as I see them going, the criminal consequences should fall squarely on him. Your name is not associated with those purchases or the insurance on them. However, if he assigns a portion of the business to you or transfers title of the art and books to you, then you will share the liability and possibly need to defend yourself against an insurance fraud investigation. Right now, all we need to worry about are the tax returns you signed," I cautioned.

"*Blah, blah, blah.* I don't care. I paid you a shitload of money, and I want all the books and all the art," she shouted.

"But they aren't there to divide. Richard reported books and artwork stolen. There isn't anything tangible there to fight over. We don't know if the actual books or art ever existed. I think it was all smoke and mirrors," I snapped back.

This was crazy. I believe if this kept up, I would have a stroke.

There was a knock at the door, and I moved past Vanessa to welcome the new associate Samuel Martin to join us. Mr. Martin, as he preferred being called, was approximately sixty-two years old. Excellent posture and standing at six feet two he presented as a man who brought a new meaning to the term, "stick up your ass." He chose to comb his gray and blond hair straight forward toward his forehead, emphasizing his full Dumbo-like ears. I wasn't sure how well he would relate to clients as he was persnickety and a bit of a curmudgeon. But, right now, he was my lifeboat in a turbulent sea of craziness.

"Ah, Mr. Martin, come in and have a seat. This is Vanessa Abernathy, and we are studying her assets. I understand you are a rare book and sacred texts enthusiast," I announced.

He nodded an acknowledgment.

"We are trying to get a handle on her husband's rare book collection. . He claims they were stolen. Here is a list," I added and handed him the inventory Vanessa had provided.

I watched his eyes move left then to the right across the page, and then his brow crinkled in disapproval.

"The Codex is the earliest bound bible. The Codex Sinaiticus is from around 350 A.D., one of the oldest Bibles in existence. It was written in Greek as was most of the New Testament. This was opposed to the Old Testament where portions are Greek translations from the original Hebrew. Despite uneducated people's opinion, Jesus did not speak English, but Aramaic a form of Hebrew. His words were written down in Greek decades after his death. Various Greek manuscripts were compiled into anthologies like the Codex Sinaiticus. These were later translated into Latin and then into Olde English.

"Our present-day English Bible didn't come directly from

the mouths nor writing instruments of religious figures. It was an accumulation of centuries of oral tradition, evolution, and translation. So, if Mr. Abernathy claims such a text is in his inventory, he is falsifying that information. One can only find such a rare book in a museum or library," he said.

I had no idea what his history lesson revealed, and the only thing that mattered was the word falsify.

"So, are you suggesting that if he has such that they are forged or stolen?" I asked.

"I am stating it is impossible for him to possess these documents. The Codex is now split into four unequal portions: 347 leaves in the British Library in London, 12 leaves and 14 fragments in the Saint Catherine's Monastery, 43 leaves in the Leipzig University Library, and fragments of 3 leaves in the Russian National Library in Saint Petersburg. These other books he claims to own are also housed in museums and if you'd like I can provide you with a list of where the originals reside. Anything else?" he asked. His voice never inflected, nor did he display any emotion.

The man must be some type of book savant.

"Yes. Would you please take that list and verify when Mr. Abernathy allegedly bought those books through that corporation? Go through the records he provided in discovery and track them down," I said ready to move onto the artwork.

"Not necessary for this second set," he replied remained standing.

"Pardon?" I said.

"This work is a medieval-era book and mislabeled a Bible. To some, the word Bible just meant a collection of sacred writings and Gospels specifically covering the history of Jesus. Psalters are songs from the Bible; the Books of Hours are filled with prayers and Bible quotes. Monks recreated the ancient Bibles by hand in Latin and then illuminated them with pictures and calligraphy. I assure you, these books he has listed would most certainly only be found in libraries such as the British Library or Trinity College Library in Dublin. Do you want me to explain why the likelihood of the rest he claims was in his possession is also false?" he asked.

I was dumbstruck.

"So, it would appear he assigned a monetary value to purchase these volumes, and he documented it on the list I gave Mr. Martin. However, he may have used the money for some other purpose. Alternatively, he could be hiding the cash. For all we know, he converted the money he claims he used to buy these books to gems for easy transport, or even gold bars."

"Without documentation, I could not hazard a guess much less draw a logical conclusion as to what happened to that money," he replied.

"Just so I recognize which are blatantly false, would you research the location of those particular books or manuscripts if not in his possession," I instructed.

He removed a pen from his coat pocket and made a few markings on the paper I had given him. He handed it back to me with notes next to each book or manuscript.

"I've made a note that the Magna Carta in Salisbury Cathedral remains there despite the attempted theft in October of this year," he replied.

Vanessa fanned her face with her hand as her breathing picked up in speed.

"So, are you telling me that he, we, own none of those documents?" Vanessa asked.

"The likelihood is very low he ever owned any of these

documents or manuscripts. If he physically possessed a document, it was probably stolen, and therefore you could not legally own them. Is he in possession of them? Again, the probability is so low even to calculate, because they would need to be housed in a hermetically temperature-regulated vault," Mr. Martin replied.

"What about the artwork?" she whispered as her eyes welled with tears.

I didn't need Mr. Martin to answer that, because that was my wheelhouse.

"He claims they were stolen in transport from the freeport where he said he kept them. To keep it simple, freeports are tax havens. Rest assured Jackson Evans our investigator is on it. Untangling the freeport nightmare is bad enough. Then to chase down an international theft is like staring into a black hole in space. I suggest we turn this portion over to a firm we use to investigate these types of things and let them hunt this down. These men had worked for the FBI and have contacts with Europol that will be invaluable to the investigation," I offered.

"Be honest with me," she said as a fat tear rolled down her right cheek. "These artworks and rare books, they are probably part of a scheme to inflate his net worth, aren't they? Something he could use as collateral to borrow real money against, right?"

I was reasonably impressed she could draw that conclusion.

"Yes, and in the end, we may have to do some fancy footwork in the divorce to indemnify you against his tax evasion and insurance fraud charge," I said.

"If he was to die suddenly would that end my problems?" she asked.

It would undoubtedly end mine.

"No. It will take a while, but we will work through this mess. The net worth you may have planned to walk away with probably has decreased by several zeros. Luckily, the house has a lot of equity, the cars are paid off, and I believe I can find some offshore accounts," I told her.

"What about the eight-million-dollar life insurance policy," she blurted out.

"If it's universal or whole life, it might have some cash value," I said.

I noticed Mr. Martin was studying her and hoped he wasn't going to ask her what I was thinking. *Why? Are you considering bumping your husband off?*

"Let's table that for now. This has been a rough two hours. Why not go home and rest? I'll have Mary call you for a return visit once Mr. Martin goes through all the financials we have. Does that sound like a plan?" I asked.

"Yes. Still, I want you to investigate the life insurance," she said. That garnered a raised eyebrow from Mr. Martin.

Great.

CHAPTER FIVE

Poppy

THOUGHT I WOULD LEARN SOMETHING ABOUT THE CASE OVER THE weekend, but apparently, the firm was true to their word that they followed a forty-hour work week. That didn't mean I wasn't eager to get started in my new job, nor that I couldn't wait to hear the update of the case. I trolled the internet for further information, but nothing popped up. So, did that indicate Dr. Blackwell remained in a holding cell over the weekend? *Odd.*

Our staff meeting set for 8 a.m. was pushed back to 10 a.m. because of an emergency that arose with a client of Tallulah's. What a nightmare family law is, and I was glad I would not have to be a part of that regularly. Mary had shared a hair-raising story that involved Tallulah, well Lulu as everyone calls her, being attacked by a client's husband. Had it not been for Mary shooting the man point blank they both could be dead. The world was devolving into a cycle of chaos where everyone was fair game.

"Where's Dalia?" I asked Mary.

I wanted to get an update on the case but didn't want to appear like I was snooping.

"She'll be here before long. She had to meet with Ms. Blake this morning to go over the details of the bond hearing for this afternoon," she said, shuffling through some papers.

"Wait. What? The district attorney wouldn't sign off on a consent bond on Friday? Why in God's name not? I've had people arrested for drug deals out on bond an hour after an arrest."

This argument over bail was almost unheard of with wealthy clients in this county. The purpose of the bond is just to ensure that defendants will appear for trial and all pretrial hearings for which they must be present. The amount of bond is set by weighing certain factors such as the risk of flight, the type of crime alleged, the "dangerousness" of the defendant, and the safety of the community. Surely the district attorney could not argue Dr. Blackwell didn't have a steady job, roots, or say he would have a reason to believe he would flee.

"I'll let Dalia give you all the details, but two things were clear. We can assume the D.A.'s office is going to grandstand with this case because it is such a high profile. Also, the client appears to be cash poor with limited liquid resources. The couple has lived a high-flying lifestyle with lots of 'stuff,' but it's all mortgaged or leased. They have invested a great deal of money into promoting themselves as a power couple, but are living above their means. When it came down to the wire, a lot of the actual funds they have, are in Ms. Blake's name as family money. Moreover, she wasn't keen on tapping into two million dollars of her trust fund asset," Mary said raising her eyebrows.

I could certainly understand that. I'm not sure if my hubby was a philandering sleaze, I'd want to invest my separate money into helping him either.

"What about a property bond?"

"Their home has two mortgages against it so they couldn't

come up with any equity from that. And before you ask about a bail bonds person who requires only ten percent up front, they were struggling to raise the two hundred thousand cash over the weekend," she said.

"So, isn't Dalia afraid that if they can't come up with the funds for that, then how could they pay her remaining fee?"

Actually, this wasn't any of my business, but fighting for payment of my legal fees made me aware of the struggles, and it just popped out. I'd have to work on filtering my thoughts.

"That is something we will need to discuss. Here's Dalia now. Let me get everyone into the conference room. Would you stick your head into Mr. Martin's office and tell him we are ready? Lulu's client left, so I'll grab Lulu," Mary said.

I knocked on Mr. Martin's door, and a curt "Enter," was his reply.

I opened the door and was surprised to see a workspace that appeared to have been in use for years instead of just two hours. Until this morning I wasn't even sure Mr. Martin had accepted the job offer. But somewhere between 7 a.m. and 8 a.m. this morning, the man brought in fifteen books, two computer monitors along with a laptop. There were no personal items to make the area his, but that wasn't something I expected of him anyway. I wonder if he was married or had any grandchildren? He wasn't the type to chitchat, so I suppose that would remain a mystery until he decided to divulge a morsel of personal information.

"Good morning. Mary asked me to let you know they are ready for the staff meeting."

"Right," was his response.

He stood, picked up a pad, and walked past me without even a morning salutation.

Jerk.

Lulu and Dalia filed into the room. Mary told us two more people might join us in a bit. Cillian O'Reilly and Jackson Evans, the men who ran the security firm that offered investigative support to the law firm might be at the latter half of the meeting. They had started their part of the investigation and would bring Lulu up to speed on background information about Mrs. Abernathy's husband. I discovered that somehow Mary was an equity partner with that organization and lent her sleuthing skills to both places. At ninety it was a wonder she could get out of bed in the morning, much less run two offices. But hey, Dick Van Dyke, Betty White, and Angela Lansbury were older than her and still active in the entertainment field. It stirred me from my thoughts as the bang of a gavel hitting a striking block startled me.

"For the love of God, Mary, put that thing down," Lulu said as she strained to grab for the gavel. Mary was quicker and placed it out of her reach.

My eyes cut to Mr. Martin, who wasn't even trying to hide a sneer.

"I'd like to welcome our two new members, Poppy and Mr. Martin. I can speak for all of us and say we hope they will have a long and prosperous association with our firm. To make this a little more efficient, I've prepared a list of open cases and wrote a brief account of the posture of the open cases for the benefit of our new associates. Over the next few days, I want to meet with each of you separately to determine which I can slot you into as the second chair. Before we start is there anything pressing?" Mary inquired.

Mr. Martin stood and smoothed his jacket.

"I have an issue," he said as all eyes moved toward him.

"Go on then," Mary said. "And you can remain seated."

He continued to stand at attention.

"You assured me when I interviewed, I would not be involved in matrimonial cases. And yet the first thing this morning, Ms. West interrupted my morning preparations, to take part in some such a case," he complained and pointedly looked at Lulu for an explanation.

The room went silent, waiting for a response. One was not forthcoming. I couldn't tell if Lulu's body language was emanating shock or anger, but something was brewing.

"Lulu?" Mary interceded.

"Well, yes, while I requested you participate in a specific piece of a divorce action, the information you provided proved invaluable. Did you have a problem with being asked about financial issues in the case? Because your extensive knowledge about books greatly impressed me, and it was an immense help," she said.

The compliment didn't seem to hit the mark she was hoping for.

"There's nothing impressive about it. That was information I regularly used for my last place of business. Be that as it may, it still involved a domestic law client, who based on her outburst, obviously had some unresolved emotional issues. I specifically questioned if interacting with such clients would be a condition of my service. Now if the answer is yes, then I will need to terminate my employment," he said and adjusted his shirt cuff.

I watched Lulu struggle not to erupt with a curt answer, and she did a good job keeping a lid on it. I was sure if I was the target of his nonsense, I'd have tossed him out. *Good riddance,* I'd say.

"Your point is taken." Mary nodded. "Is it the face-to-face contact that is disturbing? Or do you have a blanket aversion to anything that has a whiff of divorce attached to it?"

"I don't want to deal with the emotional output that surrounds these people," he replied.

Shocker. The man had absolutely no people skills.

"So, if there is a case that involves your particular skill set are you okay with reviewing the information if you don't have to interact with them?" Mary inquired, attempting to negotiate a resolution.

Why were they coddling this jerk?

"Wait," Lulu interrupted. "What if the client needs an explanation about the conclusion he draws or has an issue with the final report?"

"Unacceptable. No contact means no contact," Mr. Martin answered, waggling his finger at her closing down the discussion.

"Well, ladies, he's pretty clear. Do you accept these terms?" Mary asked.

Dalia tapped her index finger against her cheek.

"What if I have a client charged with financial fraud and I need your expertise of sifting through financial reports? I might not know the exact question to get at the answer quickly, but with your education and professional background you may be able to cut right to it," Dalia asked.

He turned his head and crinkled his brow.

"I thought I was clear in my delineation: no family law clients, no divorce cases. Criminal defendants do not fall in that category. Does that answer your question?" he asked.

Dalia shrugged her shoulders and nodded.

"Whatever," Lulu replied with a dismissive wave. "We have

other people we can use. Still, I think you owe us an explanation of why you refuse to work with family law clients."

"No, I don't. I was clear when I took the position," Mr. Martin stated. "If it was a deal breaker, you could have rescinded your offer."

Mary tapped the gavel on the wood block again, startling all of us. Except for Mr. Martin.

"He's right, so can we move on?"

He sat, and Dalia stood.

"To give you a rundown on Blackwell, we have a bail hearing this afternoon. The D.A. won't budge on an 'own recognizance' bond and will not come off a two million cash bond. Nevertheless, I'm sure the judge will order a workable amount. The charge of murder I understand, but unlawful termination, quite frankly, I think is overreaching. My opinion is, once the fact they are playing hardball becomes public, they poison the jury pool. If we go for a change in the venue, it will be a fight to the finish. Something feels off about this case, but until I get discovery, I feel as if I'm missing something big," Dalia said.

"Does he admit the baby could be his?" Lulu asked softly, wincing.

"No. As a matter of fact, Gabriel said he had a vasectomy years ago, and although things can happen, he refused to open that line of discussion at all," Dalia said.

"Then maybe that opens your suspect pool to other men who have had access to her and a motive for some other person," Mary offered.

"Or a motive for him, if he was jealous and found out," I said.

Mr. Martin drummed his fingers on the table, and it diverted our attention to him.

"After a vasectomy, the rates of pregnancy are around one in one thousand after the first year, and between two to ten in one thousand after five years. A seminal report in 2004 and other reports that followed indicate that following a vasectomy a couple has a less than one percent chance of getting pregnant," he stated.

Dalia stared at him with her mouth slightly gaped open.

"Right. Okay then. I'm certain the pathologist will do a DNA test on the baby to rule Gabriel out. If he's ruled out that might open the door to an alternate suspect. Nevertheless, we need to hop to it and try to start closing the loop to show he did not have the means, motive, and opportunity to commit this crime," Dalia said making notes.

"Except he did," Mary said, twirling the gavel.

"Did what?" I asked, leaning forward.

"Have means and opportunity. Motive is still on the table," Mary replied shrugging one shoulder.

"No shit, Sherlock. I'd like to think after we open a line of investigation, we can offer alternative theories of the crime and offer other suspects. Reasonable doubt is what we want. Also, let's not forget we don't have to disprove the case. The state must prove the elements of the crime," Dalia said.

"That's BS, and you know it," Mary jumped in. "Juries want to have everything tied up in a bow, and they want you to show why the accused could not have done it."

"Mary, it goes both ways. Look at Casey Anthony and OJ. The jury didn't feel the prosecution met its standard of proof and came back with a not guilty without the defendant offering a realistic alternative," Dalia returned. "Right now, we don't know enough about the case to start making assumptions. I am going to have Mary interview the hospital colleagues of the victim. Her little old lady act deserves an award and people seem to open up to her. I'd like you to get on that today, Mary, so I can determine how hard I will have to worry about character assassination. I won't say I'm not concerned. Let's not forget Alex Clarke, who is sitting in jail because circumstantial evidence made it impossible for him to get a fair trial."

"Alex Clarke?" I asked. That was a name I wasn't familiar with.

"I'll fill you in on that case when we have a chance. Or Google his name. So, unless Lulu has something pressing, I'd like to ask for an early adjournment," Dalia said.

"Actually, I have one concern," Lulu said.

"Go on," Mary encouraged.

"I had to meet with Vanessa Abernathy after reviewing some records that just came in. There appears to be exposure to tax evasion. I'm pretty sure the feds can make a case against her husband, and I didn't want her dragged into the mess. And well, she seemed a little focused on a life insurance policy which was recently taken out on Mr. Abernathy's life. It's a key man insurance policy through the corporation. However, there is a subordinate beneficiary clause naming her personally as the chief beneficiary. How that got past the partners, I don't know, but ..." she said as her eyes cut over to Mr. Martin.

"And?" Mary asked.

"Well, desperate people do desperate things. I'm just a tad worried," she replied.

I guess this validated Mr. Martin's adamant decision of not being involved with family law clients.

"Look, Lulu, you likely still feel the aftermath of that Lansing case, that crazy husband nearly murdered you. Has Vanessa indicated to you she has a plan to do something to harm her husband?" Mary inquired.

"Well, no. Why even bring it up?" she asked.

"Who knows? You have enough on your plate as it is. Until she asks what poison to use, what caliber gun would work best, how do you hire a hit man, or how much antifreeze is enough to kill her husband, I'd back burner it," Mary said.

Lulu shook her head and stared at the table.

"I envy you, Mary. You're the one that shot Mr. Lansing. How do you get past that?" Lulu asked quietly.

"Shot him. Whom did Mary shoot? Was it a client? Also, why was she armed?" Mr. Martin asked with alarm in his voice. Mr. non-emotion actually raised his voice an octave.

"Enough. Find a way to deal with it and let's not make an issue out of it. If it becomes an ethical concern, then we can talk about it," Mary said.

"No one answered my question. Do I have to worry about violence in the workplace?" Mr. Martin persisted.

"No, you don't. I shot the man while he held us captive in Tallulah's car. Case closed. We stand adjourned," Mary announced, tapping the gavel to the block. "I'll let Jackson know to catch up with us later."

As we filed out of the room, Mr. Martin remained seated. He probably was deciding if he should leave now or quit at the end of the business day.

CHAPTER SIX

Poppy

DALIA LEANED HER SHOULDER AGAINST THE DOORJAMB OF MY office.

"I have three clients I am working on this week to determine if we should take a deal that the D.A. has offered. Cases start out so promising to win and then certain facts come to light and boom, it all falls to shit. I need to bring you up to speed and get you involved, and we can decide which to handle first. Do you want to jump into the most unusual case or what I consider the easiest? It will be up to you."

"Great, step in and take a seat. I'd like to hear about the most interesting first, for sure," I said.

There was nothing to clear away on my desk or chairs, and I welcomed the work.

"If you have that list Mary gave you, get that, and you can make notes. The top three are the ones we'll need to discuss today and tomorrow. Then we have to go. I want to talk to Gabriel before the bail hearing."

I pulled out the sheet that had twelve cases listed.

"Let's discuss Peter Laters today. He's charged with fraud, forgery, theft, and embezzlement. The D.A.'s office is calling the case *Pretty Boy Pete*. I think somewhere in their office they have him on a *Most Wanted* poster. It's a fact-driven case filled with juicy details. I guess they decided to play hardball because they wanted to focus on some of the dangers of dating sites. Everyone from *Dr. Phil* to *20/20* has produced shows about this topic, so now it's their turn to jump on the bandwagon, I suppose. This is my favorite case.

"According to the D.A., Peter dated a large number of women from several dating sites. He doesn't dispute that. No crime there. However, they state that in doing so it wasn't for companionship, but rather to determine who owned their property outright and unencumbered by a mortgage or car loan. They allege he targeted the most vulnerable women. The offenses the D.A. charged him with involves a twenty-eight-year-old woman, Lilian Mathers. The woman's grandparents left her well off financially as she was the only surviving member of the Mathers family. She lived off her investments rather than work and had limited life experience. From all accounts, she was what some people might call a susceptible person, but an adult nonetheless.

"The investigation was extensive. Lilian's version of the story was that he didn't trick her into giving her home to him as one would think. However, instead, she said she never transferred the residence in question to him period. Peter's story is, she signed the property over to him and thus made him the sole owner. He considered it a gift in contemplation of marriage. They lived together in the house for six months as a couple and here's where their stories go down a different path. Lilian reports Peter suddenly filed an eviction with the court to have her removed from the home. She filed a response stating that she owned the property and the court should dismiss the case. Our client says her behavior had become so erratic over time that he feared for his life. Peter filed a petition to evict Lilian, and she states that was when she discovered the alleged falsified transfer of property.

"He refused to leave and stayed in the home. Peter likewise claimed all the furniture was his as well. The luxury car in the garage in his name also is part of the dispute as a gift. The total value of the gifts? Two point one million dollars. Lilian says it's not her signature on the deed, and the handwriting analysis is inconclusive. Witnesses we've interviewed say they appeared to be a loving couple; others labeled him a snake charmer. I'll get you the file and see what you think.

"The other two are not as colorful as *Pretty Boy*. One is from a stop and search and I am challenging was an illegal stop. So, I would consider anything from that subsequent search the fruit of the poisonous tree and tossed. I've already moved to suppress the drugs they found. Our client claims the drugs found in his car were not his but must be one of the passengers'. The amount of drugs found could put him away for ten years.

"Our other case is larceny and an identity theft allegation. Because it involves a senior, the D.A. is going after the client as if she was Satan herself. Our client says her mother-in-law was dying and gave her permission to use her credit cards to refurbish her home with expensive furniture. A parting gift as her mother-in-law left this life. The mother-in-law agrees yes, she thought she was dying, but never gave her permission to use the cards. Once she recovered, she realized the woman had run up sixty thousand in credit card charges she is now responsible for paying. She had her arrested."

"So, is *Pretty Boy* pretty?" I asked.

"He'd have you throwing your panties at him," she shared.

"His story seems solid. The morally right thing to do would be to return the house, furniture, and car if the engagement and marriage plans dissolved. Until they can prove a crime, in my estimation the property is his, and this is more a matter for the civil courts. My concern is that the jury won't see a distinction between moral and legal," she replied.

"I see. Well, I'm looking forward to digging into it," I told Dalia.

I could understand the alleged victim's angst. I had a knack for picking losers in the romance department.

"Grab the Blackwell file and let's go," Dalia said, checking the time.

Once we were on our way, I waited for Dalia to get comfortable with the flow of traffic and then asked her what was happening today.

"Over the weekend I met with Gabriel and Ms. Blake several times. That's a couple that needs to employ Lulu and just sever their connection, in my estimation. Nevertheless, for whatever reason, they've found a comfortable point in their relationship, that to this point has worked for them and kept their marriage together.

"Moving past that, here's the financial snag. Dr. Blackwell has no property in his name. He divested himself of any property so that if he was ever sued and lost a malpractice case, then no one could attach any property. Yet, even beyond that, there is no equity in their mansion to satisfy a property bond. Next, Ms. Blake is adamant she doesn't want to turn a large sum of money over to a bail bonds person because there is no recouping that money. If she were amenable to putting the whole amount up in cash, which she isn't, she'd recover that money when the case ends. However, she'd have to invade the corpus of the family trust, and that would involve a lot of red tape and time.

"So, if we can't get him out today on his own recognizance or a reasonable bond, then he will sit there for a while until the time is right for a bond modification."

"Surely he must have other people he can ask for help? Or what about a go fund me page?" I asked half kidding.

"His partners in the practice are giving lip service to raising money. However, I'm getting the vibe they have had it with his personal issues and would be happy to cut him loose under the 'for cause' portion of their partnership agreement. I'm not seeing any of them digging into their personal funds to help him out. They'll just spread his patients amongst themselves. The defense he is using for his bad behavior is that he's a sex addict and has undergone therapy and taken medication to control his impulses. Now that all this might become public, more women may come out of the woodwork to tell their own stories of how he ruined their lives. His partners feel he's a liability and their insurance might consider his actions as intentional rather than negligent. If sued for keeping him in the practice over time, they'd be on the hook for any out-of-pocket liability."

"Okay, I see everyone's point. However, the bottom line is, does the D.A. have enough facts and evidence to pass a probable cause hearing?" I asked. "I know this is a bail hearing and we're not at the P.C. hearing, but what do you think?"

She blew out a breath that reeked of exasperation.

"Until the arraignment, they aren't obligated to give us any discovery. However, we have some contacts leaking information to us. That stays in the car. Understand?" she said, turning toward me for acknowledgment.

"Right now, all we officially know is that he's charged with murder and the termination of the life of a fetus. As the case evolves, I can see where they could add kidnapping. The investigation is ongoing, but one thing is clear; it looks bad. Moreover, his attitude and demeanor do him no favors. I'm going to have to be honest with him. Short of an OR bond, he'll be cooling his heels in detention for at least three weeks before I can request a bond modification."

"Look, he seems to be a world-class prick, and I understand why Ms. Blake is upset over this whole thing. I'd be furious as well. She picked him, she stayed with him, and she had to know about his bad behavior. He certainly didn't hide it," I said.

I realize I should be the support team for our clients. Nevertheless, sometimes you had to put yourself in the place of what the public would think because those were his peers and the ones to judge him as potential jurors. He deserves some type of punishment for his careless behavior and for being a dick. And I'm sure when his behavior got out, he would be judged harshly.

"Between you and me, I suppose it will come to light and get out in the papers that three years ago she had had it with him and left. He begged her to reconsider, and they struck a reconciliation agreement very much in her favor. As part of this arrangement, if he cheated again, there was a clause that triggered all tangible property he owned became hers. Additionally, eighty percent of his future income stream automatically went to her, as part of any subsequent divorce. That money would flow to her for the next fifteen years and taxed to him," Dalia said.

"Whoa. That's motive right there, isn't it?" I asked.

"I'd like to say I could keep that document out, but…"

We both were silent.

"I feel like right now we're giving too much credence to

circumstantial evidence. What really, does the D.A. have as direct hardcore evidence? I mean, at this point it just feels like they are building their whole case on his bad character," I reflected.

"And normally I could move to exclude his character being brought into play, except that agreement if it comes to light will point to a motive," Dalia said. "We're getting ahead of ourselves. Today, let's focus on the bond and getting him out so we can mount a defense. I don't relish this being dragged out for three years waiting for a jury trial. Also, I am uncertain that demanding a speedy trial would work in our favor right now."

"I have a friend whose client was a chiropractor charged with child molestation of his daughter from his first marriage and arrested in 2014. The chiropractic partnership excluded him from practicing with them while the police investigated the allegations. He had no way of making a living. The judge ordered he couldn't live with his present family because he had two young children, and while the case was ongoing, the judge wanted to protect the children. The guy had to live in a separate place from his second family, had no job, and this stress ultimately led to their divorce in 2015. Anyway, in 2016, he went to trial and was acquitted of the charge of aggravated child molestation, but the judge declared a mistrial in the two other child molestation charges. We are now going into 2019, and he is still waiting for a retrial on those other charges. You're probably wondering what my point is," I said.

"No, I see your point. Gabriel in about three hours might be at a place where his entire world implodes. He'll have no job, an unsupportive wife, and tied up for the foreseeable future in the legal system," she said. "And if that happens, you can count on him to blame me for that occurrence."

"What's your plan?" I asked.

"Until we have what the police have gathered, we don't know the evidence and the case they are building. However, I believe the pivotal point of the case is the D.A. believes he is the father of the child and murdered her to keep this quiet. Why? So that clause in the reconciliation agreement would not be triggered. Because once triggered that would allow Ms. Blake to obtain an uncontested divorce, financially crippling him. We have to find a crack to plant reasonable doubt and exploit the hell out of it. Then widen the crack until it's a sinkhole of suspects."

"Do you think he's innocent?"

"Until proven guilty, yes. Right now, I don't see the evidence. If Dr. Blackwell stood accused of being a philandering piece of shit, then yes, guilty as charged. However, until that's a crime, we keep the watch on the system assuring it works fairly, and defend his constitutional rights," Dalia said as we pulled up to the courthouse. "The only thing that stands between him and spending the rest of his life in jail right now is us."

CHAPTER SEVEN

Poppy

"**A**LL RISE!" WITH THE SMACK OF A GAVEL, THE MOOD OF THE courtroom changed. An air of formality enveloped the room. The judge held most bail hearings in the jail; however, capital felony cases played by different rules. The state treated Dr. Blackwell to a bus ride from the adult detention center to the courthouse. Not in his usual luxury ride, and I'm certain Dalia would hear about that later.

"Please be seated." And so began the fight to regain Dr. Blackwell's freedom.

It surprised me that the prosecutor was a seasoned one. For a bond hearing, I was sure the D.A.'s office would send in a rookie. This didn't look good. They really meant business. What did they know that we didn't?

"James Bradshaw for the state, Your Honor."

"Dalia Grey for the defendant Dr. Gabriel Blackwell."

"This is a bond hearing and not a determination of whether the evidence will stand the test of a trial. We are here today for the defendant's request to set bail for his release. In my court, I base bail on the severity of the alleged offense, the likelihood of additional crimes after being released, and the chances the defendant will flee the jurisdiction before trial. I can set bail at any amount not objectively unreasonable or deny bail altogether. Now let's begin. Mr. Bradshaw, do you have an objection to bail being set on Dr. Blackwell's own recognizance?"

The man dressed in a charcoal pinstripe suit and black shoes pushed up from his chair, and responded, "I do, Your Honor."

"If the court reporter is ready, you can proceed," the judge replied.

"Dr. Gabriel Blackwell is charged with the crimes of murder and unlawful termination of a pregnancy. As the state investigates the case, it may amend those charges. The state contends that the defendant was in a short-term relationship with the victim that became a problem for him. When she became pregnant, he decided to end her life and the life of their child. This act was a premeditated, cold-blooded crime that also involved the life of an unborn child. A child he wished to dispose of in the most heinous manner—"

"Mr. Bradshaw, you can bypass the theatrics. What I want to know is do you have any reason to believe the defendant will not return to court when summoned, will flee the jurisdiction, or harm anyone while he is out awaiting trial?" the judge interrupted.

"Judge, the defendant and his wife have access to a large amount of money. If he wants to disappear, he can. Might I add we look to our doctors to save lives, not snuff them out."

Dalia could have objected to these viperous statements, but she was ahead of the game right now, and that last statement would only inflame the judge more.

"Ms. Grey, I'm certain you have something to say," the judge said looking toward Dalia.

"Yes, Judge. My client is a respected member of the

community. He is not only a practicing physician whose skills are needed to save lives, but he is also a devoted member of many charitable institutions. He has no criminal record, not even a speeding ticket, and vehemently denies these charges. The defendant had a vasectomy many years ago and therefore contends he could not be the father of this child, thus, negating what the state is hinting at is motive. My client asks the Court to release him on his own recognizance, and should you wish an ankle bracelet as an extra layer of protection,; he has no objection. He very much wants to return to work, and should you remanded him to jail, his standing in the medical practice will suffer irreparable financial loss. People who need care will be deprived of his skills, and the charities he serves on will suffer. There is no reason to believe he will tamper with witnesses nor is he a threat to the public," Dalia offered in a calm, even voice.

"Thank you. I've reviewed the financial information provided by the defendant to support his request. I am concerned that the defendant has shifted all his property to his wife's name. This action normally would signal that someone has no financial reason to remain in the area. However, on balance, that is something frequently done in the medical community. I will set a bond at one hundred thousand dollars, and no ankle bracelet is necessary. He is to surrender all firearms. Further, he shall have no personal contact with any witnesses that involve any discussion of this case. See the clerk for the arraignment day," he said.

Score one for our team. He'd only have to put up ten thousand dollars for the bond. I knew Dalia had already determined the upper limits he could afford, and this fell well within those limits. A bonds person sat in the last row ready to write the bond immediately. This presence assured Dr. Blackwell would be free within the next few hours.

As I turned to see how the prosecutor reacted, I noticed Ms. Blake's face reflected disappointment. Was she disappointed in the amount? Or his release?

"You think she'll file for divorce while the case is pending? That could deal a blow to our defense," I said.

"Oh hell no. She'll wait until the trial is over. If he's acquitted, she'll invoke the reconciliation agreement and capture eighty percent of his future stream of income. If he's found guilty, she'll file and get his equity portion of the practice outright. It's a win-win for her," Dalia whispered. "Let me catch Gabriel before they take him and tell him we need to meet tomorrow to start planning the strategy."

I took my seat to wait for Dalia to return when I felt a tap on my shoulder. It was Ms. Blake.

"Please tell Dalia that Gabriel is not to return to the house. I have to think about the optics of this and what it will look like to the public and how it could affect my practice. He needs to find someplace else to live. He can come by later today and take what clothes he needs. I'll leave the checking accounts in place so there will be no disruption in the household bills. Also, tell him his little whore's family has filed a wrongful death action against him that they tried to serve on me, and I refused service. That was the last straw because now it involves me personally. I have no intention of being a witness in a civil action where my life can be picked apart in public. Please don't count on me for any support in this matter emotionally, or financially. He's on his own. I am done! It would not surprise me if he killed that woman and I refuse to have any further interaction with a murderer," she said.

My mouth probably gaped. I know my right eye started

blinking quickly, a nervous tick I had. What could I say but, "Okay." Who was I to argue with a woman who had every right to feel deceived and betrayed? Before I could even let out the breath I was holding, she turned and walked away. What could have changed her mind about his innocence? Should I run after her and try to find out? Instead of making a move I remained dazed and frozen in my seat.

When Dalia returned, I gave her the news to which she replied, "Shit!"

I waited for her to process the information and then she said we'd have to discuss this with him later.

"I'd like to keep the wrongful death suit in-house to co-ordinate on all fronts. I'll speak to Lulu and see if she's willing to take on the civil litigation part," she said. "The fact that the standard of proof is much lower in a civil court can hurt us in the criminal case. If they can get the case through the civil courts before ours, then evidence out of reach in a criminal matter could hurt us if obtained through the wrongful death action. Moreover, it also assures that the public will have access to way too much information. They probably will want to take a deposition of Gabriel and his wife, which they never would be allowed to do in the criminal arena. Shit, shit, shit!" Sshe said as her hand went to her forehead.

"Surely Lulu can quash the deposition subpoena and get a protective order, so his fifth amendment right not to be forced to testify against himself is protected," I offered.

"With what just happened to the wife, I'm more worried about what she will say in a deposition. Spousal privilege only goes so far. Okay, let's first discuss it with Lulu and see if she is willing to get involved. When we have more facts, we can discuss it with Gabriel. Let's stop by the clerk's office and get a copy of the lawsuit before he gets served, so we have the gist of it," she said.

With that, we headed to the civil clerk's office to get the copy and then back to our office. I hope Tallulah assigned Mr. Martin this case. It indeed held the promise of making his head explode.

CHAPTER EIGHT

Tallulah

"THANK YOU FOR BRINGING ME A COPY OF THE LAWSUIT. I'VE looked it over so let's decide if we want to accept it," I said.

Mary, Mr. Martin, Dalia, and Poppy all sat anxiously waiting for me to start. Everyone except Mr. Martin was poised to take notes.

"We're taking it," Mary said and slapped the table with her hand for emphasis.

Her role as office manager afforded her the right to offer an opinion about potential cases. The position also awarded her the authority to seek out new associates and offer jobs to them. But it was my final decision to sign my name onto the court documents as the attorney of record. Lucky for her I had already decided we should take it. It would get my brain out of the soul-sucking family law matters that took up way too much space in my head.

Moreover, I saw no merit in the lawsuit. Plus, if these two decided to divorce later neither could hire me. I could declare a conflict of interest.

"I agree. We will need to do a lot of damage control in

this civil action to protect the criminal matter," Dalia offered. "I can't take the chance of someone screwing up the civil litigation so that it might bleed onto the criminal one."

"I don't see anything explosive in here," Mr. Martin responded. "I'm not on the criminal matter, but it appears to me that there is nothing new here. In fact, this gives you a lot more leeway to get information about the woman's past and exploit it if necessary, here. You might not be able to use a character flaw of the plaintiff victim in the criminal trial, but you can certainly do so here. Frankly, I think it's a blessing."

"Unless our client is guilty. Then her flaws could give him a motive," Dalia said.

"Mary, you've done some investigating on the case, what have you come up with on the victim Marsha Anderson?" Dalia asked.

"Marsha Anderson was a twenty-six-year-old, single white female who shared an apartment with another woman. She had been a nurse at the hospital for two years and highly regarded by her colleagues. I have an appointment to meet her roommate tomorrow to see what background I can get from her. No lawsuits, no arrests, but she was heavily in debt. Her nursing school student debt alone was staggering, and those were co-signed by her parents who are now stuck with the obligation. Even in death, student loans don't go away. The girl had expensive taste. She leased a Mercedes and paid about eight hundred a month for that and was almost two months behind on payments. It was in a position to be repossessed. Trolling the outstanding indebtedness, she had maxed out her cards. She was one step away from bankruptcy," Mary observed.

Well, this was good news. We could see why the parents jumped on this lawsuit so quickly. Now that Marsha was dead the loan company passed the student debt down to them. They now had the burden of the debt for the next eight years.

"How did you come into such personal information about her finances when discovery hasn't started?" Mr. Martin inquired.

"Don't ask, trust me," Dalia jumped in. If she hadn't, I would have. Mary played fast and loose with the privacy laws, and with Dalia's new cybersecurity skills, I worried Mary might try to exploit those.

Poppy took the hint, moved on, and asked, "Information about past or present relationships?"

"Yes, Poppy, interesting question. As far as I could tell, she did not have any meaningful relationships, male or female. When I interviewed her colleagues, they said she liked to play the field, and many men had briefly entered her life. As yet I haven't discovered other men's names, but I'm on it. And no, Dr. Blackwell's name did not come up. Maybe the word is out from administration to put a lid on the flow of information," Mary said.

"So why involve herself with a man such as Dr. Blackwell? I can understand from his end why he would get entangled in a risky relationship with her. Sort of. Still, it would seem that for Marsha, he would be nothing but a dead end. Surely, she would have been privy to hospital gossip and innuendo," Mr. Martin offered.

I suppose it was a valid question, but the answer also was pretty obvious to me and probably every woman at the table. Wealth, a power position in the community, and good looks, it was hard to look away from that trifecta.

"Hope springs eternal, Mr. Martin, for women. Possibly she hoped she would be the one enchantress to tame the beast.

She was in debt, and he's a thoracic surgeon, she might have felt she could cash in on their affair somehow," Mary said.

"I disagree," he replied.

Mary bristled at his response, but Poppy got there first.

"Why?" Poppy asked.

"The man had a reputation for being a womanizer. Leopards don't change their spots. Surely, her colleagues warned her about his fuck 'em and chuck 'em attitude. The fact he had chosen the O.R. suite to have sex with a sex partner instead of a hotel room speaks to his unwillingness to part with additional money. If his wife kept a watch on the finances the way you believe, then I doubt he took his companions away for lavish weekend getaways or expensive meals. Unless she was completely delusional, I can't imagine she thought he would leave his wife based on the string of women that preceded her," he suggested.

There was a knock at the door, and Jackson entered with a pile of papers in his hands.

"Oh, sorry to interrupt your meeting, folks," he said. "I didn't see the watchdog sign Mary usually displays to ward off intruders."

"More like warding off evil spirits when it comes to you," Mary shot back.

I had to get a handle on this before it became the war of words. Mary and Jackson took great pleasure in aggravating each other and at times could escalate to a near-nuclear detonation.

"Poppy and Mr. Martin, this is Jackson Evans. He owns the security firm we associate with, and he is Eloise's husband," I said. "He's also an attorney and former FBI agent."

Mr. Martin stood and rounded the table to offer his hand in

greeting. Poppy leaned across the table to shake it. Mary looked irritated he broke into our meeting.

"Lulu, I have all the material you requested me to review for the Abernathy case. I've pulled all the details about each of the books and paintings you asked me to track. I've reviewed the history, provenance, invoice of sales, and location. Here is everything I could find along with all the shell companies he owns and moves his money through. It looks as though he tried to clean his act up when we filed the divorce, but really, it's too late, the information is out there. Once you have a digital footprint, it is nearly impossible to erase," he said.

"Okay. Can you leave it and let me plow through it and get back with you?" I asked.

"Sure, here's a flash drive with a Power Point presentation and Excel spreadsheets." Jackson reached in his pocket and placed it on the table.

"How many shell corporations did you identify?" Mr. Martin inquired.

Well, what perked him up, "Mr. no matrimonial cases"? Could I dare hope to lure him to the dark side?

"Four," Jackson said.

"Where?" Mr. Martin inquired as he lightly touched the stack of papers.

Jackson smiled.

"That's where it gets interesting. You would think it would be somewhere like Panama or the Caribbean. But not so. He incorporated one in Delaware, one in Switzerland, another in Luxembourg, and a highly unlikely suspect in China," Jackson replied.

"All places where he can hide a collection of valuables in a freeport storage facility away from the US customs control,"

Mr. Martin responded.

"What's a freeport?" Poppy asked.

"In one sentence, people use them as storage facilities that also offer you the opportunity to evade taxes legally—a tax suspension zone. While the valuables are parked there, taxes are not due until they leave the facility. There is also a stigma that it is a place where you can hide stolen properties, because regulations are lax, and subpoena power for searches are a nightmare," Jackson said.

Mr. Martin tapped his index finger on the table and appeared deep in thought.

"If indeed the information about the property the husband provided declares they were truly in his custody in one of the facilities, then he's hiding something. The fact that our judicial system cannot force the storage facility to let someone in to inspect what he has there offers something of a conundrum. How do you know if he owns the property or is even still in possession of it? What if he has smuggled it out and sold it without paying taxes? Or if there never was anything there, then the information he gave the insurance company is all paper transactions," Mr. Martin said. "There would be no way to prove the property had been there or somewhere else. Moreover, reporting it stolen would mean the insurance firm would have to believe it was there to start."

"Is that the sound of interest I hear?" Mary chided.

"Hmm," Mr. Martin answered.

"Enough interest to look at what Jackson prepared?" I asked.

"I do enjoy a good puzzle. Yes, leave it all to me," Mr. Martin said.

"Call me with questions," Jackson replied. He slid the flash drive toward Mr. Martin and left.

Mary shuffled her papers and looked behind her at the whiteboard deciding whether to use it.

"Okay, back to Blackwell," Mary interjected.

"Let's put everything on the table, the good and the bad, and decide where we go," Dalia said. "But first can we all agree we will take the civil matter? I would feel much better if we kept it in-house."

We all agreed.

"This case is all about Marsha Anderson, but why? Why her and no other women before her? Why would Dr. Blackwell have a reason to kill her? We don't know if she was trying to extort money from him. Based on her lifestyle, that might be a consideration. If the baby were his, then in today's day and age that would not be a career killer for him. And I'm not convinced the police can assign that as a motive," Dalia started.

"Except if his wife found out, and that triggered the detonation clause in the reconciliation agreement," Poppy said.

"Yes, there's that," Dalia agreed. "It would wipe him out financially and curtail his activities."

"It would seem until the DNA test comes back and verifies if the child was his or not, then that might not be the motive," I said.

"I disagree. If Marsha presented to Gabriel the baby was his, waiting for a paternity test after birth left a lot of months for her to extort money if that was her goal," Mary said. "Nine months is a long time to wait, and she could do a lot of damage to his career and marriage. What if every month she came to him with a demand for more and more hush money?"

"The wrong premise," Mr. Martin interjected.

"Pardon?" Mary asked.

I wonder if she was second-guessing her pick in him as an associate. The indignation in her voice was palpable but didn't faze him.

"Using a noninvasive DNA prenatal paternity test, he could have determined paternity at eight weeks of pregnancy. This analysis requires only a blood sample from the mother and a simple cheek swab from the possible father. There would have been a definitive result, and unless you can ascertain that someone performed the test and he was the father, your theory is poorly constructed," he replied.

We all sat there stunned.

"He's correct that these tests are available. I've never used one, but they are out there. He could have run it through the lab under a false name. Easy peasy. I'm just wondering, Mr. Martin, how you know so much about it with the hatred you have for family law," I said.

"I read a lot of medical journals. I have a keen interest in stem cell research which led me to this path of laboratory testing." He shrugged.

"Okay, let's fast-forward. The fact that the police took Dr. Blackwell's DNA upon arrest, they will now have a sample to compare with the baby from the autopsy. So that could go either way for us while we are in the dark," Dalia said.

"Which is all starting to make my head ache because you are all going into the realm of what-ifs. If Marsha Anderson was pregnant and told Dr. Blackwell it was his, that may be a motive. If he found out she was pregnant and two-timing him, that may be a motive. If Dr. Blackwell didn't know, and there was a random argument that escalated, that could become a problem. Alternatively, maybe he didn't have anything to do with this at all, and therefore had no motive," Poppy said throwing her hands up in exasperation.

We all sat there silently agreeing, but knowing we had to put a plan together.

"That is too simplistic. You are trying to pigeonhole this into either a Cinderella story or a Faustian bargain. Might I suggest you go down the path of your garden variety motives for murder," Mr. Martin said, not turning, or making eye contact with anyone.

He stood, walked to the whiteboard, picked up the marker, and wrote a series of words upon it. He put the cap back on the marker and returned to his seat.

"Love, lust, loathing, to keep a secret, revenge, frustration, hate, money, greed, sex, jealousy, a property dispute, personal vendetta, political, drugs and an urge to protect, start there. Next to each motive, assign a person who might have a reason to kill the victim. Then, you may have your list of alternative suspects. Now I'd like to get started on the documents that Mr. Evans delivered. May I be excused?"

"Yes, yes, you may," Mary said. She seemed to stutter over her response. Had someone actually been born that could throw Mary off her game?

"Okay, you heard him, let's start this separately and agree to reconvene back here after Poppy and Dalia meet with Dr. Blackwell to discuss strategy. I think we've teased out a lot of information today," I said. "I want to be in on that meeting with Dr. Blackwell so I can craft an answer to this lawsuit."

"Any other suggestions, Mr. Martin?" Dalia asked.

"Not until I see the autopsy, toxicology, and forensic reports," he said. "I believe in the aphorism: Never trouble trouble till trouble troubles you. The proverb is actually a rewording of an earlier adage found in John Ray's 'A Handbook of Proverbs' published in 1670. John Ray was a clergyman, biologist, and naturalist, and called the Father of English Natural History. The maxim upon which we base this proverb is this: Let your trouble tarry till its own day comes."

"Swell. Meeting adjourned," Mary said and slammed the gavel on the strike block.

CHAPTER NINE

Poppy

I T SEEMED AS IF AN ENTIRE WEEK HAD FLOWN BY SINCE I STARTED THIS wonderful new job, and the darkness I had felt over the last few months had lifted. That is until Eloise knocked on my doorjamb. Eloise Evans, a partner in the firm, dealt with the estate portion and taxation matters. She was married to Jackson, a member of the investigatory arm of the firm, and best friends with Lulu. I liked how everybody had a personal connection with each other.

"Poppy, Dalia asked me to grab you. We have an emergency staff meeting, and we're in the conference room," she declared.

"Sure, be right there. Just let me save this work," I responded.

By the time I got there, everyone was seated, and the vibe was one of agitation. A man who looked like a law enforcement agent was speaking in hushed tones to Dalia in the corner. As I slid into the seat beside Lulu, I asked who he was, and why he was here.

"That's Declan Murphy; he's a Detective in Major Crimes and Dalia's fiancé. I don't know why Declan's here, but for Mary to call an emergency staff meeting it must have something to do with a case," she whispered.

When everyone gathered, Mary called the meeting to order.

"Okay, people, let's get right to it. Mr. Martin and Poppy, this is Detective Declan Murphy of Major Crimes, and he has some information for us about the Blackwell matter. Lulu, would you pop your head out and see if his partner, Detective Stow, is waiting in the anteroom, please," Mary said. "We'll just wait a minute for Lulu to get him."

Lulu returned with an older man, dressed casually, almost disheveled. He reminded me of Columbo but older.

Once everyone settled, Detective Stow took a subordinate role and stepped back a few paces.

"Dick, my partner, Dick Stow, will take the lead on what I am about to tell you along with the Marsha Anderson matter. Nevertheless, I will remain on the case. Dalia and I have built a Chinese wall vis-à-vis information that passes between us concerning the investigation. My lieutenant has signed off on it, and we're good to go," he said.

Okay. Awesome. Good to know. But, why did they have to call an emergency meeting for that tidbit?

"This morning someone found the body of Sandra Blake floating in her pool."

That got everyone's attention.

"Now, I realize you will have a million questions. Let me cut you off and tell you what I know, so everyone isn't coming at me at once," he said, leaning forward and placing his hands palms down on the table.

Dead. The news grabbed me with such a force I felt the front of my body tip forward. I didn't like the woman at all, but this hit me as if I had known her my whole life. I had just completed the motive map that Mr. Martin had laid out, and she had ticked a lot of the boxes as Marsha Anderson's murderer.

Detective Murphy looked around the room, gauging the temperature of emotions and tried to determine if we were ready to hear the rest. Mary sat forward prepared to engage him, but he stood, rather than wait for her to say something. He lifted his hand indicating she should wait.

"Here is what we know. Ms. Blake departed work yesterday at six p.m. and told a colleague she was meeting her husband at the house so he could remove more of his belongings. It seems he had vacated the house earlier in the week, and she insisted on a cooldown period before he could return. No one heard from her after she left. We have tracked her phone calls, and she didn't make any that evening.

"By the pool, we found a variety of tablets scattered about on a small glass table. There were no bottles associated with those pills; we are inventorying the house now. Until we get her medical records, we can't identify what medication she was on. Until the autopsy is complete, and the toxicology reports released, we won't know what was in her system. We are having a pharmacologist identify the pills. However, until we can determine what tablets were on the table and then learn what drugs she ingested, we won't treat them as anything but collected evidence. In other words, we are not making the leap that the pills were any part of her death," he said.

"So, was the cause of death drowning?" Mary asked.

"We won't know that until the autopsy. The ME will have to evaluate her lungs to see if there's water in them and if so, was it chlorinated water from the pool? Alternatively, someone killed her elsewhere and then dumped her there trying to make the scene appear like a suicide or an accidental overdose," Detective Stow said.

We all let that sink in. I watched each person process the information.

"Killed. Killed as in homicide?" Lulu gasped lightly touching her chest.

"We can't rule it out." He shrugged.

"So why are you here having a meeting with us?" Eloise asked.

Yes, good question. We aren't immediate family and have no legal involvement with her.

"Because her husband was supposedly the last one to see her that evening. You are representing him on the Anderson murder, so unless it's my lucky day he'll speak to us without a lawyer, we figured we should talk to you first," Detective Stow responded.

Dalia let out the breath she was holding, and she and Mary traded glances. An unspoken language passed between the two.

"Okay, I realize I'll have to wait for your preliminary report, but can I get some basic information from you?" Dalia inquired.

"Shoot," Detective Murphy replied.

"Do you have a cause of death?" she questioned.

"No. Ms. Blake had a gash on her head, but we don't know if that came before she went into the pool, during a fall, or when she got it. All we know is it looked fresh. Until the autopsy is complete that just remains a relevant piece of information. At this point, I have no idea if there was water in the lungs or not. There were no indications of strangulation, no gunshot wounds or signs of a stabbing," he replied.

"Has the ME narrowed the time of death down?"

"Nope. Just somewhere between eight p.m. and six a.m. You know how it is when water is involved. He'll have more—"

"I know, after the autopsy," Mary said with a tone of irritation.

"Did the house have a security system?" Dalia asked.

"Yes, and we are searching for the hard drive," he replied after referring to his notepad.

"So, correct me if I'm wrong. The only reason you are looking at my client is that some person at her place of work claimed she said that he was coming over to remove his belongings. You really have no idea if someone came after he left. Or for that matter, if he even went over that evening," Dalia said, tapping her hand on the table.

"We noticed your client, or someone, removed a bunch of suits from his closet along with ties and shirts from his dresser drawers," Detective Stow added.

"Yes, but you don't know if he took them last night or several days ago. Correct?" Dalia asked.

"Correct," Detective Murphy confirmed.

"And I suppose you want to ask Dr. Blackwell about where he was last evening and interview him about any conversation he had with his wife. Would that be accurate?" Dalia asked.

"That was the plan in coming here. We could meet you later today with your client instead of at the station," Detective Murphy offered.

Mary looked at Dalia with a raised eyebrow I took to mean, "Is he crazy?"

"Declan, let me speak to my client, and I'll let you know. At this point, I am hearing you say he is a person of interest because he may have been the last one to see her. Is that right?" she asked.

"You didn't hear me declare him a person of interest. Right now, we're treating him as a possible witness," he replied with a shrug of his right shoulder.

"Was there a suicide note?" Mr. Martin asked.

"We retrieved no note," Detective Stow answered.

"Was alcohol involved?" Mr. Martin continued.

"Yes, there were two glasses of scotch in the living room. One was half full, and the other empty. We have bagged and tagged those," Detective Stow responded.

"Was there any blood at the scene to determine where or how she received the gash?" Mr. Martin pressed.

"No," Detective Stow responded.

"Any marks on her arms to indicate she struggled, or someone restrained her?" I asked.

"Not as yet. However, often bruises surface several days after death," Detective Murphy responded.

"Robbery?" I questioned.

"Still to be determined," he said.

Dalia looked around the room. "Anyone else?"

"When will you release the house as a crime scene so we can do our investigation," Mary inquired.

"Give us until tomorrow evening, maybe the day after. We might need to take pool samples. Also, we're still trying to find the security hard drive, if Dr. Blackwell knows where that is, let us know. We have a safecracker ready to break into the safe unless your guy wants to give us the combination," he said.

"Thanks, Declan. I'll get back to you later today. Do you need an escort out?" Dalia asked.

"Seriously? See you later," he said and placed a large cowboy hat on his head.

He and Detective Stow walked through the conference

room door, then shoulder to shoulder down the hall. We heard a door close.

"Are they gone?" Eloise asked, tilting her head toward the door.

"I think so," Mary said.

"Mary, go lock the front door and everyone stay seated," Eloise told us.

Mary left the room and returned in a few minutes.

"Does this warrant another pot of coffee?" Mary asked.

"Most likely yes, but you've had your quota" Eloise replied.

That got her a middle finger salute from Mary.

Um, okay, what's that all about?

"Okay, what's up?" Dalia asked, ignoring Mary, and moving the discussion forward.

"While we were meeting, I just received an email from your Gabriel Blackwell," Eloise said.

"You? Why? You're not involved in the case," Dalia said as a frown set upon her face.

"Strangely, after the police contacted him, the first thing he thought of was to make certain he secured Ms. Blake's last will and testament. He went to the bank and retrieved it from their safe deposit box." She stopped and looked around the table.

"One guess who's the beneficiary and executor of the will?" she asked with what appeared a smirk crossing her face.

"Dear God. Don't tell me. He is," Dalia said, dropping her head into her hands.

"Look, Dalia, I seriously do not want anything to do with this character. You know he's going to want to probate the will immediately, and this will turn into one hot mess," Eloise said, pressing her finger hard against the table.

"Not necessarily," Mr. Martin interjected.

"Oh, so now you're an expert in probate matters?" Eloise asked sarcastically.

"No. However, I completed law school, and I assume you have a concern over the slayer rule," he said.

"Slayer rule?" Mary questioned, looking between Eloise and Mr. Martin.

"In the common law of inheritance, it is a doctrine that prohibits inheritance by a person who murders someone from whom he or she stands to inherit. This rule applies to civil law, not criminal law. So, this means that even a person acquitted of the murder in the criminal court, can still be divested of the inheritance by the civil court administering the estate," Eloise explained. "I've watched you people struggle with this case, and frankly, I've always thought from the start that the good doctor had something to do with the Anderson murder. So now with another woman close to him murdered, and might I add with a motive, my guilty needle just moved up to the red zone."

"Hmm," Dalia said and expelled a loud breath. "I know this looks pretty awful. Also, why did he contact you and not me?"

"I have no answer. Moreover, I don't want to even try to get in that man's head," Eloise said, crossing her arms in front of her.

"Look, people, I'm starting to feel a bit overwhelmed here. I want to keep all of this in the firm. It would be a disaster if we had to coordinate with other firms. You never know if there will be leaks that will hurt us in the criminal or civil cases," Dalia held.

"Well, if your guy would stop whacking the people who get in his way, that might lighten your burden," Eloise said.

Lulu let out a quiet laugh that was cut short by a harsh glance from Mary.

"Well, if that's how you truly feel you can't be part of the case. You'd be unable to represent your client zealously," Dalia said annoyed.

"I'd like to take the case," Mr. Martin said as he folded his hands in front of him.

"You've never been involved in such a complex legal matter," Mary said.

"I've been closely associated in probate matters with the life insurance portion through my previous job. I might not know my way around a courtroom, but I've been a working member involved with probate administrative hearings where we refused to pay out on policies," Mr. Martin said.

Everyone's eyes turned to Eloise for a response.

"What?" she said.

"If Mr. Martin does all the legwork, will you oversee him?" Mary asked.

Eloise sat back, crossed her right leg over her left knee, and stared at the wall.

"Here's what I am willing to do. I'll let Mr. Martin run with this if Dalia is also on this portion as well. If we get a whiff that Dr. Blackwell is guilty of her murder, then I have the right to pull out. Period," Eloise stated, making eye contact with Dalia.

"Works for me," Dalia agreed.

"You respond to his email, Dalia. I want limited contact with him; he triggers my creep meter. Mr. M, you can run the probate and if you need me to review the paperwork, I will. But read my lips, *no unnecessary contact with Dr. Blackwell.*"

"I'll need to get with him tomorrow to have him sign a retainer for this matter, preferably right before your meeting. For now, it appears his money worries are over," Mary observed with a lifted brow.

"Or just starting," Eloise opined.

CHAPTER TEN

Poppy

"ALL RIGHT, DOES EVERYONE HAVE WHAT THEY NEED FOR their meeting with Dr. Blackwell?" Mary inquired.

"Should we call him Gabriel as he requested?" I asked.

"Poppy, the only people I call by their first name are folks I trust, so you call him what you want," she said and studied something under the table.

I couldn't help myself. I mimicked Mary, bent over and looked under.

"Jesus Christ, Mary, is that a gun bolted to the table?" I yelled.

Suddenly everyone was bending over to see what was under there.

"Mary, what the hell are you thinking?" Dalia yelled rolling her chair away to get a better look.

"What am I thinking? I'm thinking the man who is about to walk through our doors has people dropping like flies around him. I, for one, will be your line of defense in case he goes postal on us," she announced.

"Oh my God. Then why did we take on the estate portion?

Why not cut our losses and drop him like a hot potato?" Eloise said with disgust. "And I know all about that gun. Jackson has one exactly like it. That bad boy is basically a Colt 45, and can blow someone apart."

"Look, everyone, calm down," Mary said, tapping her hand quickly on the table to get our attention.

"You realize if you shoot from that point, you'll blow our legs off," Mr. Martin commented calmly.

"Of course, I realize that, and I'd have to cock the hammer to shoot it. It's not an automatic firearm, for God' sake." Her voice now had a tinge of anger to it.

"I'm with Mary. If it weren't for her being armed when Mr. Lansing had broken into the car and tried to kidnap us, we'd be dead. Keep that fucker handy, Mary," Lulu said with an affirmative nod.

Mary gazed at the screen which monitored the exterior door. Dr. Blackwell had just come off the elevator and was making his way to the entrance.

"I'll greet him, you all stay here. Also, Mary, don't you dare touch that gun. I am sure you're breaking a multitude of laws. We need to talk!" Dalia exclaimed.

"It's not an assault weapon, Dalia, so don't over-dramatize this," Mary said.

"It appears to be a Public Defender Revolver, a small shotgun that fits in your pocket," Mr. Martin added.

"What, are you crazy? Put that thing away in your office," Dalia ordered.

"Too late, he's at the desk and walking this way," Mary said with a Cheshire smile.

"No other weapons? I'm disappointed," Lulu said, returning her smile.

Mary leaned over slightly, unhooked something from the leg, and placed it on the tabletop.

"What are you going to do, beat him to death with a flashlight?" Eloise asked sarcastically.

"Flashlight, Taser, stun gun," Mary responded.

I love this woman—a real, honest to God arms dealer.

The door opened, and Dalia walked through with Dr. Blackwell. He looked around and took the empty seat at the end of the table, directly across from Mary.

"Gabriel, we are all sorry for your loss," Dalia said, extending the firm's sympathy to him.

"Thank you. And thank you for meeting with me. As you can probably understand I feel overwhelmed by the events that have occurred and find it nearly impossible to work. I had no idea how depressed Sandy was, and I didn't identify the symptoms in time. I hold myself responsible," he said making eye contact with me.

If he thought I was young, dumb, and could tap into me for sympathy, then he was so wrong. Over this last year, I had heard every sob story. All my clients had one to tell. Also, for people I didn't know personally, my heart had become a hardened shell. Sort of.

"If you are up to it, we need to form a strategy to protect you on several fronts. I will continue to work on any criminal matters that arise. Tallulah is working the wrongful death aspect, and Mr. Martin is in charge of the estate portion. Let me start with Tallulah; she can discuss the plan on her end," Dalia said and took her seat.

"What about Poppy?" he asked, staring at me.

"Poppy?" Dalia questioned, tipping her head to the side.

"What is she doing for me?" he asked, holding my stare.

"She's floating between the cases as needed. I am still the point person," Mary stated and gathered her papers.

I was beginning to understand why he triggered Eloise's creep meter, despite his exotic good looks. Ted Bundy was wholesome and handsome and also quite the lady killer.

"Okay. Well then. I have done several things on the wrongful death action," Lulu stated sliding each person a folder with papers clipped inside. "On your behalf, we are filing an answer to the petition for the wrongful death action, interrogatories, a motion for a protective order, and a motion for summary judgment. I also have someone digging into Ms. Anderson's background. I want to know everything I can about her: friends, enemies, lovers. Whom she owed money to and if she had a dark side."

"In English, please, on what you are filing," Dr. Blackwell said, turning toward her.

"We must respond to the accusations, and that is what we've done. They have served notice to take your deposition immediately, which means they can ask you any questions they wish which are even tangentially relevant to the case. It's a fishing expedition. I need to stop that from happening, so I moved to quash the deposition and requested the judge to issue a protective order, so you don't have to sit for the deposition. I don't want them using something they can obtain in the civil realm against you in the criminal matter," Lulu said.

"Will the fact that Sandra is dead help us?" he asked.

Well, I had not seen that coming. Neither did Lulu, who looked startled.

"The fact that they cannot elicit information from her which might hurt your case certainly benefits us," she carefully phrased her response.

"Such as your reconciliation agreement you had with your wife. That document had the potential to cause some serious damage. Without her to authenticate it, the prosecution will not likely be allowed to use it. In fact, I'm sure they will never be able to find it at this point." Mary threw out and waited to see if her grenade exploded.

"Ah yes, that agreement. I did not keep a copy, and I don't know what became of Sandra's original. However, the legal counsel who reviewed it before I signed it, assured me he would easily deal with it if necessary or I would never have signed it," he said with a tone of smugness.

We all waited for someone to respond, but the statement was left unchallenged.

"Anyway, I think they jumped the gun on suing. Be that as it may, I will do everything in my power to delay and challenge it moving forward," Lulu assured him.

He then looked at Dalia.

"The police want to take your statement concerning the death of your wife. You don't have to cooperate. And frankly, as you may have been the last person to see her alive, I would at this point discourage you from giving a voluntary interview," Dalia said.

"I had no intention of cooperating with them," he told her shifting to the left in his seat.

That's odd. Dr. Gabriel was more than willing to sit for a first and second interview on the Marsha Anderson murder, but not his wife's investigation. I'd be down at the station demanding hourly updates. I am sure they would accuse me of micromanaging whatever investigation the police undertook if it was my relative.

"You realize that by not cooperating with the police as to

who may have murdered her, could throw you in a bad light," Mary taunted.

"Murder! Who said anything about murder? They found her in the pool, and the pills were on a table. I assume she killed herself," he said with flatness in his voice that troubled me.

"How do you know there were pills on the table?" Mary asked, flashing right back at him, not giving him a moment to think.

"We had a drink, and I left through the back gate. I didn't say anything when I saw the tablets. Sandy's a grown-up," he said.

"The detectives said they found two glasses. One empty," Dalia followed up.

"That was hers, which I'm sure the police will discover when they fingerprint them," he opined.

"Not necessarily. Cut crystal might prove difficult for prints," Dalia added.

"Ah, yes, true. Well, that's what they get paid for, right? It's their job to chase down clues, not ours to deflect. Now I'm more concerned about probating the will," he said turning to Eloise.

"Mr. Martin is overseeing that," Eloise responded.

"What can I expect?" Dr. Blackwell asked.

I held my breath waiting for Mary to say something snide, but she kept her tongue.

"Everything appears to be in order as far as the will construction. You are the only beneficiary, and there are no other heirs. The court should appoint you the executor to administrate the estate. I will notify any creditors and ask you to take an inventory of her personal and tangible property and real estate holdings. We'll deal with taxes as they rise. The court will issue an order transferring any titles accordingly. Insurance will pass outside the probate court as well as her retirement funds or cash and mutual accounts," Mr. Martin advised.

Dr. Blackwell reached into his coat and produced an envelope and slid it toward Mr. Martin.

"On that flash drive is the entire inventory of her estate. I cataloged everything she owned. I also listed the value of the tangible, personal, and real estate property."

Dr. Blackwell sat back and placed his right ankle across his left knee.

"How fortuitous of you to have this ready," Mary said with a raised brow.

"Not really. I was prepared for Sandy to pull the pin on the reconciliation clause and start divorce proceedings. I just wanted to be one step ahead to mount a valiant fight," he answered with a shrug.

Everyone was silent. *That man was one cold bastard.*

"Now bring me up to speed on the Anderson matter," he requested brushing his pant leg.

"The arraignment is in three weeks, and we are collecting information. By the end of the week, I should have the police record. We have permission for an independent forensic evaluator to look at the car. The full autopsy report takes a while, and the fact she was pregnant complicates things," Dalia said.

"You know they can test the fetus for paternity?" Mary said.

God, Mary had some balls to be taunting him. If I were him, I'd wonder if she was on my side.

"I went to medical school you realize? I welcome it. I'm waiting patiently for the results to be released, so I'm exonerated. Then their theory of my motive will be as dead as her.

There is no way it was mine," Dr. Blackwell shot back.

Mr. Martin remained silent and didn't attempt to argue with him about a probability and statistics issue. Undoubtedly a good move. He seemed confident it wasn't his. I wonder if he had run a test already and kept that from us.

"Now, how much do I need to make the check out to fill the coffers?" he asked.

"Another twenty thousand," Mary said.

"That seems a little steep for an uncontested probate matter," he said as he reached for his checkbook.

"That includes our representation on the investigation front for your wife's death," Mary returned.

"What? That was clearly a suicide. They can't tie me into that. Moreover, once the DNA comes back not mine, they should dismiss those charges in the Anderson matter," he said waiting for a new number.

"It's up to you. If you want us to work with the police on both matters, that's the number," Mary insisted.

"I guarantee there is no way they can tie me into Sandra's misfortune," he said. "Trust me."

"Let's keep that good thought," Dalia said, trying to defuse the escalating situation.

"So, we will hasten this probate matter, right?" he asked.

"I have all the paperwork ready, and with your inventory, that should speed things up substantially," Mr. Martin advised him. "I reviewed the will, and it sets out the specifics of the insurance policy information in the body of it so I will contact the company directly. Once the ME releases the death certificate, we can move forward."

Dr. Blackwell ripped the check from the booklet and slid it toward Mary.

"Why do we have to wait on the death certificate?" Dr. Blackwell asked with a puzzled expression.

"If the ME records the cause of death as a homicide, then I suppose the insurance company may put the check on hold. Ten million dollars is a large payout," Mary answered leaning forward.

"Homicide. That's ridiculous. The woman drowned," Dr. Blackwell argued.

"She had a gash in her head, which probably red-flagged something to look at closely," Dalia said.

"Well, I'm paying you people a lot of money to grease the wheels. Let's close these matters out quickly." He stood and tugged at his coat.

"We'll do our very best," Mary replied and smiled. The smile never reached her eyes.

"I can see myself out," he said, picking up his manila folder.

"No worries, I have to lock the door anyway," Dalia said and left with him.

When Dalia returned, Mary broke the overwhelming silence.

"Do we cash this check?" Mary asked, waving it around.

"Of course. Look, no way that man would win a popularity contest. Right now there is nothing concrete to prove that he has been a part of anything sinister. We all have a lot of ideas and questions floating around. However, until test results come back, we owe him the benefit of the doubt," Dalia lectured.

Mr. Martin raised his elbows on the table and leaned forward. He folded his hands together in front of him and touched his nose to his bent knuckles. Was he praying?

"Having second thoughts, Mr. Martin?" Eloise asked with

a slight laugh.

"Ask me after the toxicology report comes out on his wife," he replied.

"Everyone get busy. We stand adjourned," Mary stated.

"Mary, get rid of the gun," Eloise said as she left the room.

CHAPTER ELEVEN

Poppy

THE REST OF THE MORNING WAS A BLUR. I SIFTED THROUGH THE witness statements that Mary had transcribed from hospital personnel who would talk to her. It appeared the nurses and the ancillary staff was a chatty bunch. However, the doctors and administrators had circled the wagons and were stingy with their information. Even though we were helping one of their own, nobody wanted any involvement with a murder. I could understand the fear of being called into court to testify.

One nurse, in particular, who gave the outward appearance of being a good friend of Marsha the victim, gave answers that were inconsistent. It made me wonder if she was another of Dr. Blackwell's paramours. God knows how many we would find once we started turning over all the rocks.

"Are you ready to talk to the witness?" Mary asked.

"Yes," I replied.

I was very excited to be a part of talking to the roommate. When gathering information, it was critical to study a person's body language and demeanor. And it was often what someone didn't reveal that was as important as what they did.

"Mary, I'm looking at the nurse Wesley's statement, and it's riddled with inconsistencies. For example, she stated she had not known that Marsha and Dr. Blackwell were lovers, yet, made a point to tell you she saw her sneak out of the hospital with him a time or two. And here, let me find it, she attended a weekend seminar with Marsha where Dr. Blackwell was a keynote speaker. On that Saturday night, she indicated Marsha hadn't returned to her room. It's almost as if she wants to tell us but doesn't want to betray Marsha's memory or something," I said.

I know when we women wanted to be catty you could always leave it up to someone's imagination once you drop enough breadcrumbs. Or, my all-time favorite was to preface a spiteful revelation with, "bless her heart," then let it rip. As if that would mitigate the damage your sharp tongue would inflict.

"Good point. Yes. You're reading the transcription without the benefit of seeing Wesley. She fidgeted, wasn't able to maintain eye contact and probably drank a gallon of water. I want to come back to her once we have more material so I can ask her to confirm things rather than pull information out of her. There's a fine line between interviewing and interrogating," Mary said.

"How did you get your private investigator license?" I asked.

I was amused yet somewhat in awe of Mary's colorful background which involved being a private investigator at ninety.

"It's a long story; the short version is I worked with Jackson and Cillian on a case when they were in the FBI. I knew that's what I wanted to do, the challenge it offered energized me beyond anything I've done before. The government got in the way, as it often does, and said I was too old and would be a risk to others. I sued on an age discrimination claim, won, and the jury awarded me a pot full of money. And, as much as I enjoyed the course, it's your gut that matters. You can study gestures for years. As the Supreme Court said about obscenity, you can't really define it; but you know it when you see it. So much of what I do requires that I rely on instinct instead of trying to study the signs you learn in courses," she said.

Before we could continue, Dalia had texted Mary, she was waiting out front for us.

Before the passenger door even slammed closed, Dalia turned to Mary.

"Best behavior, don't try to badger her. After we finish the interviews, I'm turning them over to Lee. I want him to look them over to make sure we didn't miss anything."

"Who's Lee?" I asked as she eased away from the curb.

"Lee Stone," Mary replied, turning around. "Lee works more with Jackson's group as an investigator when needed. He was a police officer with the Chicago P.D. and spent his last few years in the homicide division. Lee worked a case with us and stayed on when we needed him. He does wood sculpting full time, and the furniture in the office is some of his work."

"Oh, wow. That is awesome. I had no idea what a complete complement of personnel you had at your disposal. This firm is an exciting place to work," I told her.

"His wife, Belle, was a New York homicide detective before she married him. She had also been part of the case Lee worked on for us. She writes novels full time now and earns a good living at it. Once I have the pieces, I need to put a defense strategy together, and I'll tap into her expertise," Dalia said.

"So why didn't she join your firm? It seems like it would be a great fit," I said.

"She couldn't walk across the bridge to what she calls the dark side. To be honest, I have days when I question my choice myself. I have just completed a degree in cybersecurity, and that's where my heart is, but I have to get some practical experience to make use of my book knowledge. Cillian and Jackson will bring me in on those types of cases. However, for my level of experience they are few and far between right now," she said.

"Cybersecurity! You would think that would be the hot ticket," I replied.

"It is if that's all you do. There's a lot of competition out there, and honestly, I'm content where I am for now," she said.

"Any tips about where hackers will hit next?"

"I tell everyone to make sure they have a stash of cold hard cash available. The hackers keep taking a run on the banks. Someday they will penetrate their firewall, and you will hear the crash around the world. You'll need cash for the basics for at least a month," she said.

"Well, that's putting a gloomy spin on our day, Dalia. So, let's switch to how we're going to hit this roommate," Mary interrupted.

Mary was right, but Dalia gave me something to consider. Why couldn't the hackers just hack into the system and wipe out the student loan and credit card debt? I could get behind that type of market instability.

"I think we should let Poppy take the lead. Sometimes younger people can't relate to me and seem to feel a certain connection to their own age range," Mary said.

My stomach did a flip. I had limited experience in the area of witness interviews. My fear was I would come across more like an interrogator than an interviewer.

Dalia looked in the rearview mirror to catch my eye.

"No offense, Poppy, but I think you're a little green right now. I want you to watch a few, and then we'll set you up with something not so vital. I want to make sure we don't shut this person down, and we may have to tiptoe around her. Is that okay?" Dalia asked.

"More than okay," I responded. "I haven't taken many independent witness statements, and I definitely would be uncomfortable."

"Ladies, we have arrived," Dalia said.

The area was what you would expect to be for a person earning over two hundred thousand dollars a year. We entered a gated apartment community that hosted manicured landscaping and well-kept buildings made of brick and lots of thick tinted glass. A golf course for those like-minded and multiple tennis courses spread throughout the area. We found building B and eased into a designated visitor parking space.

"Mary, if you have your usual set of weapons in your purse, you can leave it in the trunk. Or promise me you won't open the weapon storage bag in this person's presence," Dalia said.

"Not to worry. All I have is my key chain. No guns, knives, or mace," she said.

I wondered if she was joking, but I had a feeling she wasn't. I had to have her outfit me with an arsenal just like hers. Then I'd be as badass.

Dalia led the way, and as we approached, we saw the curtains pull back from a large plate-glass window. And, before we could knock, the door opened. A well-dressed young woman in her middle twenties with curly red hair extended a hand to each of us. She introduced herself as Nancy Carlston and welcomed us.

She furnished the home with high-end furniture, several pieces of beautiful artwork, and not a thing out of place. Envy crept through me as I thought about the meager apartment I would return to later today.

"Please, have a seat on the couch. Can I get you ladies anything to drink?" she asked.

We declined.

"Thank you for seeing us. I know this must be difficult, so we'll be as brief as possible. Would you mind if I record this interview? It helps me organize my thoughts later," Dalia inquired.

"I have no objection, except if we place it on the record by recording it, I want assurance it is only for your work product. I need your promise you won't use it later for any other purpose. I don't want it falling into someone's hands, nor have it used to impeach me later." Nancy smiled and folded her hands on her lap.

Work product and impeach, both legal terms not within the vocabulary of most everyday folk. I wonder if Dalia would pick that apart.

"No, that's fine. You're doing us a favor by speaking to us, and we want this to be comfortable for you," Dalia said.

Dalia removed the recorder while Mary took out a pad and pen from her bag. I decided just to observe. She then placed the disclaimer on the recording.

"I'm just going to go through the initial background information to start. How did you know the victim?"

"Marsha and I met at a Narcotics Anonymous meeting three years ago. We both had gone down the rabbit hole of drug dependency; an addiction picked up in college. She liked her Ritalin, which she gradually branched out into different types of amphetamines. I got hooked on pain pills after a skiing accident in my junior year of college."

"And as far as you know, Marsha was clean?" Dalia asked.

"Oh, absolutely. At the hospital, they did random drug testing, and they would have caught something," Nancy said.

"What do you know about her family?" Dalia asked.

"Not much. Marsha visited them a few times a year, but they weren't really close. I think they live in Maine. And I didn't appreciate them swooping in here the other day to clean out her stuff without me being here. The day they came, they left a note on the door indicating they would be back the next day to take whatever furniture was hers and I should have everything marked."

"That seems a bit odd. Would it be difficult to identify Marsha's property?" Dalia asked.

"No, because all she owned was what was in her room. I paid for all this in the common area from an inheritance. And when they unexpectedly came ready to cart stuff away in a U-Haul, there was quite a scene. Thankfully I had all the receipts available to prove I bought everything, and still, they didn't believe me. They accused me of taking cash from her to pay for half of the property. The nerve! Her mother was spouting off that she'd see me in court. What a piece of work," Nancy said, rubbing her pant legs in agitation.

"I see..." Dalia started.

"I loved Marsha, but that girl did not know how to live within her means. I can't show you the three closets that were stuffed with her clothes because they took them all, but everything was high-end. They probably will get a pretty penny for them in some consignment shops. Her shoes ranged from fourteen hundred dollars a pair and up. And she even had a safe to put her designer bags inside. Add the Mercedes, although a bitchin' car, it was nothing but a black hole money pit," she added.

"So, she liked to live large," Mary interjected.

"Yes, well beyond her means. She was behind in her car payment; the student loan people were calling night and day. I even got a call from them because she wasn't returning their calls. Now, this may sound judgmental, but I still think it was wrong what she was doing."

Here comes the good stuff. She probably was going to go off on a tear about Dr. Blackwell and being his sugar baby.

"Selling off her body for money, that was just plain wrong," she said and shook her head.

"Wait, are you saying she was an escort or a prostitute?" Dalia asked with an elevation to her voice.

God, if that were true, then it would open a vast pool of suspects. If so, we hit pay dirt.

"Oh, no. Well, I'm not sure if what Marsha did was better or worse," Nancy said.

We sat in silence. Nancy stood and walked over to a desk and retrieved two cards and a pamphlet.

"It all started when she sold her eggs to a fertility clinic in New York. That was about two years ago. The egg donation process started with an application. Once the clinic approved her as a donor, and after a series of interviews and tests, she had to match a recipient. Some people never find a match. The egg donation cycle itself took about three to four weeks, and I helped her administer hormonal medications to help her ovaries produce multiple eggs. She had hoped for the high-end payout of fourteen thousand dollars but only walked away with eight. Marsha aspired to be labeled a high-demand egg donor, but they wound up not using her again," Nancy said.

She handed Dalia a card from the clinic and a glossy pamphlet that described how egg donation worked. I had no idea such things existed.

"When they wouldn't commit to buying more eggs from her, that's when she got involved in the surrogate program," she said.

"Now, then, what?" Dalia asked with a bit of a stutter.

"The surrogate program. Marsha became a surrogate for a family that wanted a child but could not have one. All I know is that someone placed seventy-five thousand dollars in an escrow account for her. The program paid all her medical expenses, and the money in the escrow would be turned over to her when the baby was born. That card is the OB-GYN involved," Nancy reported.

We were all in shock, no one moved. Mary was the first to speak.

"How far along was she?"

"About ten weeks. Marsha had an ultrasound, and recent blood draw to determine the sex of the baby. It was a boy. In fact, she found out two days before someone murdered her," she said.

"Do you know if she had shared her plans with Dr. Blackwell? I mean to be a surrogate," Dalia asked.

"No, I have no idea," she replied with a shrug.

"Well, this puts a whole new spin on our investigation. Thank you for the information and the cards. Once we can digest all this, we may have more questions. Would it be okay to call you again?"

"I'd really rather stay as far away from this as possible. I'm certain her parents have no idea about the surrogate business, and I don't want them coming back demanding information. I'm just waiting for them to serve me with a lawsuit to try to get their hands on my furniture. What a nightmare those people are!"

"We'll keep that in mind," Dalia said.

We thanked her and left knowing motive may have just been removed. Except if she had tried to extort money from Dr. Blackwell telling him the baby was his. Had we moved forward or just stepped sideways.

CHAPTER TWELVE

Poppy

MY STOMACH DID A FLIP AND ROLL. IT FELT LIKE THE ONE TIME I drank too much rum and Coke and puked until I couldn't stand. The opening scene of *Look Who's Talking*, where millions of sperm were talking smack rushing at an egg to fertilize it kept playing through my mind on a closed loop. Only now I saw it in reverse. The eggs were chasing down one lone sperm.

Marsha must have had emotional issues far beyond my comprehension to put her body through what she did for material gain. Of course, it wasn't about the actual possessions. It was more an internal emptiness she filled up with things. This was a Ph.D. in psychology level head case.

"Can we stop somewhere for a cup of coffee, please? My head is feeling a little woozy. Is it a low blood sugar attack or the visual of dozens of eggs being mass produced in some clinic causing me to have an issue? It's a toss-up," I said.

"I'm always up for coffee. I have a bag of jelly beans, here, take it. If it's low blood sugar, it will pick you right up," Mary said.

At some point, I would have to ask Mary if I could look

inside her bottomless bag. And maybe even set up a duplicate one for me. *Weapons and candy, every girl's dream.*

"Wow, that was some bombshell." Dalia blew out a long breath.

We took a moment to reflect on what we heard. I staved off an internal battle of what I felt. Who was I to judge people's choices? Oh hell, that reel kept playing.

"Yes, it most certainly was. Now the question is, do we let the prosecution know or keep that to ourselves? If we tell them will they try to brush over it? I'm concerned they might attempt to paint it as an irrelevant issue," Mary said.

"You know we won't be able to get a copy of her medical records, especially the clinic ones, without good cause. I'm not convinced if the pregnancy alone without more information will buy us a ticket to them. And I am confident that the doctor and clinic will refuse to talk to us voluntarily. We'll need a court order to get past the privacy issues," Dalia said.

"So, we just wait to see if they produce the records during discovery, and if they don't, then we should start the fight?" I asked.

"No, I have an idea. Hold on, let me get Lulu on the phone," Dalia said as she used the onboard service to dial Lulu.

Within two rings Lulu answered, and we heard her through the speakers.

"Lulu, I have you on speaker," Dalia said.

"What's up?" Lulu asked. I heard her ink-jet printer spitting out paper.

"We just came from a meeting with the roommate. She told us that Marsha Anderson was selling her body parts for money," Dalia informed her.

There was dead silence.

"You mean like selling a kidney on the black market?" Lulu whispered.

"No. Marsha was selling her eggs to a clinic in New York. Then when that didn't earn her the pot of money she hoped for, she went down the surrogacy road. The baby Marsha was carrying was for an infertile couple. After the delivery she was to net seventy-five thousand dollars," Dalia responded.

"Oh," was all Lulu said breathlessly.

"Any comment?" Dalia asked.

"Well, that totally caught me off guard. I don't know what to say. The law hasn't caught up with technology, so there aren't many legal opinions out there about this issue. Do we know if it was a gestational surrogacy? Or if she had a contract with the couple or a pre-birth order? I think Colorado is somewhat gestational surrogacy friendly, but no laws govern it. So that leaves both parties fairly exposed," Lulu said.

"Right now, I have no idea how they set anything up to make it legally binding. All I have is this small piece of information from the roommate."

"Geez, that's not much if it's even true," Lulu offered.

"We don't know if the D.A. has any of this information yet, and it might be critical to our defense. I'm back and forth on telling them now. Or should I wait until the arraignment when I move to have the charges dismissed? However, I thought you might be able to get her medical records by setting up a deposition with the doctor involved with the surrogate program. We need to determine if it is a legitimate program and not some baby-selling scheme. I looked him up, and all it says is he's an OB-GYN that specializes in fertility issues. Getting her records from the clinic might be even more difficult because they are out of state. So, since you can start discovery right away in the civil case, I thought maybe you could jump in and track down the medical records," Dalia suggested.

"Since the whole basis of the wrongful death claim is that Dr. Blackwell is the father, and the motive was to get rid of the baby, I'm sure I could make an argument for those records. Otherwise, that pesky little Health Insurance Portability and Accountability Act might prevent that based on confidentiality," Lulu said.

"Great. You get to work on that, and I'll think about how best to drop this on the D.A.," Dalia replied.

They disconnected.

"Are you feeling better, Poppy?" Dalia asked looking at me in the rearview mirror.

"Much. I must have had a blood sugar drop. I can wait for the coffee."

"Good. I was hoping you could do some background research about the clinic in New York, and the doctor here in Colorado. See if there have been any state or federal lawsuits or malpractice claims filed with the Medical Board of Examiners. I don't know how we can find out about any contracts except through the OB doctor. Hopefully, Lulu can discover that through the wrongful death case. I don't know why, but this whole thing doesn't sit well with me. I understand if you feel a calling to help someone to conceive, don't get me wrong. But to reproduce for money feels like a slippery slope on a moral and legal front," Dalia said.

"I think that's a little sexist," Mary said turning her head to look out the window.

"How so?" Dalia asked with a hint of anger.

"Men have been selling their sperm for years. You saw that Washington Post piece that revealed the astonishing number of related siblings from one donor. That particular donor sired at least twenty-nine girls and sixteen boys, now ages one to twenty-one, living in eight states and four countries. If those sperm banks keep using the same guy over and over, there's a worry he'll father so many kids they could marry their relative," Mary said with a shrug.

"Not that this moral argument isn't of great interest, but I want to follow up on what you need me to do in my research," I said.

"Oh, right, sorry. I already said find out what you can about the clinic and doctor. Also, see what the standard requirements are for the surrogate. You know, like do they have to pass a psychological evaluation, are there any physical requirements, does the place do a background check. I want to see if this doctor is doing this independently or going through an agency. I still can't wrap my head around this seemingly well-balanced woman doing something so extreme to put her money toward material possessions," Dalia said.

"Would you rather she sells her blood?" Mary asked.

"I'd rather her work a second job," Dalia responded without a pause.

"Why does this bother you so much?" Mary asked.

"There are so many things that could go wrong. What if the child develops some chromosomal abnormality? Then who is responsible for the child? If Marsha slipped and did drugs that harmed the baby, then what…" Dalia said.

"Again, sorry to break in but I think we are going off track. I want to make sure I cover anything you need," I said.

"It's just a hot button. Okay, back on track. Now Nancy said they met at Narcotics Anonymous so check the nursing licensure site and see if Marsha's ever been in trouble with the nursing board," Dalia said.

I was quietly thinking about the whole process.

"Something wrong?" Dalia asked.

"I just feel icky, like we are tarnishing the victim's character or memory. She wasn't doing anything illegal. It wasn't her fault someone murdered her," I said.

"Please don't feel that way. I am trying to get a handle on who this person was in life. Did she do something to piss someone off who came after her? Did she try to back out and want to keep the baby or maybe she tried to up her remuneration? Had she told another man he was the father to double or triple dip? This is an unusual circumstance, and we owe Dr. Blackwell a duty to leave no stone unturned. He says he didn't do it, and we have to believe him," Dalia said.

"How long for the lab to process the DNA to determine the parentage?" I asked.

"They can push it through in two hours if they want. However, it depends on when they finish the autopsy," Mary said.

"Do you think they'll drop the charges if the paternity test comes back disproving him the father?" I asked.

"That's their cornerstone for arrest as far as I know. But I don't have all the evidence yet. So too soon to guess," Dalia stated.

"I would hope after this mess that the man slows down on his wayward ways," I sighed.

"Don't count on it," Mary said with a sarcastic laugh. "If you gave him the green light right now, I guarantee he'd be trying to have his way with you."

"Um, not a pleasant thought," I said.

And his wife would roll in her grave.

"We're almost back to the office. I'll drop you two off, and I want to swing by Lee's. I have a few questions for him, and I want to bounce some things around. Okay?" Dalia asked.

"Sure."

"Wait, I just got a text. Stay by your phone because Declan indicated they are releasing the car for us to look at later today. I'll meet you back here in about an hour and a half," Dalia said.

CHAPTER THIRTEEN

Poppy

"**P**EOPLE, GRAB YOUR NOTEBOOK, AND I HAVE MY NIKON camera. We're heading to the police impound. They've released the car for us to inspect. Lee and Gabriel will meet us there," Dalia told us.

"This should be interesting. I am anxious to see how Dr. Blackwell reacts to the scene of the crime," Mary said.

We took almost thirty minutes to arrive at the impound. Lee was on the scene, and Dr. Blackwell had yet to arrive. Dalia let the officer on duty at the gate know we were waiting for him.

We parked and found Lee, who was already moving around, camera in hand taking photos of the vehicle. It was apparent the luxury Mercedes was the scene of a violent crime. The rain had washed the blood from the driver door on the outside, but it was the inside that told the story. The interior was intact, and a bloody roadmap of where Marsha spent her last dying moments.

"Ladies, there's really not much to see you haven't looked at in the crime scene photos," he said.

"Can you tell if someone forced the driver's door open

from the outside or was it voluntarily opened?" Dalia asked.

"No. So let's start making some observations. If you start with the driver side, you'll see the seat is not pushed back to accommodate a larger person. My guess is someone about five-four, maybe five-five was the last driver which is consistent with Marsha Anderson. Now walk around to the passenger side. What do you see?" he asked.

We walked around to the door, he already opened and looked in.

"The seat is fairly level with the other side. So, it doesn't look like someone very tall was in the passenger seat. I'm new to this, but I'd say if someone made her drive to the place it wasn't a man unless he fixed the seat back to the original position before he left. What I'm saying is I don't think a man was in the car with her," I offered.

"Excellent. Now, what do you also notice about the driver's side?" he queried.

We walked back around.

"Okay, I'll take a stab at this and just give you my impressions as they hit me and tell you how the story unfolds as it comes to me," I said.

Lee nodded, and Mary smiled her approval.

"The window is three quarters down. So, I would suggest that someone may have pulled up next to Marsha, and she lowered the window to speak to the person. Because it's November, and the weather has been cold at night, she probably wouldn't be driving with it down that much for fresh air. Leaving the parking deck at night she wouldn't lower it except to swipe her card to exit, and then for a safety factor would put it back up.

"I believe she may have spoken to someone through the open window. From the crime scene photos maybe she got out, perhaps to talk to them face-to-face. Which would suggest she knew the person. From that point, I think the person may have been standing more toward the front left of the door, you know, here, where there's the hinge. I believe that is the place where someone may have hit her with an object. She stumbled back and was either stunned or dying at that point. She probably lost her balance and fell back into the car and sat. Then I think the assailant hit her face to stun her and get her under control. Her head fell forward and then came the final blow on the top of her head," I said.

"How did you reach that conclusion?" Lee asked.

"The pictures of Marsha showed someone hit her on the right side of her head and the top. So, I think the right-side blow stunned her. However, the top blow that breached her skull killed her. Also, she had blood smeared on her right palm. Maybe she grabbed her head after getting hit. Then, like I said, stumbled back, and fell backward into the seat. The left side of her face also had abrasions. So, maybe someone came around, faced her, then hit her to stun her when she tried to get out. It was then someone struck the final blow on the top of the head," I said.

"Yes, that's exactly what I think happened. There's not much blood, which would be consistent with a closed head injury. The trauma to the right side was probably the one that stunned her. While the pain gripped her, her hand reflexively grabbed the area, and it threw her off-balance. That gave the person enough time to walk around the open door, maybe punch her in the face if she raised her hand to protect herself and then strike the killing blow. I'd say the person was left handed if the object was a small murder weapon. Only if it was bigger and needed two hands, then it's up for grabs," he stated.

"So, the reason there's not a lot of blood as most head injuries produce is…" Mary started.

"Probably because she died instantly from the blow to the top of the head and it was fairly self-contained," I offered.

"I guess she stood outside the door while it was open. She faced the person who stood on the opposite side of the door. If you look at the placement of the wound on the right back of the head, it would be my guess the person was about the same height as she was, possibly an inch or so taller, but the arc of a swing would indicate a level height. If the person were very much taller the hit would be higher up," Lee said.

"Then, does that rule out Dr. Blackwell?" I asked them.

"Nothing rules anyone out yet. Marsha could have turned to her left and tried to duck as she saw the weapon coming at her from her right and that would give a taller person the ability to land a blow from above. Until we get the autopsy report, we have mostly supposition," he said.

"Why leave the car door open after they left?" Mary inquired.

"Maybe they panicked, or maybe they hoped some form of wildlife would find the body and destroy the evidence. Who knows what goes through someone's mind? Still, I think this was a premeditated murder only because they brought the weapon with them. And the person probably concealed it in their left hand," Lee said.

"What if she was the one with a weapon, and the person disarmed her?" I asked.

"I'd imagine you would see signs of a scuffle, and the gravel around the car wasn't really disrupted," he said.

"What about someone hitting her from behind?" I asked.

"I believe she would have stumbled and fallen forward on

the ground," Lee said.

"No, I mean what if someone was hiding in the back seat, made her drive here, then hit her on the side of the head and then the top," I asked.

"I think you'd see more blood in the car and not on the outside roof. Also, the headrest might be an impediment," Lee said.

"Yes, good point," I replied.

"Let me get a picture from the angle we are talking about. Poppy, you be the victim and, Dalia, you be the assailant and then Lee. This way we'll have it from both perspectives, equal height and taller. Then I can apply some software and manipulate the angles and line up the wound areas," Mary stated. "And same with hitting her from the front once seated."

It creeped me the hell out to put myself in Marsha's shoes as she lay dying. Also, it made me more empathetic to her as I channeled her death.

"Well, that's it. I'm disappointed Gabriel didn't come. Makes me wonder..." Mary said.

"Don't go there, Mary, just don't," Dalia said, shaking her head and walking back toward the car.

Lee shut Marsha's car door, and we left him standing evaluating the car from the front. My gut said a woman did this, and for now, I trusted my gut.

CHAPTER
FOURTEEN

Tallulah

"I'VE TRACKED DOWN SEVERAL SAFE-DEPOSIT BOXES SCATTERED throughout the area for Abernathy," Jackson said, plopping in a chair.

He handed me a list of the banks that included when the boxes were rented and last accessed. They were all outside a fifty-mile radius. Except for one. It had been opened within the last three years and was within a three-mile radius.

"Tell me what you see that will put a smile on your face," he said interlocking his fingers across his chest.

I scanned the paper, and Vanessa's name jumped out. I circled the entire line then placed the paper on my desk.

"This looks like a box opened right after he and Vanessa married. It's the only one that has her name on it along with his and within walking distance," I said.

"And..." he encouraged making a circular hand motion.

"That one box appears used by him the most. Only him, over the last three years. However, it seems to have been dormant since the divorce papers hit him," I replied.

"I think you need to call your client and see if she remembers signing a card for the box and see if she has a key. If she doesn't, then call the bank and arrange for them to have some-one meet us to drill the box lock," Jackson said.

"Okay."

I quickly found her in my contacts and dialed her number.

"Vanessa, this is Tallulah. We have found a safe-deposit box in your name and Richard's. Do you remember going to a bank and signing a card for it?" I asked.

"No, I certainly don't. Where is this box?" she asked. Her voice came back over the phone.

"It's at the Bank of Stanhope on Mason Street. I will email the information to you. I want to get into that box and see what's inside. Since you don't remember opening it, then you won't have a key. So, tell the bank manager you have lost your key and need him to arrange a person to drill the box. Tell him you will be there in an hour. Jackson and I will meet you there," I told her.

She agreed, and I disconnected. With three clicks the infor-mation was on its way. I then turned my attention back to him.

"What else did you find?" I asked.

He blew out a long, frustrated sigh.

"It's clear that this guy is moving money around and some-one is helping him to clean it. What I am going to tell you stays between you and me," he said.

My body went on alert, and I felt myself holding my breath.

"Of course. But can I bring Dalia in on it?" I asked.

"No, no one, not even your client or things could get com-promised," he said leaning forward.

"Okay," I said, releasing my breath.

"I've made some informal inquiries about your boy with my people at the FBI. He is firmly on their radar and is a target. Trust me."

"Anything in particular?" I asked.

"Your guy has diversified his money-laundering schemes. We know about the art and books. But he is using two methods that are rarely used in the western world. Which leads them to believe there may be a Middle Eastern connection. Any time that a Middle Eastern country on a particular list comes into play, they follow it to see if it's a potential terror cell. What he has himself hooked up with are hawalas, an underground banking system, and the Colombian Black-Market Peso Exchange," he said with raised eyebrows.

"I've heard of hawalas, but not the Colombian exchange," I said.

"It's linked to narcotics trafficking," Jackson said.

"I know you don't want this to leave the room, but I'd like to have Mr. Martin in on this at some point soon. If he's putting everything together for me, this is vital information," I insisted.

"Lulu, the fact I got this from a contact could put their investigation at risk. If even one person knows about it and makes a blunder, everything could implode. For now, let's keep it tight," he said.

"Okay, so what does this mean for Vanessa?" I asked.

"She's not mentioned in the hawala and CBMPE issues. However, because of that insurance fraud, they are probably all over his offshore banking and shell companies. So, your client is now right smack in the middle of the investigation," he said.

"They said that? The FBI said Vanessa is under investigation?" I gasped.

This problem just went nuclear.

"They didn't have to say that per se, Lulu. She's on the documents; she's on their radar," he said. "The best thing to do is get her off those right now. Do a blanket revocation."

"What have you seen that is sending up red flags?" I inquired.

"I don't know if you saw Mr. Martin's report this morning?" he asked.

"No, I've been concentrating on the Blackwell matter," I replied.

"Well, read it and let the three of us get together. Mr. Martin mentioned that Mr. Abernathy owns a racehorse, large amounts of Bitcoin, and invested in hundreds of thousands of pre-paid cards. All vehicles for money laundering," he said.

I checked the time and decided we needed to head out to the bank.

By the time we arrived at the bank, Vanessa had already managed to piss off and intimidate the manager. He had arranged for a locksmith to breach the box with a drill. After signing numerous documents indemnifying the bank and its agents for any problems associated with the loss of her key, the drilling began. It took all of ten minutes, he pulled the lock, and placed the box in front of her to inspect. Vanessa signed more papers, the manager led us to a viewing room and left.

"Before you open the box, give me a minute to get this on video," Jackson said. "I can sign an affidavit to what I saw as the contents, but it's always best to have visual confirmation."

He stepped back into a corner of the room to get a wide angle. Then he started the video and identified the people in the room. Jackson explained for documentation, how the box was breached. We were now ready to view the contents. He referenced the sign-in sheet showing that although Vanessa was an owner of the box, only her husband had accessed it since it had been rented. Vanessa affirmed that on the record.

I held my breath as she slowly opened the box, and then jumped back, as she quickly flipped the lid open.

"Oh. My. God. Do you see what I see?" she yelled.

"Shh. We don't want to create a stir," I cautioned her.

"Vanessa, here are some latex gloves. Take the contents out and lay them on the table," Jackson said.

He handed us each a pair of black latex gloves.

"For the record, have you seen the contents before?" he asked.

"No. Now can I take all this out?" Vanessa asked, lightly jumping foot to foot in excitement.

He told her to wait and looked inside the box.

"Let me identify the contents, so the information is recorded correctly," Jackson said. "Go ahead and remove the three bars."

Vanessa removed three gold bars and placed them on the table.

"Mrs. Abernathy just removed three metal bars, gold in color," he said. He picked up each and inspected it.

"The weight feels to be about one kilo, and there are no identifying numbers or markers on any of the three. If this is real gold, then each is probably worth about forty-one thousand dollars," he said.

Neither of us said anything.

Vanessa lifted the velvet bag and shook it.

"Can I dump the contents?" she asked.

"Yes, but wait a minute," he said, pulling a handkerchief from his pocket, and laid it down on the table. "Spill it onto that."

Slowly, dozens of small stones slid from the bag. Jackson

took the time to separate them and count each one.

"Mrs. Abernathy has placed twenty-eight loose stones on the table of various sizes. Some appear cut and polished and others not," he said.

"Are they diamonds?" she asked.

"Probably, but I'm not a gemologist," he replied.

She then removed twenty bundles of what appeared to be US currency. We divided the bundles between us to count.

"This appears to be US currency of one-hundred-dollar denomination. Each bundle contains one hundred bills. So, our best estimate is that the total currency is two hundred thousand dollars."

"Jackson, turn that thing off," Vanessa said.

He complied.

"Just so I am clear. We have two hundred thousand in cash, and about one hundred twenty thousand in these gold bars. Depending on the cut, color, and clarity, these stones could be worth a couple hundred grand. Is that right?" Vanessa inquired.

"If the metal bars are gold, the currency not counterfeit or traced as stolen, and the diamonds are of impeccable quality, then yes," Jackson answered.

"At this point, we should have the bank manager give us a new box and replace everything in it. Leave it where it was, and monitor his next visit," I said.

"Absolutely not," she declared and crossed her arms.

"What do you mean?" I questioned.

"I am not leaving more than half a million dollars sitting in some safe-deposit box," she said.

"I don't understand," I said and lowered myself onto the metal chair.

"This box is in my name, right?" she asked.

"Yes, yours and Richard's," I responded.

"It belongs to each of us individually, right?" she asked.

"I can see where this is going. Yes, it's considered a marital asset. However, it probably is compromised and from illegal activities. So, if you're thinking about removing the contents, I would caution you not to do that," I said.

"Why should I leave this here and let him come and take it?" she demanded.

"Well, one major reason is that you have no idea if this is legal or illegal funds. Do you want to be hauled in and have to explain why you have possibly illegal or stolen property?" I asked, hoping my tone relayed my displeasure and alarm with her plan.

"I agree with Lulu, Mrs. Abernathy. You don't know if the FBI or some other agency has this box under surveillance. It's one thing looking inside to protect your interests. To remove anything and take possession of the contents is asking for trouble," Jackson said backing me up.

"As I understand the law, you have to have the intent to commit a crime. I think you people call it, *mens rea*. Isn't that right?" Vanessa asked.

"I'm impressed with your grasp of the law, Vanessa," I said.

Apparently, she had been reading up what constitutes a crime. But why?

"You are traveling into dangerous territory, Vanessa. Some crimes take into account actions after a fact," I said. "What if this money is the end result of money laundering, related to drug trafficking, or any other variety of crimes? That would indicate to me he's involved with some dangerous people. These people might come looking for their money."

"Then let's say I'm just taking it into protective custody.

Safekeeping for everyone involved," she said and started putting the bars in her handbag.

"Whoa, whoa, whoa. I think the prudent thing to do would be to have a third party secure all of this to make sure none of it is spent," Jackson said. "What if someone comes for it and figures out you have it. You've heard of the horrible things cartel members are accused of doing, right? Well, I'm here to say it's true. So please listen to us."

"Thank you for your advice. I'm going to, what is the term, take custody of this property, like the police to protect the chain of evidence custody. It's in my name, and I'm not stealing anything, just relocating it. Now, will you let the bank manager know we are ready to place the new box back?" she said.

Shit. My criminal law was rusty, and I hope I had not just placed myself in the middle of an ethical dilemma.

"What if Richard comes back and finds everything missing? Aren't you afraid you will be placing yourself in danger? Or what if he's holding it for someone and they decide to track you down?" I asked.

"I don't see Richard being a problem," she said.

I decided not to ask why.

CHAPTER FIFTEEN

Tallulah

U PON RETURNING TO THE OFFICE WITH JACKSON, I ASKED MR. Martin to join us. I was facing a quandary of how I should proceed with the new information about Vanessa. Jackson made the mistake of asking Mary to brew a fresh pot of coffee. Soon our group grew by an extra person. Mary.

We all took a seat around the table. I noticed Mary positioned herself next to Mr. Martin so she would have a bird's-eye view of what was in his possession. I retrieved his memo from the pile of papers I had to review and gave it a cursory review.

"Mr. Martin, the gist of what I've read is that for lack of a better term it appears Mr. Abernathy is actively laundering money through some creative sources. How could that be in today's day and age of heavy regulation? Wouldn't the SEC pick up on that?" I asked.

"Abernathy's been doing it for years, and over time, changed things up. That's what kept him under the radar. Until now. Now he's become bolder and careless. I've prepared a flowchart for you so you can see how he does it," he said.

He gave us each a legal-sized sheet with interconnected color-coded boxes and lines.

Mary placed the original in the table's center, engaged a projector, and suddenly its projected image appeared onto the whiteboard.

"I think the flow is self-evident from the schematic I drew. However, I found Mr. Abernathy appears to have a new partner in crime. Let's start with the premise that it now seems he has a girlfriend who is helping him spread his money around.

"Some earlier shell companies were in his name alone. When he married his wife, you can follow the grouping in blue where he shifted those original corporations into his wife's name. This would appear in an audit of the enterprises and on paper show she owned them and had authority over them. Digging deeper, they were just shell companies that allowed the flow of money from one place to another. The funds just traveled through them but didn't stay; like a pipeline. Once the cash passed through those companies she owned, they landed back in a business he controlled. However, by this time he had transformed the cash into some form of tangible property. That's how he bought the art, real estate, racehorse, and investment in a casino. So, it started as currency more than likely, passed through the shell company owned by her on paper, and then came back to him in a different form," he said.

"Okay, back up. When you say girlfriend, you mean a mistress-type person?" I asked for clarification.

"Yes. This is something recent, within the last year. I thought you'd want a background check done on her, so I had Mary pull the available information. There are pictures as well in the folder," Mr. Martin offered, pointing at the red three-ring binder he had prepared.

He reached across and handed me the binder. Jackson and I paged through it. The photographs proved the most interesting.

"If I'm reading this report correctly, last year this woman came into a large sum of money. She met Mr. Abernathy, maybe through his investment firm. Then bippity boppity boop, they started an affair, and now they are working together like a hand in a glove," I suggested.

"Boiled down to the simplest terms, yes. The way he wove the money in and out of his various investments is extremely complex. If you look at the red lines, those are the ones he and the wife own; and the blue lines the ones he and the girlfriend own. What is notable is that last month he took out a key man policy on the wife's life and girlfriend's life for twenty-five million dollars, and one on his own life to benefit the wife for eight million and one to benefit the girlfriend for eight million. Which means if the wife or girlfriend dies, he gets the payout and vice versa. It's not at all unusual to have a key man policy in business situations. However, this type of arrangement appears highly suspect. Throw in the disparity and enormity of the payouts and the timing during the divorce, and I'm not sure how anyone would write such a policy. It's a perfect recipe for murder. And if there is nothing actually in this warehouse, but only on paper, he hits the jackpot if the wife and girlfriend die. He'll collect fifty million and can say he had nothing to do with the disappearance of property," he said.

This was a lot to digest.

"So now he has two women involved with his money. Both worth more dead than alive," I surmised. "When you talked about the art a moment ago. Is that the art that was supposedly stolen when in transit from the freeport?"

"Yes. As a claims investigator in my previous job, this, along with the rare books theft, would raise a red flag. Personally, any robbery during a divorce would have me questioning things a little more, but that's just me. However, it might not ring any fire alarms, because it was in route from one place to another. With this set of facts, there will probably be arguments between the company which insured the actual property and the moving company that moved the inventory. I have a theory," he added.

"I do as well. You first," Jackson said with a sly smile.

"I don't think that art ever existed. Well, let me step that back. It existed at one point because an agent would have to see it to value it and insure it. However, because he has his valuables stored in a freeport, he can move them as he pleases. There is no regulation or reporting of what goes in or out of these places. What if he put them in the freeport, to delay taxes and duty until sold? Then he slipped them out for a private sale without registering the sale, saving on the required taxes due at that point. He could replace the art piece with some fake nonsense as a place holder. Then, in cahoots with a moving team, arranges for the robbery, and they split the proceeds. The artwork, because of the theft, disappears in the eyes of the regulatory body before the government can collect the taxes and duty. He probably already sold the art, so everything from the coverage received from the theft is pure profit. Think of it as double dipping," Mr. Martin offered.

"It certainly would take a lot of coordination, but doable," Jackson replied.

"Mary, what about the girlfriend?" I asked.

"Mr. Martin hasn't seen this yet, and I just printed this out. Tamara Downing, thirty-one, came into a substantial amount of life insurance money after her husband's death a year and a half ago. He had some on-the-job accident on an oil rig that paid out, and he also owned a few personal policies. So, she was flush with cash and wanted to invest it. Fast-forward and check the binder, there are a few cozy pictures of Mr. Abernathy and Ms. Downing after he helped her invest her money. Other than that, she led a quiet life," she said.

"Nothing rang any alarm bells?" I asked.

"None whatsoever. It seems like Ms. Downing was an everyday person married to a man with a dangerous job. When her path crossed Abernathy's, he saw a money-grabbing opportunity, and she saw a handsome, charismatic man," she said.

"It's always far more complicated than that, but that's where we are working until we flesh it out. Well, it seems we have our hands full here," I said. "Jackson, do you feel comfortable working on this with Mr. Martin and keeping me in the loop? You're a lawyer with experience in this, and I'm sort of drowning in the financial part," I added.

"Absolutely, I love a puzzle and a challenge," Jackson replied.

"Do you need any more surveillance from me?" Mary asked.

"My first thought says no, we have what we need. However, was this woman the cause of the breakup of the marriage? That might change things. If so, possibly we can get a better settlement for Vanessa. So, use your discretion," I replied.

"Any way we can get a peek at what the insurance companies are doing on the theft?" I asked.

"I have a request for the police report out there and will follow their investigation as best I can. Law enforcement to law enforcement, people usually get chatty. On the other hand, with the insurance company, getting access to internal investigations will be tricky. I am going to nose around some databases I still have access to. I want to determine if those artworks popped up anywhere, even for a short time," Jackson suggested.

"Okay, thanks, everyone," I said.

"And, Lulu. You and I are on the same page. Any remnants of the companies still left in Mrs. Abernathy's name, she needs to divest herself. I can see the light coming down the track on heading toward a train crash that can't be avoided with these financials. On the other safe-deposit boxes, maybe get an order from the judge to view them but file the request under seal. I'm afraid once he sees the request, he'll clean them out, and without an order stopping him from entering the box, it's fair game," Jackson offered.

"I'll see what I can do," I said. "Have we got the documentation tracking down the shell corporations? In other words, the actual incorporation documents?"

"I'll coordinate with Mr. Martin, and we'll get them as quickly as possible. Some are friendly countries he incorporated in and shouldn't be a problem. But China, well, I don't hold much hope for cooperation," Jackson said.

"Thanks, everyone. Mary, could you hang back?" I requested.

After everyone left, we started a fresh brew of coffee, and after the gurgling and hissing stopped, we filled our cups and relaxed in Mary's office. I set out what we discovered and the events that transpired.

Mary shook her head.

"That woman is playing with fire. I hope you are documenting everything so that if the government gets involved, you can have a record. In fact, I would have her sign a paper saying you told her not to take it, or in the alternative, give it to a third party to hold," she said.

"Either way it's an ethical mess. Because unless I know there is a plan for a future crime, I can't talk about any of this even on the stand. The property was in a box she owned, so she wasn't stealing anything. Could she reasonably assume it was the fruits of illegal activity? If it were me, I'd say yes. Her? Well, I don't know. Jackson recorded everything," I said.

"You know this is a case that will wind up going to trial. Why not hand it off to a big firm that deals with these train wrecks of a case?" Mary said.

"That's not a bad idea. Once we have all the information together that might be the best plan. Those law firms have experts they can tap into and probably would have a partner and three associates working on it. I'll give it another week and then regroup," I said.

"I'll see you later. I have a motion to draft to keep a subpoena under seal," I said and left with my coffee.

CHAPTER SIXTEEN

Poppy

VOLTAIRE SAID, "*TO THE LIVING WE OWE RESPECT, BUT TO THE DEAD, we owe only the truth.*" I will always remember that quote from a seminar about forensic investigation issues I attended during law school. From that, I learned the course of the death investigation had several phases and finalized in three documents: the death certificate, the investigator's statement, and the postmortem report. It usually took between four and six weeks to release an autopsy report, but we had just received the preliminary report and eager to go through it.

Mary called a meeting to review the autopsy results of Marsha Anderson. I looked around and saw a face I wasn't familiar with, but Mary remedied that.

"Poppy, I'd like to introduce Belle Hughes, Lee's wife, and an author of several gripping novels. Both she and Lee come from a homicide background, and both work with the team," Mary said nodding toward Belle.

"I am turning this meeting over to them. This is their area of expertise, so take it away, Belle," she said.

Belle, a short, attractive woman, stood and passed papers counterclockwise around the table. She waited for us to review the document.

"Let's go through this and pick it apart so that your client has the best representation possible. The general content format of the autopsy report consists of: diagnoses, toxicology, opinion, circumstances of death, identification of the decedent, general description of clothing and personal effects, evidence of medical intervention, external examination, external evidence of injury, internal examination, samples obtained - evidence, histology and toxicology, and microscopic examination. We have a preliminary, and they should publish the final in a few weeks. However, I believe we can glean some important information from this preliminary report," Belle said.

The document was twelve pages. My focus skipped immediately to the opinion section of the forensic pathologist, which contained a summary of the cause and manner of death.

"Let's start with the final diagnosis. It states: blunt force trauma; cranial cerebral injuries; multiple cranial penetrations to the back of the head concentrated on the right rear lobe; a linear fracture on the right side of the skull; abrasions of left cheek; abrasion on right forearm, and from this he deduced the cause of death to be from blunt force trauma. I'll let you pick through the sections on the external examination and external evidence of injury. However, I would point out: The top of the skull has a star-shaped break with some pieces of skull and scalp missing. This same pattern is present on the back-right side of the skull. Livor mortis on this side of the face makes identification difficult. Which in plain English means someone beat her with an instrument that cracked her skull. She was so badly beaten it was hard to identify her," Belle said shaking her head.

"In that same area of external evidence of injury on page three, it reports: Blood is smeared on the palm side of the right hand but no abrasions within the hand itself. Do we know if that was her blood or her assailant's?" Dalia asked.

"Excellent question. If you look at the addendum, it appears the lab ran that blood, and it is not the victim's," Belle responded. "I believe they also ran it through the regular databases with no hits."

"Excuse me, Belle, but I'd also like to point out on the external evaluation it says, below the level of the top of the head are two dried purple abrasions, and the sclera is red-lined with the left eye containing a significant amount of blood. Which indicates someone may have hit her that was right-handed and walloped her so hard that her eye bled. Also, Dalia, this might put a hitch in our original theory that she grabbed her head after being hit if it's not her blood. It leaves only one conclusion. It was her assailant's. So, we need to regroup and rework a new theory," Lee said.

"Okay, next, if you look down to the internal examination, breezing past the description of the organs, let's zero in on the genitalia, which describes the size of the uterus and verifies that she was pregnant. Now here is the explosive news, so hang on. Go to the first addendum. Look at the report. If you want to study it further for your education and compare the alleles and markers be my guest. All I want you to do is look at the conclusion. Based on the DNA sample provided by Gabriel Blackwell pursuant to an arrest, he is not excluded as the biological father. Moreover, the probability of paternity is ninety-nine point ninety-nine percent. Skip down a few paragraphs, and there is a statement that the pathologist reviewed the victim's medical records. He noted her enrollment in the surrogate program under Dr. Steven Masters. Based on her OB-GYN records, the fetus was being treated as the child of the couple who donated their egg and sperm," Belle said.

"Shit," Dalia blurted.

Shit indeed. And now it had hit the fan.

"Before we pick this apart, I wanted you to note what it said about the brain. Brain: Sections from the areas of contusion disclose disrupted blood vessels of the cortex with surrounding hemorrhage. It also identifies that she suffered a subarachnoid hemorrhage. Cortical neurons are surrounded by clear halos, as are glial cells. Someone did a number on her head, I'd say it reflects a great deal of force and rage," Belle offered.

The room was dead.

Total silence.

Eyes moved from side to side as brains engaged trying to assimilate everything in the document.

No one said another word for about ten minutes. We read pages, highlighted them with markers and made notes on our pads. Often investigators and attorneys review a report with the anticipation of it stating what you want it to reveal. Not so this time. This time it put Dr. Blackwell back in the frame.

"Well, I better get a hold of Dr. Blackwell and get the rest of the retainer," Mary said nonchalantly.

"Not so fast, Mary. I want him to get his records from the physician who performed the vasectomy. If he was lying and knew all along there was a probability that he was the father, then I'm dropping him like a hot potato," Dalia announced, and hit the table with her hand.

"Let's approach this today as if he can prove he had reason to rely on the vasectomy. I know how you feel about clients that lie, but I have a gut feeling this will catch him by surprise," Mary offered.

Dalia slumped back in her chair and nodded. I hadn't

noticed it before, but she looked exhausted.

Lee stood up and looked around the table.

"Ladies, this murder was rage-fueled, of that there is no doubt. So, let's proceed. Look at the coroner and ambulance report. It says blunt force trauma is likely the cause of death, based upon the initial examination. Also, it states there are defensive wounds, facial blows, and major injury on the back of the neck. Poppy, this information might bring your theory of someone being in the back seat of the car forward. How did she sustain the back of the neck injuries? This with the vehicle crime scene description, and photos give us some good information, doesn't it?" Lee asked.

"This confirms the car was the scene of the crime," I said.

"I'd agree," Lee responded.

"Stepping through it in an orderly fashion you'll want to get a copy of phone records for that night. See who may have lured her to the place. For all we know, someone may have just wanted to meet her and talk, but then things escalated," Lee said.

"I don't know. If you want to talk, then meet at a restaurant," Mary contradicted.

"Well, yes, but this was really private, and the person who wanted to talk probably knew it would escalate at some point and brought a weapon. We still don't know if the weapon was for defending himself or herself and things got out of hand. Alternatively, someone brought a weapon with them for the sole intent to murder her," Lee said.

"Sorry to interrupt, but on the crime scene vehicle information, I don't see a report for fingerprints, do you?" Dalia asked.

"You're right. I'll follow up on that," Belle offered. "And

since they have Dr. Blackwell's DNA now, I'll see if they ran that blood on the hand against his profile."

"Okay, continuing on. On the weapons information sheet, they didn't recover any weapons. We know that someone used their hands for sure. Also, the star-shaped fracture on the skull would lead me to think about something like the rounded bend of a tire iron or a hammer. I don't know why that came to mind, it just did. The vehicle report lists Marsha's tire iron and jack in place. What we need for the weapon is the type, size, length, color, diameter, and approximate weight. Some weapons a man could use with greater ease than a woman. Next, I'd look at the witness list and check out the people on her shift she may have spoken to."

"I've already done that and didn't get any information we could use. Marsha hadn't said she was going anywhere but home," Mary said.

"So, maybe the phone log will show she got the call after she left the hospital. I'd also subpoena the phone company and get a cellular tower trace to see if she went straight to the lot or somewhere else before that," Lee said.

Belle stood next to him and reviewed her notes.

"Here's a list of what you want: the evidence list, event schedule, crime scene photo log, and the lab work request form. Now, when it comes to the car which we believe is your crime scene, get specific. You want information about the position of the doors, windows, locks, ignition position, and gear shift position. Were the lights on or off? Was there damage to the exterior, interior, or glass? What were the contents of the interior, trunk, glove box, and the ashtray? We have the wound chart already, so I can cross that off my list," Belle added.

"I'm going to bring Gabriel in and explain that the DNA

results have shown he is the father of the baby. That also will screw with the wrongful death suit. Now more than ever we must nail down his movements. I believe we need to formulate an alternate list of suspects, go back to Mr. Martin's murder map. I put people on there like his wife, maybe even the surrogate couple. Although unless we can prove they had the knowledge she wasn't carrying their child and just flipped out, then I don't see it. Right now, they are not out any money because it should be in escrow. That phone call log will be vital," Dalia said shaking her head.

"This might not be the best time to ask, but what about his wife's death?" Belle asked.

"I am actively trying to put that out of my mind right now. The pathologist has requested another pathologist give a second look at the body. He felt he could not in all good faith list the cause and manner of death as inconclusive. I suppose he felt he might have missed something. There was no fluid in her lungs. Her blood ethanol was point zero six, and the initial drug screen was negative. So, no drugs, not drunk, didn't drown, so what killed her? That should conclude next week," Dalia said.

"There are ways that natural appearing substances can kill. Like the case of Sunny von Bülow. In that case, the prosecutor tried to convict her husband for murder, accusing him of giving her an insulin overdose. Some paralytic agents like they use in lethal injections, paralyzes your diaphragm and stops you from breathing. Now if you want to get wild and crazy, how about curare, the poison they put on the tips of arrows derived from the bark of Strychnos toxifera," I said.

"Lots to think about," Dalia replied.

"Anything else you need help with let us know. I don't need to tell you it doesn't look good for the doctor. And with his wife dead, it will be impossible to get a confession from her. However, I would definitely keep her at the top of the short list," Lee told us.

"I'd get the wife's medical records to see what medication her doctors have prescribed her. Check her OB-GYN records as well. Sometimes women get antidepressants from their GYN. Maybe she was taking hormones that made her go off the rails. Though those types of medications should have shown up in the initial screen," Belle said.

"Well, Poppy and I have our work cut out for us. Thanks again, everyone," Dalia said.

"You know, if Poppy is onto something, that second pair of eyes on the wife's autopsy might pick up a needle mark the first pathologist missed. Or bruising around it might show up days later. I think your doctor client is going to make you all very rich," Belle said.

At this point, I was beginning to believe he was involved with both murders. I didn't need a psychopath in my world, cash cow or not.

CHAPTER SEVENTEEN

Poppy

APPREHENSION GRIPPED ME. IT HAD BEEN YEARS SINCE SOMEONE had invited me to a get-together where I actually could attend. Work inevitably kept me from committing to fun activities in any way, shape, or form.

Lulu was throwing a party. Not just a party, but a big party with lots of individuals from different walks of life. Freelance artists, people from her church, and even members of her book club milled about. Although it was a Saturday late in November, she had fired up the barbeque, and three men were manning the grill. One man carefully monitored steak, chicken, and hamburgers, the other apparently was in charge of grilling the vegetables, and the third just seemed to oversee the other two.

Everyone from the office attended and were having a blast. Mr. Martin, in his business attire, had popped in for a few minutes. Maybe to give the appearance he was one of the team. But I read social anxiety all over him, and he left rather quickly. A woman wiping the messy face of a sweet little girl was introduced as Emma, Eloise's best friend. The man next to her holding a wiggling boy upside down was introduced as her husband, Cillian. Ah, Cillian, Jackson's partner. I heard there was a dramatic story behind how those two met when he was an FBI agent. I was more interested in how they juggled their rambunctious twins.

As I scanned the room, I noticed a young man, about my age, deep in conversation with a woman older than him.

"Who's that over there? The cute guy with the blond hair?" I asked Lulu.

Her smile was one of real affection.

"That's Mark Willis. He's an officer with the police department, soon to be a detective, fingers crossed," Lulu said.

"So, what's his story? Married, girlfriend, single?"

"Ah, some interest. Unmarried and a very nice man. The woman he is standing next to is Margaret, a former client. Mark is the officer that saved my life when a client's husband tried to kill her and then attacked me. Margaret looks amazing after the hell she went through. Come, let me introduce you to both of them," she said with a tip of her head for me to follow.

My stomach quivered with butterflies, and I hadn't even touched his hand yet. Somehow Mark spoke to a primal place within me. Maybe it was the way his black sweater molded against his muscular chest and arms. Or, it could have been how his black stonewashed jeans hugged his thighs. Whatever it was, it was evident the man knew his way around a gym.

As we approached, his eyes met mine, and he watched me walking toward him as if locked on a target. Clear, ice blue, like the actor Chris Pine's eyes, just stunning. Margaret kept talking, but I could tell he wasn't listening. He focused on me.

"Mark and Margaret, let me introduce you to Poppy Pacheco. She's a new associate in our firm who's working with Dalia on the Blackwell case." She smiled and watched his reaction.

"Oh, wow!" Margaret exclaimed. "Are you the young attorney that Mary saw arguing a case in court and loved your fiery spirit? I'll bet you are. She had lunch with me one day about a month ago and said she had seen a young lawyer who reminded her of herself and was going to offer her a job. I'm so excited you accepted her offer," she rambled on. "I'll always be grateful to Mary. Had she not shot my husband dead, I could be dead today."

I must have looked startled, and my mouth gaped. I realized I never knew how the firm found me and now that question was answered. Many times, I had wanted to ask, but afraid if I did it would break the spell.

"I'm embarrassed to say, I had no idea Mary saw me in court, and that's why she offered me the position. At times I suppose I can get animated when I'm trying to make a point," I replied and felt a flush spread across my chest.

God, I hope it wasn't one of the times I flapped my arms around looking like I was a large, uncoordinated bird preparing for takeoff. Or worse, threw my arms up in disgust when some idiot told a blatant lie. The opportunities to see me at my emotional finest were plentiful.

A look passed between Margaret and Lulu, although quick, it was there, nonetheless.

"Mark, would you mind getting our Poppy something to drink? I want to talk to Margaret about something," Lulu said.

"Sure. Poppy, come with me. We'll get a drink, and I'll show you a quiet spot where it's not so noisy. You have to capitalize on the warm days in November when you can," he said.

His smile was just as captivating as his eyes. And chest. And legs. And I was sure once he turned, his rear end would be captivating as well.

I followed him to the kitchen where I got a drink, he

refreshed his, and we then headed to an area in the back. He was right; he was well acquainted with a small secluded area with a wood bench and an array of berry type bushes.

"How do you like working for Mary? She's a real character. She sure keeps all of us on our toes. That woman always has far more questions than we have answers. And she doesn't mind calling us slackers when we can't keep up with her," he laughed.

"I love Mary; she's my hero. When I get to be her age, I only hope I have half her energy," I said. I wasn't sure if I should add that half the time she scares the shit out of me especially when she has a firearm bolted to the conference table.

"I guess since you're working with Dalia, that means you do primarily criminal defense."

"For now. I had been under the illusion that when I graduated, I'd be flooded with opportunities to join a large firm. That bubble was quickly burst, so I had to scramble to earn a living. The only two things that produced an opportunity for quick cash were the indigent defense office where they get the overflow from the public defender's office, and the Family Violence Center," I told him.

"What type of cases did you catch?" he asked, leaning toward me.

His aftershave smelled so good, a woodsy scent, and was quite a distraction.

"Ah, low-level misdemeanors to start. Things like shoplifting, public intoxication, and simple assault. Once I got my sea legs, they moved me up to felonies. I did lots and lots of bench trials, but if the case turned into a jury trial, that was the point it was transferred to another more experienced lawyer, thank God. I'd be bumbling and stumbling my way through the first few jury trials, and probably have a panic attack halfway through. I'm certain there would have been a sitcom offer there, had the right people seen me in action."

He laughed at that and shook his head.

"So, you, Margaret, and Lulu?" I prompted.

"I met them when Margaret was going through an ugly divorce. Vicious, really. Her husband was a real control freak, a batterer who used her as a punching bag for his frustrations. Finally, after years of family violence, it exploded into a nasty custody battle and fight over every penny they owned. Margaret's husband was a total menace to her. After years of abuse, one day before the final divorce hearing, he totally flipped out. He beat her practically to death, and then when he finished with her, he attacked Lulu. Margaret was in a coma for roughly a week fighting for her life, and Lulu sustained a bad concussion. We arrested the husband for aggravated assault and battery. However, some idiot judge let him out on bond, based on a lack of credible identification and sufficient evidence. So, what was the first thing he did when released? He hunted Lulu down and tried to kidnap and murder her. She was with Mary and Mary had one of her many weapons on her, thank God. She blew a hole right in his chest. It's not a story that had a happy ending for him. Those are three courageous women."

"Wow, I knew a little of the story, but had no idea how bad it really was."

What more could I say to that sort of real-life drama? Should I share with him I probably would have peed my pants?

"With any luck, you won't see any of that kind of chaos while you're working with the firm. And if it comes even close, I'm sure Mary will make sure you are armed and ready to defend yourself. Have you seen her arsenal? Putting work aside, what type of things do you like to do on your off time?" he asked.

"Well, until Mary offered me this position, I had no free time to explore any fun opportunities. When I wasn't in court, I was working as a waitress in Trouloues on the evening shift, to earn my living expenses. However, I'm a big sports fan, and, if I had a free day, I'd kill to catch a few games. If I had the money and time, I'd be all over the Rockies when they play at Coors Field or rooting for the Avalanches as they spill some ice hockey blood. There's nothing like watching wild men whizzing by in a blur, hungry for a fight to erupt."

"Well, that was unexpected. You caught me off guard. I thought you'd say you'd go for a stroll through an art museum or maybe a quiet day at the botanical gardens. I belong to an ice hockey team, and we're pretty good. Would you like to come to our next game? One thing I can promise is lots of blood and maybe even a cracked tooth. Or if you're really lucky, possibly someone will need some stitches applied right there in the penalty box. We're a real competitive bunch and take our hockey seriously."

"Would I? You bet. Just tell me when and where and I'll be there." I smiled and clapped my hands in glee. The very thought got my heart pumping.

We heard what sounded like a captain's bell ring three times.

"That's the signal dinner is ready. If you give me your phone, I'll put my number in it so I can give you the schedule. If you're free for lunch tomorrow, I'd like to introduce you to some excellent company. And not so bad food," Mark said waiting for me to hand him my phone.

He placed his number in my phone, and his phone buzzed with my number. Wow, this had been quite an unexpected good fortune.

As we approached the seating area, Dalia motioned us over to sit with her and her fiancé, Declan Murphy. Mark and Declan appeared to know each other and soon fell into a comfortable conversation. Dinner was almost finished when Dalia leaned over and asked "Poppy, can you walk me to the bathroom?" That's a phrase I hadn't heard since high school.

Once in the hall, she motioned me toward the bedroom on the left and closed the door after her.

"What's up?" I asked, sitting in a rocker.

"This is bad. Declan said they got Marsha's phone records back under a search warrant and Gabriel's phone number came up as the last call received," she whispered.

Oh, that was indeed bad. Like, very bad.

"Are you going to talk to Dr. Blackwell about that?" I asked.

Of course, she would, that was a stupid question.

"I planned to wait until Monday to ask him to come in and discuss the paternity issue, but with this new information, I thought I'd call him now and see if he can come in tomorrow. Are you free?" she asked.

"Well, Mark just invited me for a lunch date, but I suppose I can cancel if I need to." I assume my disappointment was evident.

"No, keep your date. I'll make it for nine, and if it gets close to lunch and we aren't finished, you can leave," Dalia said with a nod.

"Great, that works." I liked that arrangement. "Dalia, this whole thing just seems too weird. He has to know the police can track phone calls. Why not tell us he could have been the last one to speak to her? I really want to be there to see his demeanor as you tell him how bad this all looks."

She scrubbed her face with her hands in frustration.

"I hate being so far behind the curve on information. Working in the D.A.'s office in my other life, we had all the material before the defense got their hands on it. That gave us a better position to deal with the case. Now I'm running as fast as I can to keep up, and every time I feel I've reached a good place to rest and regroup, I'm running again," she said blowing out a breath.

"Well the good news is you have Belle and Lee squarely in your camp helping you," I said.

"But helping me do what? I hope not to set a murderer free."

CHAPTER EIGHTEEN

Poppy

SUNDAY MORNING ARRIVED, AND WITH IT THAT WONDERFUL elated feeling which came from knowing I was going to meeting with Mark Willis. This quickly then turned into a stomach full of knots when I thought about the fact that Gabriel Blackwell was about to walk through the office doors in about five minutes. As bad as he tripped Eloise's creep meter before, I was sure now it would make it self-detonate. It was looking as if he murdered Marsha Anderson and my suspicion of his involvement with his wife's death was edging up.

"Is everyone settled and ready?" Mary asked, pounding her judge's gavel on the striker block.

Think of what she could do using that as a weapon. Weapon. Could something like that have killed Marsha? A hammer perhaps? Heavy metal end and solid wood body, a possibility.

"Do you still have a loaded firearm under the table?" Mr. Martin inquired.

"Of course. Especially now when we know Dr. Blackwell is connected with two murders. I leave nothing to chance," Mary said with an affirmative nod.

"I see. However, I would like to register my concern once

again," Mr. Martin returned.

"Noted," she responded.

Lee swung his head her way and raised his eyebrows in question. Belle smirked.

I spotted Mr. Martin as he moved his chair back, a guarantee to be out of the line of fire. Personally, I felt a certain comfort knowing a weapon was available after hearing how Mary had to kill a client's crazed husband. As I stood to get another cup of coffee, I noticed Dr. Blackwell had come into the range of the monitor and I announced his arrival. Dalia left the room to greet him and escort him back. We all settled in, reviewed our papers, and tapped our laptops to life.

Dr. Blackwell stopped in the doorway and gazed around the table. His eyes lingered on Belle and Lee, and then he took a seat. We decided Dalia would be in control of the meeting. However, with so many interests represented, it could quickly turn into a free for all.

"Gabriel, let me introduce two members of our team you haven't met. Belle Hughes was an NYPD homicide detective, and her husband, Lee Stone, was with the Chicago PD in the homicide division. We have invited them to join us this morning. Their experience in how an investigation unfolds and the best way to review the evidence will be invaluable to us," Dalia stated.

A nod toward Lee and Belle passed as an acknowledgment, but he said nothing. His face was unreadable as was his body language at this point. He sat at the end of the table across from Mary, crossed his right leg over his left, and settled back.

Smug bastard. You won't be cocky for long.

"So, am I to assume there is bad news that required a full complement of my legal team on a Sunday?" he asked, folding his fingers together and placed them in his lap.

"That would be my guess," Mary blurted.

That garnered a look from Dalia indicating that Mary should shut the hell up.

"Well then, shall we get on with it?" he asked, without acknowledging Mary.

"We received the preliminary autopsy report," Dalia said and handed him a copy. "I'll let you take a moment to review it. I don't believe I need to explain it; the document speaks for itself."

We all watched him read each page with a disinterest that is until he scanned the addendum page. The page he focused on listed the paternity results. He flipped back several pages, re-read something, and moved back to the addendum once again. By the look on his face, his expression finally caught up with his brain. He understood the implications.

"This is absolutely wrong! Someone has mixed up evidence or planted it. It is impossible that child was mine. This is all bullshit," he said with a raised voice, discarding the report on the table.

Dalia waited for him to look at her before she spoke.

"What we have learned from Marsha's roommate, is that in the past she had worked with a clinic in New York to sell her eggs. I can see you have questions, so do we. We are trying to get the records from that clinic.

"Marsha was deeply in debt. And I suppose she thought selling body parts would be a quick fix. When the program did not invite her back to sell them a second time, she appeared to go down a different path to leverage her body for money," Dalia replied leaning forward.

"Okay, stop right there. Where is the clinic Marsha sold her eggs to? Who is running this baby mill?" he inquired, raising his hand in a halt position.

"Our information says it's a clinic in New York. Now, once that road was closed to her, she discovered a surrogacy program here in town that would pay her to be a surrogate. Her roommate gave us the information she had about it, and we are investigating that angle. However, it was her OB-GYN records provided by Dr. Masters, the surrogacy handler, that the medical examiner relied on and referenced in the autopsy report," Dalia said.

"Dr. Masters, why does that name sound familiar?" he asked, concentrating on the name.

Dalia shrugged and continued.

"So, as you can see this new information changes things a great deal. Now the prosecutor's case is taking a definitive form, placing you squarely in the prime suspect box."

"Who is the supposed surrogate couple?" he asked as if he didn't hear a word she said.

"We don't know. All we know is they were paying Marsha's medical bills, and that they had set up an escrow account where they deposited seventy-five thousand dollars to be paid to her when the child was born. Right now, there are a lot of moving parts," Dalia added.

"Can I assume Marsha was on a high hormone regime when he implanted the egg? If so, could that have been the perfect storm for this fiasco?" he asked, pointing to the report.

His thoughts seemed disjointed. Why was he so focused on how this could happen, instead of what it meant?

"I have no idea. Until I get a full copy of Marsha's medical records, all I have to rely on is that the pathologist reviewed the records as part of the autopsy," Dalia said.

"Unbelievable," he mumbled. "So how are you going to deal with this mess and keep it out of the case?"

"I will request that our independent lab performs another paternity test, which the judge will of course allow. So I'm asking you to submit proof of your vasectomy to our expert. Since we built our whole defense around the vasectomy prevented fertilization, the last thing we want is for the police to prove you intentionally lied," Dalia said.

"What if someone planted evidence?" he stated again.

Lee spoke up at this point.

"I will never say never, however, the probability of that happening is miniscule. There are checks, balances, and control of evidence and samples documenting everything done. I'd say at that point you're grasping at straws. However, we will review all the evidence to make certain there was not a break in the chain of custody."

"We're on top of this, trust me. I won't lie to you; this report will be a problem in our defense. We asserted it was impossible for you to have fathered the child, therefore, there was no motive. But motive is separate from the fact the state must prove all elements of the crime. They just can't throw a theory out there and ask a jury to rely on a theory with no facts," Dalia said.

"What are the charges right now? I thought it was first-degree murder and unlawful termination of a fetus?" Dr. Blackwell asked almost dazed.

"I expect they will amend the charges when they indict you to include manslaughter, a crime of passion. Now, speaking of putting our case together and collecting information. We received another bit of bad news and will need to investigate this immediately."

"There's more?"

His eyebrows almost reached his scalp, and his relaxed hand placement now had his hands gripping the arms of the chair.

"I have not received the written confirmation. However, I'm aware that after the police executed a search warrant on Marsha Anderson's phone, your number was the last one she received a call from. After that, no calls were placed or received," Dalia told him.

The look on his face was that of utter devastation. He seemed to lose all his facial color in front of us, and I could tell his breathing sped up.

Dalia continued.

"The police can get a search warrant for your phone and probably are doing that already. Before they may not have had probable cause, but now do. I need you to sign an authorization for me to obtain all phone communication for the last six months. That would include incoming and outgoing calls, text messages and any type of voicemail recordings. Mary will provide the paperwork to you," she told him.

"But how do they know I was the last person to talk to her?" he asked, still dazed.

"I guess because no calls were coming in or going out from her phone after you," Mary said with a tone that implied, "*dumb ass.*"

"I also need you to trace your steps for twenty-four hours before the murder. Had you left your phone where someone could have had access to it? As you can conclude the prosecution will say you were firming up plans to meet her that night, and thus you were the last person to see her," Dalia said making a note.

He turned the autopsy report over and scribbled notes.

"Someone set me up," he said with a dull even voice.

"That may be so, however, if that is the case, we need to find that person and the reason why," Dalia said in a somewhat disinterested tone.

"What's next?" he said, once again settling back in the chair.

"We don't have your wife's final autopsy results. The state's ME has asked for a second pathologist to come in. He is not comfortable listing the cause of death and manner of death as undetermined. They didn't find water in her lungs, she wasn't intoxicated, and the initial drug screen was clean. Unfortunately, we must continue to wait for a final autopsy report and death certificate. So now I'll turn it over to Eloise, who will explain the progress of the estate portion," Dalia said and sat.

"Bottom line, without a death certificate I can't move forward on life insurance policies or anything paid outside the will. I can't ask for a new property deed to reissue in your name alone until we have the death certificate to trigger the rights of survivorship section. We are not at a complete standstill; however, the bulk of her money passes outside her will, so until I have a death certificate it's a waiting game," Eloise said.

"I can still live in the house?" he asked.

"As soon as they release it as a crime scene," Dalia interjected.

"I can access joint accounts?"

"As long as there is no court order freezing any assets," Eloise responded.

"What about her partnership in the law firm? Do I get her quarterly distributions?" he queried, turning a bit to face Eloise square on.

"I've asked her firm for a copy of the partnership agreement. Do you have access to that?" she asked making a note.

"I'll look in the important papers. This is a fucking night-mare, excuse my French," Dr. Blackwell said so quietly you could have missed it. "So, again, what's the plan?"

"I need your phone records, so I can see what the police are digging up. We need timelines, and we need a solid alibi," Dalia replied. "I've sent discovery requests, and we should have some responses within the month. That's not to say we aren't running a parallel investigation and doing our own interviews. Anything else?" Dalia asked.

"How worried should I be that they will drag me into Sandy's death?" he asked, studying his thumb nail.

"I'd like to say you're in the clear. However, as far as the police know, for now, you were the last to see her and…"

"I know, last to see is the first suspect. Great. Send me a to-do list, and I'll work on it. Now, where do I need to sign for authorization for my cell phone records? By the way, Sandy and I were on a family plan. I am the owner of the phones and plan. You want one for hers as well?" he asked, reaching into his jacket for a pen.

"Yes, that's an excellent suggestion," Dalia said. "Just fol-low Mary to her desk, and she'll print something up."

"I'd like copies of everything as they come in. Also, any-thing harmful to me; I want a second and third test run. If you need more money from me, let me know," he said. "I can't prove I didn't do it other than tell you I did not kill Marsha."

"If you get us everything on the list I give you, it will help. Can you get that to me within the week?" Dalia asked.

He agreed to comply. The way he stood and rapped his knuckles on the table made him appear distracted. He said nothing more and left. He was no longer the cocky, arrogant person I had first met.

Dalia closed the door after he left.

"Thoughts, anyone?" she asked.

"He seemed genuinely surprised over the parentage."

"Yes, I don't think he faked that reaction," Lee agreed.

"There's not much for me to do at this point," Eloise said.

"You've been pretty quiet, Mr. Martin," Lulu noted.

"I have nothing of consequence to add so why offer some irrelevant comment? However, just a thought. Why would he bludgeon her to death when there are so many other civilized ways that would be less traceable? If he wanted to get rid of the baby why not slip her a large dose of oxytocin in a drink? Or an overdose of vitamin A? I don't think he did it. But that is just because I can't find any logical reason for such a messy death," he said and sat back ramrod straight.

"He's a cocky son of a bitch, but I don't think he killed the Anderson woman. Now his wife, well, I'm not so sure. I can't wait to get my hands on the final autopsy report," Belle said.

"No love lost between those two," Lee agreed.

"Every time I see that man, I want to slap the smug right off his face," Eloise said ready to leave.

"Between him and Vanessa, I don't know who I dislike more," Lulu said.

"Oh, clearly him," Eloise immediately responded.

"Yeah, you haven't met the Queen of Darkness yet, so hold that thought," Mary said.

"Well, we all have our tasks to work on. So, I'm sure some of us are eager to get out of here," Dalia looked at me and winked. "See everyone tomorrow."

I left the room as if my pants were ablaze with fire. I had places to go, people to meet. Maybe sex to be had. Hope springs eternal.

CHAPTER NINETEEN

Poppy

THE PLACE MARK CHOSE FOR LUNCH HAD JUST THE RIGHT AMOUNT of rustic charm yet had an air of sophistication. First dates always presented a quandary for me. Should I eat like a bird and pretend I was nothing but a delicate flower? Or should I order a gigantic greasy cheeseburger cooked rare with bacon and mushrooms? Greasy cheeseburger it is. If he can accept my fierce love of ice hockey, then he could deal with my passion for cheeseburgers.

"Dalia told me you are in line to move over to the detective division. That's very exciting," I opened the conversation.

"Yes, I officially start tomorrow. It's something I've been working toward for my entire career. Don't get me wrong; I enjoyed being on patrol, there's an excitement about meeting a new challenge several times a day. However, the thought of doing in-depth investigations, well that sends a buzz through my body," he said.

"Never wanted to join SWAT?"

"I never considered it. Some of those guys are hot dogs, and the egos you must deal with are massive. I'm very happy wading through the minutia to get a result, well, one that's rewarding," he said unraveling the silverware. "I hope this won't be a problem, but I'm slated to work with Declan on Blackwell. Actually, it seems like everyone in the department is working on either the Anderson woman or his wife's investigation."

"Yes, Dalia is in charge of the case, and I'm assisting her," I said. "Let me ask you. You said you're assigned Sandra Blake's matter. Are you investigating that as a murder?"

"Right now, it's listed as 'suspicious.' I mean, come on, there's no fluid in her lungs, so she didn't drown, and no drugs in her system. All her organs were healthy, no heart attack, no signs of stroke, and no aneurysm. That's the kind of puzzle I want to be a part of solving," he said, moving close enough I could smell his woodsy, oh so masculine essence. A scent now implanted in my olfactory memory.

"So, you've seen the preliminary report?" I asked. Would he notice I was almost inhaling his wonderful aftershave?

"No, we had a brief meeting with the ME The guy's gut says homicide, and that's why he's bringing in another guy to go over the body, inch by inch," he shared.

I felt like he was waiting for a response from me. So, unsure how to wade through this new territory, I used a reverse conversation tool I had picked up along the way.

"How do you feel about that?" I asked.

He blew out a breath and leaned back.

"Without revealing too much, I can say it's quite a conundrum. Dr. Blackwell is an enigma. On paper, he is a pillar of the community, a well-respected physician and active in lots of charities. However, if you scratch the surface, the man seems to have a dark side," he said.

"Dark side? How so?" I asked, surprised.

Had he picked up on the psychopath vibe? No, he never met him so how could he?

"This will all come out when the prosecutor gives you the discovery package, so I'm not telling you anything that is confidential. It's no secret that the man is a dog. I know he's your client and all, but he is constantly in trouble with women." He lowered his eyes and faked a cough. "And then there's the fact that Dr. Blackwell belongs to a sex club."

Whoa. This could be huge. *Now how to play this?*

"There are a lot of kinds of sex clubs. What type was his flavor?"

Okay, I was a little embarrassed but didn't want to come across as naïve.

"The BDSM type that charges a hundred-fifty-thousand-dollar membership fee," he replied, watching for my reaction.

"Wow, that's a lot of moolah. I have to say up front, not my brand of fun and games. And someone hits me, they better be ready for a roundhouse kick," I assured him.

Unfortunately for us, I bet the prosecution will try to muddy the waters by implying that inflicting pain on women gives him pleasure and he's sexually stimulated by it. I can see where they could get a ton of mileage out of this revelation.

"However, from a legal standpoint, unless he purposefully injures people from this activity, I'm not sure that a judge would even let that in. For all we know, he might go there to be a submissive. You're just assuming he takes on the role as a dominant or at worst a sadist. Lots of powerful men like to have control taken away from them so that others can do the thinking and work," I said, placing the powdery content of a package of Splenda in my iced tea.

He chuckled. I responded with a raised eyebrow.

"Well, that was unexpected. Dare I ask how you know so much about *the lifestyle?*" he inquired.

"I know you're expecting I'll say *Fifty Shades of Grey*, but no, that's not it, not it at all. It goes back to my constitutional law classes. Many of our constitutional rights were defined and expanded as our world changed. Anyway, as part of the course, I chose the challenge of picking apart what freedom of speech meant and how the right to assemble impacted it.

"There was a place called Plato's Retreat in New York, the first swingers club and the forerunner of sex clubs. Long story short, in law school, I took part in a mock trial challenge that involved its forced closing by Mayor Koch in 1985. I was the defendant's counsel, and my theory of defense was the constitutional right of peaceful assembly. Some people argued that the type of activity wasn't a peaceful assembly but instead was *illegal per se.* They argued that the BDSM involved simple battery, and by law, you can't consent to a crime. It was a viable argument, but open to challenge, if you include boxing and cage fighting as legal activities. Anyway, I argued our constitution protects this activity as freedom of expression. I relied upon how although lawmakers tried to criminalize nude dancing, our courts said 'no, no' stripping is a form of dancing, an artistic expression. So, my argument was that the people assembled were expressing their sexual urges through a different way than most people did." I shrugged and took a sip of the tea.

"That is an unusual comparison." He smiled. "Pretty out-of-the-box rationalizing."

"Now it doesn't always hold up. There have been places that have been closed because of health concerns. Just like the government couldn't get Al Capone on racketeering, so they nabbed him on tax evasion. If the government wants to close something, they will find a way," I said.

"Sometimes I think you have to get creative to protect people from things they don't know can be dangerous," he said. "Maybe that upscale sex club has highly educated members who can make an informed decision of the risk involved. Or maybe they are damaged people who happen to be rich. What happens if an easily manipulated person meets up with someone rich and charismatic? A man with a title can fool and exploit vulnerable people."

"You've made your mind up about Dr. Blackwell, haven't you? You think he did it." I wanted to know.

"How did you get that from what I said? If you mean, am I convinced he committed a crime? I don't know yet; I haven't seen the totality of the evidence. But his moral compass is off. I think he's a complex man, a misogynist, incapable of forming relationships. Some women look at him and see a great catch. I sense he's an unfeeling sociopath. Moreover, some sociopaths find taking that leap into murder relatively easy," he said.

"Wow, this has taken a dark turn. How about we put our jobs on the side and run through what normal people talk about? I hope you're a Game of Thrones fan." I smiled with a flirty wink.

"Winter is coming," he replied in a Jon Snow British accent.

Great, a yes.

How would Dalia treat this new BDSM information? Would we get to interview members of the sex club? *Sign me up!*

CHAPTER TWENTY

Poppy

T HERE ARE MEMORABLE TIMES IN YOUR CAREER. THE DAYS THAT make you question your belief system. Today was one of those.

I had barely taken my messenger bag from across my chest when Dalia burst into my office, almost in a panic. Mary was right behind her.

"I got a call from Declan; they are going to the hospital to arrest Gabriel." She struggled to say it with a level voice, but it came out in a stuttered fashion.

She bent over slightly, and I wasn't sure if she would vomit or pass out.

"Dalia, breathe. In and out, in and out," Mary said as I rushed to her.

"I tried to arrange to surrender him at the police station. However, his chief was adamant he wants him arrested immediately. Clearly, to humiliate him and taint him in front of the public, the people who will comprise our jury," she said on the verge of tears. "I failed him in my duty to protect him."

"Here, sit for one minute, and tell us what's going on. Then we can meet Dr. Blackwell at the station after they book him in. They won't let you see him right now. Then we need to get a plan together because, surely, they will revoke his bail," Mary suggested.

Thank God someone had their wits about them.

"I have ammonia in my drawer if you need me to put it under your nose," Mary offered, rubbing Dalia's back. Dalia waved her away, easing her way into a chair.

"Okay, first, why is he being arrested? Until you get it together short answers will do," Mary said.

"First-degree murder of his wife," she said.

"Well, although that's an Oh Shit, it's hardly unexpected," Mary replied with a shrug.

"What?" Dalia blurted in almost a scream. "What are we dealing with here?"

"I feel I'm missing something here. Why did the police arrest him? And why under such Draconian circumstances? Did they feel he was on a murderous rampage? Or was it for a pure publicity tactic?" I asked, sitting across from Dalia.

"I'll give you what I have. The two MEs worked together, and they took eight hours to do a second autopsy. Maybe because so many days had passed or maybe two sets of eyes using magnifying glasses was the ticket. Whatever the reason, they found a needle prick," she said.

"A needle prick?"

"A hypodermic mark that broke the skin, and a definite bruise around it," Dalia affirmed.

Silence blanketed the room.

We heard the front door open and heard footsteps approach. Mr. Martin. He glanced into the room, stopped, and appeared to be deciding whether to speak.

"Good morning, Mr. Martin," Dalia offered.

"Is it? You ladies look as if it's a terrible morning," he returned.

"The Blackwell case," was all Dalia said.

"I see," he replied.

I suppose he couldn't decide whether to keep moving or step inside, so he stayed planted on that spot.

"I was saying, Gabriel is being arrested for the murder of his wife. The new autopsy revealed a hypodermic mark, and the theory is he injected her with something," Dalia told him.

He placed his briefcase by his right foot, unlatched it, and bent over to retrieve something. From the case, he produced a file about an inch thick. It was filled with papers clipped at the top and Post-it note stickers hung from the side of the papers. Mr. Martin walked over and handed Dalia the folder.

"Not surprising. The man is clever, and that's why I don't believe he killed that first woman, Marsha Anderson. That was rage-fueled, messy, and frankly overkill. The wife's death, however, another story altogether," he said.

"What's in the folder?" Mary asked.

"I did some research on ways to kill someone that is nearly foolproof," he replied.

"You better hope the government never confiscates your computer," Mary said.

"I use an incognito masking program to guard my searches," Mr. Martin told her.

That produced a nod from her showing she approved.

"Wait, before we go into his research, what did the ME find?" I asked.

"Once they found the hypodermic mark, they went back to the brain and took more samples and looked for something specific, Declan told me. And they found it..." Dalia said.

"Succinic acid," Mr. Martin replied.

We all swung our bodies toward him.

"Yes, how could you possibly know?" Dalia asked.

"Wait," Mary said. She placed her hand in the air to cut off any further conversation. "Let's move this to the conference room. I need coffee, and I want to take notes."

I ran to the bathroom, and Mary moved to the conference room to start a pot of coffee. Mr. Martin helped Dalia gather her papers, and they arrived together. Once Mary had her coffee, and we were all settled, she gave the nod she was ready to start. Thank God it was a nod and not the strike of the gavel. I think Dalia would have lost it.

"So, what's your theory?" Mary asked Mr. Martin.

"I believe he used succinylcholine, a neuromuscular blocking agent, a medication that paralyzes the muscles in the body. In short, once injected, it paralyzes the muscles such as the diaphragm. Muscles you need to breathe, can't move and you suffocate to death," he said.

"So why didn't it show up on a tox screen?" I asked.

"It works within seconds to a minute after it's injected. Then, once injected, it immediately breaks down into metabolites, and the body quickly absorbs it. The way the body breaks down and absorbs the metabolites, the body finds it nearly impossible to distinguish it from naturally occurring acetylcholine. So, a blood sample would be useless. The brain, however, is a different story," he said.

"How did you zero in on that particular drug?" Dalia asked.

"I started with a Google search of drug-related deaths and homicides," he explained. "From there I chased down a few different paths and came upon a case. The Carl Sadow case happened in the mid-sixties. Carl Sadow and his wife were both physicians. He was an anesthesiologist, and she was an internal medicine physician. Carl had injected his wife with SUX, short for succinylcholine. He waited until he was sure she was dead, then to bypass an ambulance coming, he called Dr. Barrett, a friend of the couple. The doctor was asked to certify the death. It appeared to be a heart attack, and that's what he recorded on the death certificate. After the death certificate was completed, everything went smoothly, until Carl jilted his mistress and married another woman.

"Here's the ironic twist. Carl had given his lover a syringe filled with SUX to kill her husband. However, she botched the job, called Carl to help her, and he finished off the husband by strangling him. Carl returned home to his wife, Marjorie. Shortly after that night to cover their tracks, Carl's lover called the Sadow home and told them her husband had died of a heart attack. Marjorie, Carl's wife, also a doctor, went over and certified the death.

"After Carl married someone other than his lover, the lover ran to Dr. Barrett, the doctor who certified Carl's wife's death, and spilled the beans. She wanted him arrested for murdering his wife and her husband. Dr. Barrett went to the authorities. After they exhumed the bodies and did an autopsy, they found the succinic acid in the brain. From there the wheels of justice moved slowly and finally convicted Sadow of second-degree murder. I then snooped around a little more and found succinylcholine in other cases. I can go on, but it would appear redundant," he said.

To say I was impressed was just not nearly enough of what I was thinking. I was gobsmacked.

"So, give us the theory of how you think he did this. Because what I hear is you think he did it," Dalia said.

"I didn't say that, did I?" he replied, taking a cautious sip from his cup of coffee.

"I'm confused," Dalia said.

I could tell by her voice inflection there was a tone of irritation mixed with frustration.

"Yes, he was the last person there that night. Correct?" he verified.

"Unless they can find a breach in the security system that puts another person there, then yes," Mary replied.

"What do we really know about Sandra Blake, except she appeared to be a control freak? A woman who needed to have her hand on the wheel steering everyone's life," Mr. Martin speculated.

We all remained silent. He had thought about this and wanted a Socratic exchange, like law school. However, none of us were really in the mood for a rapid-fire question-and-answer session.

"Did she know about Marsha? Had they interacted in some way? Did she know about the baby? If so, would it matter? Her husband was a well-known Lothario, she knew it and tolerated it. She could clean him out financially with the reconciliation agreement. Was she depressed? Was she being treated through counseling that didn't involve drugs? Could something have tipped her over the edge to kill Marsha Anderson?" he inquired.

"What about the phone conversation between Gabriel and Marsha before her death?" I asked.

"Unless he says yes, he spoke to her, how do they prove it?" Mr. Martin asked. "Could Sandra have cloned his phone number?"

These were all great questions, but out of my field of expertise, so I remained silent.

"Okay, putting Marsha's death aside just for the moment. What about the wife's death?" Dalia asked.

"Since we don't know her frame of mind, how do we know it was not suicide? What if she got her hands on the SUX, stood by the pool, and injected herself with a large dose and disposed of the syringe? And then she threw herself in the pool to kill herself with the thought of framing him? Maybe she didn't want to live any longer caged in a mind of torment. But she wanted to frame him, so he'd live in a physical cage for life. Maybe this was her ultimate revenge for the torment and humiliation he put her through," Mr. Martin postulated.

"If it's used for anesthesia where can you buy it?" I asked.

"I went on the black web last night and could have purchased and had in my possession enough to kill an elephant this morning before I was at the office," he replied.

"He's right about that; everything is for sale," Dalia said.

"So, she snaps. Kills his girlfriend and then herself?" I asked.

"The only question is, is it possible? Could you sell it as reasonable doubt?" he inquired. "That's what you get paid to do. Protect your client."

"But do you think he killed either one?" I asked.

"Is that really a relevant question?" he scoffed.

"Well, I think it is," Mary interjected before I could answer.

"That's the difference between a lawyer and a lay person. I would not ask that question of my client. All I want to know is can the state prove their case. Then, based on the strength of the evidence, I'd advise my client, either to go to trial or accept a plea if they were guilty. So, based on the information I have available do you want my theory of the crime?" he asked nonchalantly.

"Yes," we all chorused together.

"Based on the injuries inflicted on Marsha Anderson I think it was a crime of passion. Someone other than Dr. Blackwell killed that woman. Dr. Blackwell strikes me as a man who calculates all the risks and weighs his options carefully. My opinion is he would have dealt with her another way if she became a problem. I believe Dr. Blackwell would be worried trace elements left at a crime scene would give him away. However, the person who killed Marsha was not thinking straight and worked from a primal rage," he opined.

"Go on," Mary encouraged.

"Based upon the information we have available I believe there is a good chance he killed his wife. However, I have suggested an alternate theory of her death that might work in the case."

By the way, he sat and folded his hands; he appeared done with the matter.

Mary stood to get another cup of coffee and Dalia stretched.

"Do we want this case?" Dalia asked.

"I think if you're going to win the Anderson case, you'll have to take this one," Mary said, placing her saucer and cup on the table.

"Why?" Dalia asked, combing her fingers through her hair.

"You have a better chance of getting an acquittal in the wife's death. There's not a good motive. As Mr. Martin said, you've got at least one alternate theory. If you get an acquittal in the wife's case, I think it will send a message to the Anderson jury. The police got it wrong in one case; they got it wrong in the other," Mary said.

"Like they were on a witch hunt," I offered.

"A witch hunt," Dalia repeated. "So, am I setting myself up to help a murderer go free on one case to save an innocent man serving time for another?"

"A true dilemma," Mr. Martin said.

"No, it's a fucking nightmare," Dalia replied.

CHAPTER
TWENTY-ONE

Poppy

S OMEONE TIPPED THE PRESS ABOUT DR. BLACKWELL'S IMMINENT
arrest, and the harbingers of doom were waiting for him
to do the perp walk. The police had the good graces
to wait for him until he completed the surgery, instead of
dragging him from the operating suite. After he finished and
deposited his paper booties and cap in the trash along with his
gown, they slapped the handcuffs on him.

It took two hours to book him into the adult male detention center before we could see him. Since this wasn't his
first rodeo, he knew to remain silent and speak to no one. The
charge was murder in the first degree, and they could add other
charges as the investigation unfolded. This was an action that
begged us to invoke the speedy trial statute. Once the defendant made a speedy trial demand, the judge was forced to hear
the case within six months or dismiss the charges. Why allow
the prosecution time to dig up more evidence or a chance to
build a stronger case?

Dalia and I sat in a tiny room with a table and four chairs.
It was nothing more than a box to make it uncomfortable for
an attorney and their client to speak. The police provided Dalia

with the arrest warrant, and she was reviewing that when they brought Dr. Blackwell into the room. He had traded his navy-blue scrubs for an orange jail jumpsuit and his Rolex for silver manacles. He looked as if he aged ten years in one day, and the smugness that seemed to be his trademark look was gone.

The correction officer removed Dr. Blackwell's handcuffs, and he took a seat across from us.

"Buzz me when you're done," the guard advised.

Dalia acknowledged him with a nod and didn't make eye contact. Dr. Blackwell spoke, but Dalia gave him the signal to wait until the guard left. Then he exploded.

"What the hell is going on? No one will tell me anything. Everyone keeps saying 'ask your lawyer.' Well, now I'm doing that, asking my lawyer," he said in a tone filled with rage.

"Calm down, Gabriel, and keep your voice down. I don't know how secure this room is for sound. The guard doesn't need an excuse to stick his head back in to see if everything is okay," she told him.

My hat was off to Dalia. She remained cool as a cucumber on the outside, but I could tell under the surface, she was hot as a volcano. If I was lead counsel, and he spoke to me like that, I'd want to leap across the table and grab his shirt and shake him hard. My question to him would be, "what the hell is wrong with you?"

"If you're ready, we can go over the arrest warrant and talk about how this has come about. As I signed the attorney visit register, the prosecutor left a package for me. So, let's buckle in," Dalia told him.

"I'm pissed, but ready to talk," he said.

"They have charged you with first-degree murder, which is premeditated murder with malice aforethought. What that means is you thought about it and carried out the crime with evil in your heart. It wasn't an act done in a fit of passion or intense and uncontrolled anger," Dalia started, but he interrupted.

"I don't need a short law lecture on homicide. What do they have that should worry me?" he demanded.

I really wondered what any woman saw in this prick.

"Right now, all they have is the supposition that you were the last one to see her. And they believe the administration of succinylcholine killed her." Dalia let that sit.

That bit of news evoked a look of surprise. Dr. Blackwell sat back almost in a relaxed posture. His body language read he was open to receive information.

"Tell me about the succinylcholine," he replied.

"The pathologist completed the first autopsy, and his findings were inconclusive. He could not find a cause or manner of death which he felt comfortable putting on a death certificate. So, he asked for a second pathologist's opinion, which is rare. The state wants to limit its budget, so this is something out of the norm. The second pathologist found a pinprick-sized mark which he suspected was a hypodermic needle mark on her right outer thigh. Nothing relevant showed up in the blood that could be traced to why she would have a needle mark. There were no drugs, legal or illegal, in her system. The second pathologist decided to re-examine the organs and test some brain sections. Once they did that, succinic acid showed up in higher than normal levels in the brain," Dalia stated.

Dr. Blackwell leaned forward and slammed his hand on the table. It startled me and made me jump.

"That's it? That's all they have? What utter bullshit. I can think of a dozen uses for succinic acid that has nothing to do with a murder." He leaned into the table.

"Again, Gabriel, you need to get yourself under control. That guard hears another table slam, and we're done. Now, take a moment, then tell me its other uses," she replied.

We both were ready to take notes and try to understand what might turn out to be an organic chemistry lecture.

"Succinic acid has special properties that relieve stress and anxiety. The acid aims to eliminate the root causes of stress by stimulating your brain and kick-starting it into functioning normally. It's an anti-inflammatory and regulates cardiomyocyte which helps the heart pump blood properly. Did they check if her GYN had prescribed it for menopause? Jesus. Am I sitting in jail because of some incompetent doctor who made a leap from some high levels of a metabolite?" he said with disdain.

"I think it's a little more than that, Gabriel. They always look at the spouse first, that's just the way it is. The two of you had separated because of the Anderson murder, which hurt us. It gave the unwanted impression she was afraid to have you living at home. Add that the fact you were the last to see her, well that just made it worse," Dalia said.

"What else?" he asked, tapping his hand twice on the table.

"You have no alibi. You mentioned you went home alone," she said.

"Well, if I thought I'd need an alibi I would've stopped by a bar or went out to dinner, so I'd have witnesses and a credit card receipt," he said shaking his head.

"Sex clubs," I blurted.

God, they must think I have some neurological disorder. And once my eye started twitching they'd be sure. Wonderful.

Dalia whipped her head around so fast I thought she might have injured herself.

"What about them?" he asked, his tone more subdued.

"Do you belong to a sex club?" I inquired.

I should have given Dalia the heads-up about what Mark had told me, and now it was out there just dangling.

"Yes, and what does that have to do with anything?"

"Would you say it was a club that allowed more violent role-playing to occur?" I inquired.

"As opposed to what?" he responded with a shake of his head.

I didn't like deflection and word games.

"As opposed to a swingers club. You know, where role-playing and restricted physical activities are allowed," I said.

"It is a place where consensual adults meet to enjoy their proclivities not embraced by mainstream society," he hedged.

"So, yes or no to physical activities that might involve pain? And the parameters would encompass either someone inflicts it or receives it," I asked.

"Yes. Again, what do my extra-curricular activities have to do with a succinylcholine overdose?" he demanded.

"Did your wife accompany you to this place?" I pressed.

"No."

"Why not?"

He sat back and appeared to struggle with what he wanted to reveal.

"She had been a very active member at one point."

"Did something happen that made her stop? Or did she just lose interest?" I continued.

Again, he was still thinking about the best way to couch his answer.

"There was a time that chemical bondage interested me," he shared.

"I'm sorry, what exactly is that?" I asked.

"It involved me injecting Sandy with a level of insulin that would place her in a light coma. She in effect could not feel or respond to what I was doing to her. One evening we were running late, and both skipped dinner. Her blood sugar must have been below sixty. When I gave her the normal dose of insulin subcutaneously as I always did, she had a hypoglycemic reaction. It plunged her into hypoglycemia, well actually into hypoglycemic shock, and the club had to call an ambulance. It was stupid. I should have had a vial of glycogen with me, but I always had the dose under control. The fact it happened in front of numerous people made the club nervous. They didn't want the police to come snooping around. We agreed never to do it again, and Sandy was too embarrassed to return," he told us.

"Was she badly injured?" Dalia asked.

"She remained in a coma for about twenty-four hours, but she didn't have any residual effects," he replied.

"And there is a medical record documenting this?" she inquired.

"Yes."

"When did this happen?"

"About eighteen months ago," he answered.

"And you continued to frequent the place after this?" she asked.

"Sure. Why not? It was a mistake, an accident. However, now I stick more toward the mainstream bondage with my submissive slave," he told us.

Both our pens paused.

"Tell me about this submissive. Is it someone that is a regular person you use?" Dalia probed.

"I don't use her. She's not a prostitute. We have a contract that governs our agreement. So yes, to use your term, she's a person with whom I interact regularly," he replied with a bite to his tone.

"Do you see her outside the club?" she asked.

"Never. It's not like we're having an affair. We confine our activities to the club."

"Have you ever injured her during these activities?" Dalia questioned.

He blew out a breath and slumped in his seat.

"Why do you need to know about this? What has this to do with Sandy?" he asked.

"Well, it probably has something to do with both cases. The prosecution likely knows about your membership. They will want to get any information they can to make you appear abnormal. I'd say they'd like to paint a picture of you as a violent, careless deviant. So yes, everything matters," Dalia told him.

She let him absorb the implications of his lifestyle choice, let that sit and moved on.

"Were you able to track down if your phone was out of your control the time shortly before Marsha Anderson's death?" she asked.

"Ah, yes, but no. I determined I was in route home but didn't make any calls. I hadn't even looked for my phone," he said.

"That doesn't help, if anything, it hurts," she replied, her voice low and tired.

"What about bail?" he asked.

Was he joking? Had he totally lost his ever-loving mind? Clearly, he had.

"Considering the prosecutor believes you committed

another murder while you were free on bond, I doubt that will persuade the judge to let you out again," Dalia informed him.

"You're saying people have prejudged me and assume I'm guilty?" He raised his voice again, along with his eyebrows.

"I'm saying that some people hear gossip and innuendo and will accept it as truth and evidence. Right now, my phone is blowing up with calls from reporters wanting statements. I've also received a call from your medical partners who want me to call them back. We have an enormous mess on our hands. It won't get any better while there is a feeding frenzy for salacious news going on," Dalia told him.

"So, you are not asking for a bail hearing?" he inquired.

"I haven't decided. The chances the judge will grant bail are probably zero. But if granted, the money you would have to post would be astronomical. Someone will place an ankle bracelet on you, and the judge would likely confine you to your home. What I am concerned with is that this will give the prosecution a platform to tell the judge they found a large amount of succinic acid in the brain. It would give him the opportunity to explain it was a byproduct of succinylcholine, a neuroparalytic agent. While the judge and the rest of the world are googling succinylcholine, I won't have an expert available to explain the other reasons succinic acid might be in her brain tissue. Cameras from TV stations will be there, and they will splash your failure to win a bond motion across the news," Dalia told him as she tossed her pen on her pad.

"Christ, every crackpot relative of a patient that died will run to a lawyer to start a lawsuit. I can just see it, the Slayer Surgeon behind bars. So, what's next?" he asked.

"I'll meet with the team. Everyone will work around the clock, getting and sharing information. My thought is to file for a speedy trial. This tactic will give the D.A.'s investigators less time to dig around in your life," she told him.

"Will you do it for both trials?" he asked.

"I have to make an individual determination of the pros and cons of running a speedy on Anderson. However, they will be separate trials. I want to win an acquittal on your wife's trial first. However, the whole sex club thing has thrown a little speed bump in my thought process. Well, I'll get started immediately. Also, Mary will want an additional retainer," she told him.

"When I heard the police were on their way, I transferred two hundred thousand from one of my accounts to her. I hope it went through; I don't believe they froze that one," he stated.

Did I want to know where what appeared to be newfound money came from? Previously he claimed he was broke, and everything was in his wife's name. He was clear he was cash poor and depended on her to play ball with him financially. My mind wandered to the house that night where a murder took place. Had he killed her and removed money from a safe?

"What about the estate portion?" he asked.

"The judge will likely stay the proceedings until the trial concludes. However, the judge may appoint a special master. He would administer the day-to-day needs of her estate, and make sure someone pays all creditors," she said.

"But what about the life insurance policies and her part of the partnership?"

"The insurance company has a right to put a freeze on the funds. Under our law, people aren't supposed to profit from their misdeeds. So, until you are cleared it might stay put in a reserve fund," she advised him.

Apparently, the man didn't watch *Dateline* or *20/20*. Thank God Nancy Grace no longer had a TV show, or she'd make an hour-long study out of him.

"Dalia, Marsha never told me she was pregnant. Besides, if she had, that would not be a reason to kill her. I would have paid her off in a lump sum or paid monthly child support. She meant nothing to me. Also, the fact she was pregnant would hardly be a scandal. What a fucking mess," he said, shaking his head.

"Indeed. What I need you to do is think about what we have discussed. We will talk to medical experts, chemists, and pharmacists. I don't want you to write anything down or discuss your case with anyone. The team will tear apart the phone records and scour the area you traveled home. Hopefully, there will be a camera from some street or business that can place you on your way home. I won't be back for a few days. I've got a lot on my plate. If you call me, remember they record conversations. If it's urgent, say it's urgent, and I'll be out within the hour if possible," she promised.

"What are your thoughts?" he asked.

Good thing he wasn't asking me. I'd have said, "*Buddy, you are toast.*"

"It's too soon to tell, and I never like to commit this early in the case," she replied evenly.

"Poppy, knock on the door and let the guard know Gabriel's ready to return," Dalia told me.

He looked defeated. His shoulders slumped, and instead of walking he shuffled. After a handshake between him and Dalia, he left. The guard asked us to remain, and he'd be back for us.

"You notice he didn't vehemently proclaim he didn't kill his wife and demand justice?" she asked as her gaze remained fixated on the table.

"Yes, I caught that," I said, feeling somewhat low.

"How did you know to ask about the sex club?" she questioned, returning her pad to her briefcase.

"Mark let it slip, and said the prosecution was going to alert you to it," I said.

I should have made that a priority to tell her, but things had moved so fast this morning.

"That was a vital piece of information, Poppy. Next time, don't hold it so close, that's what phones are for."

I nodded my acknowledgment.

I looked up from my lap when I heard her making a motorboat sound with her lips, followed by a frustrated breath. "We're so fucking screwed."

I couldn't disagree.

CHAPTER
TWENTY-TWO

Tallulah

THESE WERE THE KIND OF MORNINGS I LOVED. NOTHING WAS ON my calendar that required my attendance at court, and not even a mediation until next week. The petition for the name change of a client was complete, and the draft of a complex qualified domestic relations order to transfer retirement funds was ready to mail to the plan administrator. Maybe I could leave early and do a little shopping. I deserved some me time.

Then the phone rang. That changed everything.

"Vanessa is cooling her heels in the waiting area, get out there before her head explodes. She has a copy of a restraining order the sheriff served her. She is convinced her husband called the police and plans to have her arrested for stalking him," Mary told me.

"Jesus. All right. Can you bring her to the conference room and then call the magistrate and determine if they issued a warrant? If not, then figure out if there's a pre-warrant hearing application pending."

I slammed my head back against the cushioned headrest and closed my eyes. I did not need this drama and chaos today.

God only knows what she did to provoke her husband to take such drastic measures. These are times I wish I could get the hang of meditation or maybe comfortable enough to keep a bottle of Jack Daniel's in my drawer.

Grabbing a legal pad and pen, I made my way to the conference room. I heard her before I saw her. She was yelling at somebody. I only hoped it wasn't Mary, or there would be a bloody battle to contend with.

Her phone to her ear, she paced like a caged animal back and forth in front of the table. Thank God Mary was gone, and she was channeling her ire elsewhere. I walked in and sat down waiting for her to finish her call. Better if she gets the rant out of her system. Within a few seconds, she disengaged from whoever she was speaking to.

"Look at this," she yelled, tossing the stapled papers at me.

I picked up the document titled *Petition For Temporary Restraining Order*. Attached to it was another document titled *Temporary Ex Parte Protective Order*. There had been an emergency hearing. After reading Mr. Abernathy's affidavit to support the restraining order, the judge decided to conduct a hearing without notifying Vanessa. That wasn't good at all. The court judged her without even being able to tell her side of the story. Although this was common practice, it still smacked of a violation of due process.

"Why wasn't I notified of this?" she demanded. "What type of messed-up legal system takes someone's liberty away just like that? This is utter bullshit. Is this going to affect the divorce? I mean, look at this, the judge thinks I'm some crazy psycho stalker."

Well, if the shoe fits.

"The court often conducts the first hearing *ex parte* which means without one party being present. The judge hears from the petitioner and errs on the side of caution and signs the order. If you look on the last page, there is a date set to hear the trial in its entirety and determine the case on the merits. It's set for one week from today. Now give me a chance to look at the accusations," I said.

I reviewed the document line by line. Twice. If these allegations were true, there was no doubt the judge would issue an arrest warrant for stalking.

"Have a seat, Vanessa, and let's go through these, one by one. Would you mind if I invited Mary and Dalia to join us? Mary will take part in investigating the allegations and Dalia may have to represent you for any criminal charges," I said.

"Whatever," she mumbled as she slumped into a chair. "And can you ask Mary to prepare a soy, vanilla latte, extra foam, one sweetener?"

Right. I'm sure Mary would get on it.

"Be back in a jiffy." I smiled. Entirely fake, and I didn't care.

I strolled to Mary's office where she and Dalia were huddled deep in conversation. I tapped on the doorjamb and walked in.

"She's a real piece of work, isn't she?" Mary smirked.

Vanessa just hit every one of Mary's hot buttons. More than once I heard Mary mimic Vanessa under her breath. The way she boldly mocked Vanessa when she turned her back, although entertaining, kept me on edge.

"You've read the petition no doubt," I replied rolling my eyes.

"How could I resist?"

"I'd like you two to sit in on the rest of this meeting with me. Mary, you'll need to investigate the claims and talk to witnesses. Dalia, it looks as if a felony stalking is coming our way. I asked Mary to see if there was a pre-warrant hearing scheduled or if the judge already issued a warrant for her arrest," I said.

Dalia's eyebrows lifted. Mary nodded her head.

"Let's go, ladies," Mary ordered.

"And, Mary, don't even reach for your gavel and strike block. I don't want any potential weapons in this woman's reach," Dalia told her.

We marched the few feet into the conference room in a single file, and when we entered, she was on her phone again. I sat at the far end of the table, and I gave her the wrap-it-up signal.

"Vanessa, you may not know Dalia. She handles our criminal defense cases, and I wanted her in on this, so if this case escalates quickly, we can be ahead of the curve," I said.

"You two finish talking about the order while I review it," Dalia said.

I handed her my copy and Mary sat quietly using the time to make a list of forms we needed to file.

"These are serious allegations, Vanessa. His documentation goes back several weeks where he caught you following him and his girlfriend. From this it appears you had him under surveillance and provided a sample of you taking pictures of him, with a large camera," I said.

"It's a free country. I can walk wherever I want and take pictures if the mood strikes me," Vanessa said and shrugged.

"That's not altogether true. Yes, it's a free country, but Richard's alleging you are invading his privacy and stalking him. Your husband says he felt threatened by your unusual behavior. Well, to use his words, your bizarre behavior. Is it true you followed him into a restaurant and sat a few tables away and pointed a steak knife at him?" I inquired.

"Maybe," she replied, twirling her pen in a circle.

"How many pictures are we talking about?" I asked.

"Altogether?"

"Yeah."

"About four hundred," she responded, picking the pen up and repeatedly tapped it.

Mary let out a long breath.

"Why?" I asked.

"To let him know I was watching him, and he couldn't hide any more property from me," she said leaning into the table.

"And did you whip-cream his windshield?" I asked.

"I may have. Well, yes, damn it, I did. So, what of it," she said getting agitated.

"That's criminal damage," Dalia interjected. "Unless the car is in both your names."

Vanessa waved her hand dismissively. "So, what the fuck can he do? Tell me to leave him alone? I'm not going to leave that shit alone until he gives me my just due of the property. And I'm keeping everything from the safe-deposit box. He's not getting any of that back. That was in both our names. He can put that in his pipe and smoke it."

I sincerely felt as if my head would explode. I could just see it now. The top of my skull blowing off from the intense pressure building up from the insanity I heard. Dalia must have read my frustration and gave me a short wave indicating she had this.

"Vanessa, we have stalking laws that carry serious consequences. If found guilty of breaking these laws, which by the way are felonies, you can face heavy fines and some long jail time."

That got her attention. But for how long?

"This restraining order he applied for is a civil matter,

which, at this point, would not involve any possible incarceration. The judge ordered you to stay away from him. Should you choose to disregard that directive then you can be held in contempt of the court order. At that point he could jail you indefinitely to get your attention," Dalia said.

"What! How? Why? All I'm doing is protecting what's mine," she yelled. As she slammed her hands on the table, her multiple bracelets jingled.

"Let me read you the legal definition of stalking: *if you repeatedly follow, approach, contact, place under surveillance, or communicate with someone or that person's immediate family or intimate partner, in a manner that would cause a reasonable person to suffer serious emotional distress, and such a person actually suffers serious emotional distress then that's stalking.* What you did hits the definition of stalking square on," Dalia said.

"You can explain to the judge why I did it, he'll understand."

"I can explain you didn't *intend* to put him in fear of his safety. We may be able to fly that flag on the criminal end and win. However, all the surveillance on a civil litigation front, well, the judge may issue a mutual restraining order just to keep the peace. For now, you must stay a thousand feet away from him and don't contact him," Dalia told her.

"Or?"

"He can file for a contempt charge, and you could go to jail."

Mary sat forward with her forearms splayed on the table and then tapped her right hand quickly to get her attention.

"Look, Vanessa, I don't think you love this man, and I don't believe it's a jealousy thing either. You are angry over the money. He gained a lot of wealth while you were married for that short time, but it's illegal. You are playing with fire. I have no idea what length he will go to protect his secrets. Why he went for a restraining order instead of killing you, I can't tell you. But he is cooking up a plan. Maybe he needs you behind bars. Or, did you ever think he wants a legal excuse to kill you. If you continue to do this, he might try to say you broke the order and threatened him and then BAM, he shoots you. You're dead."

That got her attention.

"What if I told you I put a tracking device on his car?" Vanessa asked.

Dalia looked at me, and I looked at Vanessa.

"Tell me you are joking."

"No, I'm not," she said.

"Where is it?"

"Front right undercarriage of the car."

"Can someone just bend down and remove it? Or did you get under the car and place it back where it would be hard to reach?" Dalia asked.

"Right under the bumper. In fact, I worried if someone detailed his car, they would find it. I figured he might think it's someone in his criminal world trying to follow him. Now he'll think of me first."

"I'm speechless. Anything else?" I asked.

"No."

"I'll talk to one of the guys we work with and see if they can follow him and remove it before he finds it," Mary told her.

"Vanessa, this is an extremely complex case because so much of the money and property is invisible. He is a criminal, and how dangerous, I don't know. However, if you keep pushing like this, Mary's right, you may wind up dead. I'm worried this has become an obsession for you and obsession leads people to do careless things," I warned her, but probably to no avail.

"Here's the bottom line. He's caught you breaking the law. You might be a victim of his immoral behavior, but now he's turned that around on you, and in the eyes of the law he's the victim. We are trying to put together a case to show he broke the law and is laundering money. It's like trying to nail jello to the wall; he's very slippery," Mary said.

"Let me call his lawyer and see if I can persuade him to drop it. If he won't, I'd like to ask if he'd consider a mutual restraining order to keep us out of court. Then, if he rejects that, we'll have to take our chances with the judge," I told her. "We're getting close to unraveling some of the illegal money. If he finds those funds gone from the box, I'm worried about your safety," I said.

"Okay, I'll lie low. However, I'm not putting the money, gold, and diamonds back."

"Where are they?"

"Safe. I have a gun, and I can protect myself if Richard comes after me for them."

"According to this order, you have to surrender any registered guns," I cautioned.

"It's not registered," she replied.

I was exasperated and exhausted. I didn't want to go any further as to why Vanessa had a gun, but Dalia did.

"When did you come into possession of it?" Dalia asked.

"Two months ago. Now I'm not answering any more questions. I have to go. You'll talk to Richard's attorney, right?" she asked.

"Yes."

"Call me when you have this resolved," she said and stood. "I know my way out."

Did she have her gun with her? When I was sure she left, the floodgates opened.

"Has she lost her mind? Or is there something going on here I'm not grasping? Did she do something to provoke him and it backfired?" I asked.

"If I was placing bets, she's got a plan going on, she just underestimated him," Mary said.

That underestimation could cause her ultimate demise.

It took Mary a few hours to find out that no arrest warrant was pending, nor had he applied for one. By the end of the day, I received a call from Mr. Abernathy's attorney who was smugly thinking he had the upper hand.

"So, your crazy client just can't leave him alone," Dalk Maddox said. "Jealous of the new girl?"

I hated to have to do this, but I had to go along with that line of thought. Men and their egos, they had to be stroked. I certainly didn't want him to know we were on to the money laundering. If he knew that, then there would be no place for her to hide.

"Well, Dalk, you've got her. She did go a little over the top."

"Over the top? She was following him everywhere he went and making a show of taking pictures. Maybe if she'd get a job and have a life of her own, she wouldn't find herself in this predicament," he lectured.

"All right. Mr. Abernathy made his point. How about I promise Vanessa won't do it anymore? This divorce is acrimonious enough. What can we do to make this go away?" I asked.

"I anticipated your call, and I have a small document for her to sign. Let me read you the language. *The parties shall continue to live separate and apart and each shall be free from the interference, molestation, authority, and control, direct or indirect, by the other. Further, both parties are hereby enjoined and restrained from doing, or attempting to do, or threatening to do, any act of injury, maltreating, molesting, harassing, harming, or abusing the other party of the marriage in any manner, whatsoever. Each party agrees to maintain a distance of one thousand yards from the other and not to have any contact with the other, direct or indirect.* If that works for you, we'll have them sign it, and he'll drop the petition. However, should she breach any part of this agreement then we are back on the judge's calendar," he warned.

"Email it over in a doc-u form. I'll forward it to Vanessa to sign and have it back to you tomorrow," I said.

I hated letting him think he had the upper hand, but this was a fight I wouldn't win.

"Great doing business with you, Tallulah," he said and hung up.

This has been just another volley in the bitter fight where someone surely could end up in jail. Or worse.

CHAPTER
TWENTY-THREE

Poppy

T HE FACT MARSHA ANDERSON'S PARENTS FILED A WRONGFUL
death action was a blessing in disguise. We could obtain
far more information through that case than the criminal
matter. When we subpoenaed her OB for a deposition, Dalia
attached a notice to produce her records so we would have
a full copy to comb through. We may not have had access to
those in the murder case without a show cause hearing, and
lose valuable time.

Additionally, the wrongful death action assured a face-
to-face question-and-answer session with potential witnesses
through a deposition. The state would probably call these same
witnesses as part of the criminal case. This gave us a preview of
what they would say at trial. No one volunteers to talk to the
defendant's counsel. However, now we had good reason to send
out nine notices to take the deposition of nine potential state
witnesses. Their testimony under oath, transcribed by a court
reporter, would give us an opportunity to look for weaknesses
at our leisure. The rules for questions required they only had to
lead to discoverable information. In court, questions even on
cross-examination that even smelled like we were fishing for

answers were not allowed. This way we had a head start where to look. It was like a dress rehearsal.

"Poppy, I know this is your first deposition. Here is the list of what I will ask. I expect the Andersons' attorney to object to a few, but that is just a formality. They can only object to the form of the question," Tallulah said.

"Lulu, do you have any question about what I need to be answered?" Dalia asked.

"No, I'm good with those. If you have a follow-up question to an answer, write me a note on your pad and put a star next to it. Dalia, I want you on my right and, Poppy, you on my left. I glance more right than left, so I'll catch the note quicker," she suggested.

"I've already told the court reporting company to expedite the transcriptions, so we have them eight a.m. tomorrow. That way we can comb those for inconsistencies or follow up with the next witnesses you have lined up. I still think you should have only arranged for one deposition per day," Mary said.

"Hmm, remind me again where you went to law school," Tallulah questioned.

I read the expression on Mary's face, and it did not take a genius to know an explosion of words, probably foul, would follow. Dalia must have felt the room temperature rise as well, so she jumped in.

"These are ancillary witnesses and I don't expect to get much information from them. The deponents today are staff from the hospital and the doctor's office who are helping us put together a timeline and lay a foundation for future deponents. I don't need people talking amongst themselves after, or the last person to give a heads-up to the next person about the questions. The element of surprise is vital. Unlike a judge who can instruct witnesses not to speak to each other, we don't have that luxury," Dalia told her.

"Well, I suppose I see that point of view," Mary replied. "So, day after tomorrow is the hearing to challenge the protective order to take Dr. Masters's deposition. Do you need me to do anything for that?"

"Yes, I have a list of cases I'm relying upon. Please pull them up and print them out. I hate to rely on my tablet when I'm at the podium. Come to think of it, make three copies. One for the prosecution and another for the judge just in case they haven't pulled their own after reading my brief," Tallulah said.

"Do you expect any trouble getting an order to force him to testify?" Mary inquired.

"Absolutely not. Disclosure of patient information in legal proceedings is permissible under the HIPAA laws," Tallulah answered.

"So why is he putting up a fight? What has he got to hide?" Mary asked.

"Maybe his attorney will try to limit the scope of the questions and limit our fishing expedition. Who knows?" Tallulah shrugged.

"We've already got parts of Marsha's medical records because the ME reviewed them for the autopsy. Probably Dr. Masters doesn't want to answer the hard question of how one man could be the father of the child when another couple paid him to ensure that the child was theirs. Hell, I need to know why he didn't do a routine paternity test at eight weeks to determine that. However, I haven't waded through all the medical articles about the whole implantation process. Thank God Mr. Martin finds such a fascination with the issue and is preparing a summary memo for me." Dalia sighed. "Oh, and, Mary,

I want to use Dr. Jefferson Mavery as our expert to review Dr. Masters's records. He's an OB-GYN expert that both Lulu and I could use in each case."

"One more thing, Mary. Just reach out to the attorneys we hired in New York to check if they want me there for the hearing to get the medical records for Marsha's egg donation. If so, book a flight and a hotel. I don't think they'll need me, but check since it's coming up next week," Tallulah said. "And come to think of it, Mr. Martin as well if he wants to go."

The thought of spending alone time with Mr. Martin would make drinking lots of brown liquor a necessity.

"We better leave, traffic can be horrid this hour of the day, so let's go," Dalia suggested.

My first deposition, I was excited. I hoped, soon it would be me grilling people and making them sweat.

The first two depositions were quite dull. There were no dramatic revelations or out-of-control arguments between the attorneys. No one refused to answer questions based on principle. When asked about Marsha as a person, her colleagues didn't seem to know her, much less her business. Their answers about Dr. Blackwell were guarded and appeared rehearsed. They indicated he was an excellent surgeon, his patients thought the world of him, and none of the witnesses had any personal knowledge of his bad behavior. Neither admitted to seeing the tape of him having sex with the nurse in the O.R. And in our favor no one gave credence to the gossip and innuendo about his alleged affairs. So far, so good. These people gave nothing to the plaintiff and everything to us. However, that was about to seriously change with the next witness.

Her testimony started rather mundane. The court reporter swore Liza McCarthy in as a witness with her affirmation to tell the truth, the whole truth, and nothing but the truth. Tallulah posed the usual background questions regarding her education and professional experience she had before working in the cardio-thoracic intensive care unit. Liza succinctly relayed her credentials which at first appeared unnoteworthy. Then came the revelation. She had advanced training as a nurse anesthetist. A professional with advanced training that would know about succinylcholine. Suddenly my doodling wasn't so exciting.

"Now you say you have training as a nurse anesthetist. Were you employed as one?" Tallulah asked.

She was thoughtful and took her time to craft her answer. It seemed an easy question. Yes or no.

"No, I chose not to pursue that line of nursing practice. Most surgeries are routine and go well without a hitch. However, there are times when things can crash quickly, and your mind has to work at the speed of light. As the nurse anesthetist, I would ultimately have to make the decision about the patient. I didn't enjoy being in charge of the decision-making process once I graduated. So, I took the book knowledge I had gained and put it to use in the intensive care setting," Liza responded.

"You would have had access to succinylcholine during your time as an anesthesia student, isn't that correct?" Tallulah asked.

"Naturally," she answered.

"Would you have any reason to come in contact with such a drug while working in the intensive care unit?" Tallulah followed up.

"Of course," she responded.

"How so?" Tallulah inquired.

"Urgent tracheal intubations are common in intensive care

units, and succinylcholine is one of the first-line neuromuscular blocking drugs used in these situations. Because of my training as a nurse anesthetist, the hospital extended me the privilege of intubating a patient if an emergency arose. I use it occasionally," she replied.

"I will object to this line of questioning. What has Ms. McCarthy's use of succinylcholine have to do with how she knew Marsha Anderson or Dr. Blackwell?" the attorney for the Anderson family posed.

He was correct. We were now crossing over into the death of Sandra Blake, and in truth, it was irrelevant to this matter. Tallulah had what she needed on this front. She established that succinylcholine was a drug available in the intensive care unit and that people other than Dr. Blackwell had access to it.

"I'll move on. Ms. McCarthy, do you know Dr. Blackwell?" Tallulah asked.

"Yes."

"Tell us what your association is with him?"

She straightened and stretched her neck back in a thinking position. Her eyes fixated on something on the ceiling. This probably went on for three or four minutes before Tallulah had to repeat the question. Odd.

Liza McCarthy did not like being pushed for an answer. After she shifted twice, she spoke.

"Why do you have to go into that? That's my personal business and has nothing to do with what happened to Marsha." Her eyes narrowed to slits. Suddenly she stood and leaned forward onto the table in an aggressive stance ready to pounce.

"Ms. McCarthy, please sit down. And yes, you must answer the question," Tallulah ordered.

What the hell was wrong with this person? Even the plaintiff's attorney came to attention. I guess I was getting my wish for drama.

"What do you want to know?" she snapped.

"What is your relationship with Dr. Blackwell?" Tallulah asked.

Technically the other attorney could have objected to the form of the question. However, it appeared he too wanted to hear what she had to say.

She plopped back down in her chair and pulled her hair back away from her face and let it cascade down her back. Again, there was a thoughtful silence.

"I work with him at the hospital," she replied.

Nice try. She wasn't getting away with that. No one would have that unwarranted outburst for that softball answer. I wanted to jump in and take over the questions. Instead, I lifted my butt, put my hands under my thighs, and controlled my need to move around.

"And how else do you know him?" Tallulah pressed. She smelled blood in the water. She was a real shark.

"How did you find out? This was all supposed to be confidential," she challenged.

"Please answer the question," she said not missing a beat. How great was this act? You'd swear the only reason she asked was that she knew the answer and wanted everyone to know it.

Now everyone was tuned in and on the edge. What the hell was this about? Were they part of some black-market organ-harvesting scheme?

"I am his slave," she replied.

We all sat mute trying to digest the answer.

"What do you mean? Are you saying he works you like a slave at the hospital?" the other attorney broke in. He seemed out of step and had no clue where this was going. I did.

"Mr. Jenkins, I'd ask you to refrain from asking any questions. I've got the witness on cross-examination," Tallulah snapped. "Ms. McCarthy, please explain that answer."

"Dr. Blackwell and I belong to a sex club, and I am his submissive slave. I can't say any more than that because he and I have entered into a nondisclosure agreement," she said.

Well, I hated to be the one to break it to her, but by even revealing that information she probably breached the so-called agreement. And arguably, which could be voided as an illegal agreement, depending on its contents. I, for one, wanted her to continue so I could determine what was in the contract. Mr. Jenkins seemed at a loss to where this was going.

"All right, then let me ask you the question this way. Do you have a relationship with Dr. Blackwell that is of an intimate nature? And by that, I mean outside the confines of what you'd call a slave and master relationship, do you have contact with him?"

"Do you mean other than the club and hospital?" she clarified.

"Yes."

Oh my God, lady, it's an easy question. Are you two lovers? Quit screwing with us.

Again, she sat back, and we watched her eye movement which showed she was considering how to respond to the question.

"Originally our relationship started as dating. Well, more like frequent hookups. There were no professions of eternal love, and I didn't expect him to leave his wife. But then he introduced me to *the lifestyle*. I attended a few sessions at the club and found a group I felt comfortable in and a community where I was accepted as a part of. We signed the contract delineating our roles and committed that area of our lives to each other. He insisted that our interaction remained and confined only to the club," she answered.

I glanced toward the other attorney who appeared to be hanging on her every word.

"Do you feel you have an emotional attachment to Dr. Blackwell?" Tallulah asked.

"Of course. Gabriel takes care of my every need. That's the whole purpose of these types of relationships. You have to trust and depend on your partner. Trust is key," she responded.

I could barely control myself. I wanted to jump in and ask her a million questions. Instead, I remained seated on my hands.

"Did you know he was dating Marsha Anderson?" Tallulah asked.

"Everyone did," Liza said with a condescending tone like we were the ones out of touch.

"How did that make you feel?" Tallulah followed up.

I got it, and so did everyone else. Did Liza kill Marsha out of jealousy?

"Feel? I felt nothing. I wasn't married to the man. He gave me what I wanted sexually, and I was content with that." She shrugged.

I wasn't convinced. I didn't know everything about the intimate workings of the BDSM world. However, I knew that when people got involved as married couples in the world of swingers, marriages did not become stronger. In fact, when the divorce rolled around, men often tried to use it against their spouse if alimony became an issue. Suddenly a man's wife having sex with another man was grounds for infidelity, and that launched the first shot in a messy battle.

"Did you know Marsha Anderson was pregnant?" Tallulah asked.

"There might have been some talk," she hedged and lowered her eyes to stare at the floor.

"That's not what I asked. Did you know Marsha was pregnant?" she repeated.

"Well, I overheard her telling another nurse she had had a close call at her OB-GYN's office. She had seen Gabriel's wife there. At first, she claimed it scared her to death that the wife had found out about their affair and had followed her there to confront her. However, it seems, in the end, his wife was just a patient there, and the crossing of their paths was just one of those serendipitous things. That's the first and last time I heard her talk about any pregnancy. Considering two days later she was dead..." Liza added.

Everything seemed to stop, and time stood still. The room was so quiet you did not have to look at the red second hand of the clock. You could hear its movement. Tick, tock.

"You're saying that Ms. Anderson told somebody she saw Ms. Blake at Dr. Masters's office two days before she was murdered? Can you recall exactly what she relayed?"

"Sure. Marsha told Elsa Manning, 'Man, I thought I was fucked for sure. I couldn't believe the old bitch was sitting in the waiting room when I finished my appointment. Trudy yelled congratulations on the baby being a boy as I was leaving, and if looks could kill, I'd be dead. I thought she had followed me there and would start a scene. So, I beat feet out of there and got the hell away as fast as I could.' That about summed it up," Liza said.

"Thank you, Ms. McCarthy, I think that is it for today. Although I may need to follow up on some questions after I have an opportunity to process this information," Tallulah told her.

The last deposition of the afternoon was brief. We needed to track down Elsa Manning and interview her right away. How had we not known Sandra and Marsha shared the same OB-GYN? Well, until now it didn't even seem relevant. But boy was it now.

CHAPTER TWENTY-FOUR

Tallulah

WE BARELY KEPT IT TOGETHER UNTIL WE COULD GET INTO THE car, and then we exploded in a frenzy of conversation. This was it. This information could blow this whole thing wide open. We could add two more people to Mr. Martin's murder chart.

There was no way this Liza chick could convince me she divorced her emotions from her actions. The fact that Sandra had seen Marsha in the doctor's office, and pregnancy was discussed, must have been like a punch to the gut. How to navigate this problem was unchartered territory for Sandra, there never had been a pregnant lover show up before. She couldn't know of Marsha's involvement in a surrogate program.

All this drama and chaos, and let's face it, the destruction of people's lives, could have been avoided if one man had kept it in his pants. I seriously disliked Dr. Blackwell and hoped he received his comeuppance for his bad behavior.

As we pulled up into the parking lot, my phone rang. Vanessa. God, should I answer it? Will it break the spell of what I could call one of my best days ever in the history of "what the hell did I just hear?"

I waved everyone to be quiet and tapped the answer button on the steering wheel.

"Hello, Vanessa. What can I do for you?" I asked.

I'd probably have to cut it short, or I would be stuck in the car talking to her for an hour. My mistake was not letting it go to voicemail and returning her call when I got back into the office. Well, too late. For now, Vanessa had me trapped in the fourth ring of hell of greed with her.

It took a moment to determine if she was still there. Then the loud, gut-wrenching sobbing began. The kind that leaves you breathless and your chest feels as if you have been punched, and you fight to catch your breath. I had parked the car, but no one wanted to leave. Poppy leaned forward, gripping onto the back of my headrest to get closer. Dalia turned her body to face me, and her expression said, "what the hell?"

"Vanessa, calm down and tell me what is wrong," I said.

The sobbing continued.

"How can I help you if you don't tell me what's wrong?" I had no doubt she heard the irritation in my voice, and I didn't have the time or inkling to deal with her theatrics. She had thirty seconds and counting, and then I was disconnecting.

"Richard is in the hospital on life support," she said through soft breaths filled with tears.

Oh my God. Life insurance. She tried to kill him. I should have stopped her. How will I live with myself knowing I played a part in that man's death?

"Are you at the police station?" I asked.

Well, I was glad Dalia was in the car. At least I wouldn't have to hunt her down to meet me at the station.

"Police station? What? Why would I be at the police station? No, I'm at the hospital. They called me to come down here because I am the next of kin. I need someone with me. They are asking me to make financial and life-ending decisions," she said as she blew her nose.

"Oh, okay. What happened?" I asked. Now I felt bewildered. However, if somebody was asking her to make decisions, then she wasn't under arrest.

"He was in a hit and run. Some heavy truck plowed into him from behind and crashed his car. He wasn't wearing a seat belt, and I guess he partially ejected through the windshield. When they found him, he was a bloody mess. After pulling him free they saw half his face was gone, and he was barely breathing. It took forever for someone to find him because he was on some back road. The doctors packed his head with bandages, and he's unrecognizable. Tubes are sticking out of his brain draining fluid. There are all kinds of machines hooked up to him, and an enormous ventilator breathing for him. There must be six IVs surrounding him, where they all feed into, I have no idea. They need me to sign papers for his insurance and guarantee payment. Well, I don't want to do that. I can't have the hospital tethering me to a million-dollar bill. You understand that, right? So, will you come down?" she begged.

"What hospital?"

So like Vanessa to be worried about a hospital bill instead of possibly arranging to donate his organs to another person clinging to life.

"Can I text you the information? You know, the hospital and room number," she asked.

"Yes, go ahead. I'm in the car, so I'll be there shortly," I told her and disconnected.

No need to elicit any more information. When I got to the hospital, I could at least hope someone who had the facts would be around.

"Well, you heard that. Before I leave, let's quickly put a plan together. When I return, I'll grab you, and go over what we learned. Dalia, I'm sure you will want to get Sandra's medical records or any logs from Dr. Masters to see if she was at the office the day that Liza said she was. If she overheard the exchange of Marsha and some office personnel about the pregnancy, then that gives us a thread of information to follow. I'm not sure I can get Sandra's records under a discovery request in this civil matter. She really has nothing to do with the request built on hearsay. It would be a stretch, and well, I can't see it happening," I said.

"No worries, I've got it on my list," Dalia said.

"We need to filter out the white noise in the information we received. Do we need to explore this sex club angle any further? Right now, I'd say probably not. However, the fact that Liza had a relationship of such intensity and trust with Dr. Blackwell makes me want to throw a BS flag down when she says she had no feelings of jealousy. Here's my two cents' worth. I think you should tell Declan about what we found out. Maybe he will choose to follow up and interview Liza McCarthy," I told Dalia.

"Way ahead of you. While we were driving, I texted him, and Declan wants me to call him when I get into the office," Dalia said.

"Considering she was a nurse anesthetist and trained as to the use of succinylcholine makes me wonder if she had anything to do with Sandra's death," Poppy interjected.

"I know. I have so many things running through my head on that revelation. She said she uses it for emergency intubations in the ICU. Which means she theoretically could have taken a vial from the crash cart with no one questioning her. But then the thought passed through my mind, so could Gabriel. They both had access to the cart. So, does that help us or hurt us?" Dalia asked.

"And not to be a Debbie Downer but now that we know about the feelings she's trying to deny, could they have done it together?" Poppy asked.

"Are you saying you've now put Gabriel on the active suspect list because of what this woman said?" Dalia asked with a challenge in her voice.

"Dalia, I know you want him to be innocent. I get it. You need him to be innocent in your mind, to zealously represent him. Let's face it, the more information we have, the more questions are raised. Could Liza have killed Sandra? She possibly had a motive. Did Liza have the means? Yes, she could get her hands on the drug. However, did she have the opportunity? I don't see Sandra letting this unknown woman into her home," Poppy opined.

"Well, unless she came in the back and surprised her. Or maybe she came to the front door and said she had to drop something off," I said.

"Or they could have been working together. Maybe Liza stole the drug, and Dr. Blackwell overpowered Sandra. I'm just having a tough time believing she could get close enough to Sandra to administer the drug herself, much less overpower her," Poppy replied.

"Where was the injection site?" I asked.

"Outer right thigh," Dalia answered.

"I can see where if an assailant was behind her and jabbed her in the thigh that could happen. Just saying if it was Gabriel, he could have come up behind her and locked her in with his left arm across her chest. Then he might have stuck the needle in her right thigh. If that is the case, I would think the person was right-handed since it was the right thigh. Or, you know, maybe her back was to someone leading them into the house from the door, and she was overpowered," I said.

"That still doesn't narrow it down. Dr. Blackwell could have struggled with her and moved her toward the pool and then jabbed her," Poppy said.

"Well, we aren't going to solve this any time soon, and I have to get over to the hospital. I'll catch up with you later," I said.

I dropped them off and they left chattering between themselves. When Mary found out this juicy piece of information, and they had not called her right away to share it, all hell would break loose. Yes, they would have their hands full.

I wasn't a fan of visiting hospitals, but who could say they enjoyed a good visit? There was no discernable odor to the place nor people strewn across the lobby missing body parts. Even once you reached the patient floors, most doors were closed. No one's pain and suffering were on open display. However, the ICU was different. The rooms were glass enclosures so a nurse or nurses could easily monitor patients. There were a group of nurses at the central station and one or two in a room with a doctor. Then I saw Vanessa. Pacing outside a glass room.

"May I help you?" a person in blue scrubs asked from behind the desk.

"Yes, I'm meeting Mrs. Abernathy, I'm her lawyer. She said she had documents to complete and needed help. I see her standing over outside a room," I said, pointing toward her.

"Our policy is only family members may visit. However,

I can offer you a family meeting room to talk to her. If you go over where she is and then follow that hall for a bit, the room is marked, family. You are welcome to meet there," she said.

Vanessa saw me and rushed my way.

"But wait, just a second. Here are the papers I believe Mrs. Abernathy wants you to review. She wouldn't sign them, and we need them completed for admission," the woman said.

I took the papers and met Vanessa halfway down the hall.

"The nurse gave me some papers for you to review. She wants us to meet in a room down the hall, only the family is allowed in Richard's room. However, I want to look at him as we pass by," I said.

She grabbed me by the shoulders and pulled me in for a hug. This was so unlike Vanessa. I didn't take her for a person prone to public displays of affection. Or maybe that was the point, and this was her hospital persona.

She linked her arm through mine as if she needed help walking. As if overcome by grief and it had weakened her resolve.

I lingered outside Richard's room. He was in bad shape. If he made it through the night, it would be a miracle.

We found the room and settled in.

"Give me a moment to check these papers."

Someone had evidently found his auto and health care insurance information and completed the pertinent parts.

"Let's walk down to the business office and tell them you are not the guarantor. They can't force that on you. They can coordinate everything they need to through the insurance," I told her.

There was a soft rap at the door. Before we could tell whoever was on the other side to enter, someone walked in. The man was a middle-aged man dressed in a lab coat with a stethoscope draped around his neck. He introduced himself as Dr. Newell.

"Ladies, I'm sorry to interrupt. I want to update you on what is going on with Mr. Abernathy and, I'm sorry, but it is unfortunate, but we need to make some decisions," he said removing the stethoscope from his neck.

"Please sit down," I offered.

He looked at Vanessa, I supposed, to assess if she could take in the information necessary to make a decision. When satisfied, he continued.

"Mr. Abernathy's injuries are extensive. He has sustained a catastrophic brain injury. I can explain to you about the damage to his dura mater and pia mater, however, right now, that might sound like a jumble of medical jargon. So, in layman's terms, the simplest way for me to describe his state is that we are keeping him alive by machines right now. Could he make a miraculous recovery? We never say never. However, with what I've seen on the CAT scan, I would not want to give you false hope," Dr. Newell told us.

"So, are you saying he's brain dead?" Vanessa asked.

"I'm saying that if we removed the ventilator, I do not believe he could breathe on his own, nor would his heart continue to beat," he said.

"I see," she said, and the tears flowed.

"Here is our dilemma. We don't know if Mr. Abernathy at some point signed a durable health care directive. Therefore, we do not know what his wishes would be to prolong his life based on his present state. Alternatively, if he would wish a do not resuscitate order put in place. So, as next of kin, that directive will fall to you. If you wish, you can have another family member, such as his parents or a sibling, make that decision," he said.

This probably would have been a good time to insist on speaking to her in private. I would have suggested since they were separated it might be better to have Richard's parents or brother make that decision. However, she jumped in before me.

"We had spoken about that often, and neither of us would want to linger. I give you permission to end all life support," she said with a sudden authoritative quality.

"Vanessa, do you need to think about this for a bit, and can we talk?" I asked.

"No, it's for the best. Richard shouldn't linger. We have no idea of the pain he might be in," she said, trying to muster up a sympathetic expression.

"On his driver's license, he did not have the box checked to be an organ donor. Do you know if there is any documentation which would reflect that would be his wish?" he asked.

"No, all I know was that he wanted to be cremated," she said. "No fuss, just cremate him as quickly as possible."

"Is there any family you want to notify so they can say their goodbyes?"

"No. The family is estranged," she responded. "When can we do this? You know, to pull the plug?"

"I have documents here that you may go over with your attorney and sign. If you look at the last page, Dr. Cartwright and I both signed as to his condition that would suggest there was no returning from where he's at."

"Thank you, doctor. Vanessa and I will review these. Shall we have someone call you?"

"Yes, just bring the papers to one of the nurses, and they will call me," he said. With that, he stood and left.

The tears were now gone, and I could see her mind spinning.

"So, once he's dead, then I inherit everything, right?" she asked.

"Unless a will was to surface that says otherwise, then yes, you are the sole heir. Also, the divorce goes away; the court dissolves it," I responded.

"How long will it be before I get my hands on everything?"

"I'll have to direct you to talk to Eloise about that. However, once the death certificate is issued things go pretty quickly. The house has a right of survival clause on the deed so that will pass without issue, and the businesses that are joint, as well. His hedge fund partnership might be tricky depending on the language in the incorporation documents and partnership agreement but barring anything to the contrary you would inherit his share," I said.

"The insurance claim for the books and art?" she pressed. This remained her priority.

"Would come to you. Except I must caution you, we are still investigating Richard's businesses and property as having criminal overtones. With your name on everything and if you don't repudiate what assuredly involves criminal activity, you could take on severe penalties," I said.

"They can't prove I knew anything," she replied, thrusting her arms in the air in frustration. As if I was the one throwing a monkey wrench in her plans.

"You might have been able to plead that argument before the divorce. However, we've gone over all the papers and now you know it is highly likely Richard ran a successful money-laundering scheme that now involves insurance fraud. Furthermore, once this is all yours, then you will have total access to assess if there is anything illegal. If you don't disavow it, then you are as guilty as him. God knows what type of people he was involved with. Do you want a bunch of thugs coming out of the woodwork wondering what will happen to their part of the criminal enterprise?" I asked trying to reason with her.

"We'll work that out later. I've got a plug to pull," Vanessa said.

Within the hour Richard Abernathy was no longer in this world. The mortuary sent someone to retrieve his body and within the twenty-four hours would be cremated. If he had a family who cared, they were never notified. Now Vanessa Abernathy was in charge, and everyone would know it.

CHAPTER TWENTY-FIVE

Tallulah

TODAY WAS THE DAY THAT COULD MAKE OR BREAK THE WRONGFUL death action against Gabriel Blackwell. It could also have ramifications in the Marsha Anderson murder trial. However, first I needed an update on Vanessa's case from Eloise.

"Thank you for turning over the estate matter to me. *Not.* This woman is an absolute nightmare," Eloise said.

It had only been one day since Richard Abernathy's death, and Vanessa had already arranged for his cremation. She had tried to gain access to the other safe-deposit boxes in his name but was unsuccessful. Without a death certificate and a court order from the probate court, banks she went to summarily turned her away. Surprisingly, the partnership agreement with his hedge fund named her outright as the beneficiary of his portion. Once she had that information, she spent her morning terrorizing them with threats indicating she wanted an equal say in the day-to-day operation of the business.

"That lady needs to slow her roll and realize we all don't work on Vanessa time. Plus, after meeting with Jackson and Mr. Martin, and going through the husband's records, undoubtedly he was laundering money. He made Vanessa a part of it and she is now implicated in any crimes attached to the corporations. I think I should prepare a memo with Jackson and Mr. Martin's input, which documents those corporations which appear to be a problem, and those that seem legitimate. It would point out and recommend what she should continue to control as part of the estate, and what she should not. I want her to sign a statement reflecting I gave her advice, and she releases us from any liability if she doesn't follow it. I don't want to get caught up in a RICO charge and have to hire my own lawyer to defend me," Eloise said.

I had to think about this for a minute to put all the pieces together. It wouldn't be easy.

"Can you wait on that and not put anything in writing?" I suggested.

"Sure. What's your line of thinking?" she inquired.

"Our attorney-client privilege only covers past and present crimes, not future ones we have knowledge of. So, if we know she will commit a future crime, well at least if she is formulating a plan, and gets caught, we might have to testify against her. Vanessa's entire modus operandi is based on greed. I don't see despair or grief; it's all about the money—getting it, having it, controlling it—regardless of whether or not it is legal or has a whiff of being illegal. I think it might be prudent not to put anything in writing the D.A. could subpoena outside the work product privilege. Let's talk about it. Right now I think we should meet with her and talk to her about our thoughts. If she moves ahead and takes over what we feel are illegal operations, then we should withdraw from representing her. I finished the divorce action. All we would need to do is withdraw from the probate matter and refund her retainer," I said.

"Yes, that is probably the wisest move. I don't know squat about white-collar crime. However, when Jackson and Mr. Martin laid it all out for me, it was obvious crimes were and are being committed. Some property, well a lot of it, is beyond the reach of the government because of international regulations. Once she transfers it back to the US, or converts it to another form of value and moves it around, there is no doubt they will nab her," Eloise declared.

"Here's the plan if it's okay with you. All of us will meet with Vanessa. There is no need for more criminal exposure than necessary. When will you have the death certificate?" I asked.

"I have it already," she replied.

"Excellent. I can have her sign the dismissal of the divorce and send it over to Mr. Abernathy's attorney to sign his part. Then we can forward it to the judge and once he signs the consent order that will dismiss the divorce, and it will close the case. At that time, if she doesn't want to take our advice, then we end our representation of her," I said.

"Okay, I'll meet with Jackson and Mr. Martin to review my talking points with them. You're headed to the Masters's deposition, right?" Eloise confirmed.

"Yes, and I'm a bundle of nerves. I desperately need to get the right information from him to lay this case to rest. I'm just glad that Dalia and Poppy will be there," I confided.

"Oh, and Mary said to tell you she summarized Liza McCarthy's deposition. It's on the corner of her desk. Grab it before you leave."

"Where is she today?" I asked.

"The shooting range." She smiled.

"Enough said," I chuckled. "Later."

As I walked past Poppy and Dalia's office, I tapped lightly

on their doorjamb to let them know it was time to go. I retrieved Liza McCarthy's deposition and the summary from Mary's desk. Poppy could read that in the car while we drove and highlight the most pressing points.

The man who sat opposite me, Dr. Steven Masters, appeared to be in his late thirties. If I hadn't known he was a physician, his outward appearance would have convinced me that he was a successful stockbroker. He was impeccably dressed, and probably paid as much for his haircut, as I paid for my car payment. There was something about his posture and the set of his shoulders that made it clear he thought highly of himself and wanted the world to agree with his assessment. Next to him sat his attorney, a man in his sixties, who hailed from an upscale boutique law firm. And one who undoubtedly charged a thousand dollars an hour to represent him.

"Good morning, Dr. Masters. I am Tallulah West, the attorney for Dr. Gabriel Blackwell. Just a few housekeeping measures before we start. I want to place on the record that this is the deposition of Dr. Steven Masters. It is being taken for the purpose of cross-examination, and all purposes allowed under the discovery statutes. He is here under a subpoena. Dr. Masters's attorney moved for a protective order which the judge denied. All objections except for the form of the question are waived until a later time. However, your attorney may place the objection on the record. The witness has been sworn, and I'm ready to begin. Are you ready, doctor?"

"I am," he replied.

"Could you please state your full name for the record?"

"Steven James Masters."

"You are aware you are being deposed in the case of….?"

"The Estate of Marsha Anderson versus Gabriel Blackwell."

"Have you ever been deposed before?"

"Yes."

"In your deposition, I will ask you questions, and you will answer them under oath. Do you understand this?"

"Yes."

"There are a few differences between a deposition and a typical conversation I want to make you aware of. Unlike a typical conversation, your answers today are under oath, and this subjects you to potential criminal charges of perjury for willfully giving false, misleading, or incomplete testimony under oath. Do you understand this?"

"Yes. However, it is my understanding that the answers I give are to the best of my knowledge and recollection."

"Sometimes, when I ask a question, you will have partial knowledge, but not absolutely certain or complete knowledge. I need you to answer to the best of your recollection. There are times 'I don't know' is not appropriate, but an answer," I agreed.

"Is there any reason, such as being under unusual stress, a physical or mental condition, or being under the influence of any substances, that would prevent or limit you today from giving truthful answers to my questions?"

"No."

"Dr. Masters, was Marsha Anderson a patient of yours?"

"Yes."

"I see you brought a copy of her entire medical record. I want to mark this as Exhibit A if this is a true and authentic copy. Please give me a minute to look through it, and then my colleagues will review it further as we continue." I smiled.

I took about five minutes to flip through the thin chart.

"How long was she a patient of yours?" I inquired.

"Six months," he replied without having to refer to the record.

"Do you run a surrogacy program or was she referred to you by someone?" I inquired.

"Three other physicians and I established a surrogacy program which we incorporated. Clients or patients, whichever term you prefer, come to us from several sources. The woman who wishes to offer her services as a surrogate also comes to us through various means. Once a family and surrogate enroll in the program, they then are matched based on strict criteria. Once the match is complete, and the parties agree to it, then that case is assigned to one of the four of us. That assigned physician follows the care of the surrogate, start to finish. In other words, from pre-implantation until birth. Once the baby is delivered, then the care of the baby is turned over to a pediatrician. This pediatrician is one we contract with for the first six weeks of care and evaluation. Then the family can choose a new pediatrician."

"How does a potential surrogate find you?"

"Word of mouth, clinics, a select amount of advertising and referrals," he replied.

"How did the baby's parents find you?"

"I object to this question," his attorney stated. "You are asking about a couple not a part of this lawsuit and who have not waived their privacy rights."

"Noted. Then let me ask you this, how did Marsha Anderson come to be your patient?"

"She had inquired if my office had a surrogacy program where we paid surrogates," he answered.

"And at some point, you responded yes. Is there a protocol you follow to admit a person into the program?"

"Yes. We have a minimal criterion to start. The candidate must have given birth or been a part of an IVF clinic and took part in egg donation. She also must have a healthy lifestyle, be financially stable, maintain a responsible lifestyle, and be a non-smoker. Her BMI should be under thirty-two, no history of mental illness, and age between twenty-one and thirty-eight," he relayed.

"Would you consider a person who had been addicted to drugs in the past a mental illness?" I inquired.

"It is part of the Diagnostic Manual, so yes," he replied.

"Were you aware Marsha Anderson attended Narcotics Anonymous?" I asked.

"No, she did not reveal that on her application. She did not place a mark next to the box asking about mental health issues. She also did not mark the box that indicated she had any problems with alcohol or drug dependency. However, we go an extra step. We screen all candidates for drugs," he said.

"Hypothetically, if you knew she had a previous issue with amphetamine-like drugs and was in recovery, would you have allowed her entry into the program?"

"No," he replied without hesitation.

"Did you offer Ms. Anderson a fee for her service?"

"Yes."

"How much was that fee and how was it structured?"

"I object to this line of questioning. It involves a right of privacy that extends to another party that is not part of this lawsuit," his attorney interjected.

"Turning to your contract with Ms. Anderson. Did you place a certain amount of money into an escrow account for her?" I rephrased.

"Yes."

"How much was the amount?" I inquired.

"Seventy-five thousand dollars."

"I object to any further questions about the funds as the escrow account belongs to another party, not a part of this lawsuit," his attorney reiterated.

"Let me turn your attention to an unpleasantness that occurred in your office on November second. It appears there was an altercation between Ms. Anderson and Ms. Blake, another patient of yours. Can you tell me what transpired?" I asked. *Would he take the bait?*

"There was no argument or fight. In fact, I remember that visit well. It was the day the blood results came back, and we determined the child was a boy. If anything, Ms. Blake expressed happiness for Ms. Anderson. Ms. Blake said she knew Ms. Anderson from the hospital, as a nurse that worked with her husband. In fact, she claimed they had met several times at hospital affairs and said she was a delightful woman. I agreed. She, of course, didn't know she was in the surrogacy program and it was not my place to fill in the blanks." He bristled as if he took offense.

"Speaking of blood work, let's touch on a few things. Do you have a candidate sign any papers that they agree not to have intercourse while active in the program?" I asked.

"Of course. If you look in Ms. Anderson's file, there is the signed copy, witnessed by one of the staff. However, there is no way we can be the sex police. We have to rely on our participants to follow the rules."

"Is there any reason why when you take the blood to do an analysis for the sex of the child, that you don't also do a

DNA test?"

"That's not in our protocol. Before I speculate on answering that question, I would need to have a full discussion with my attorney and other professionals as to the validity of such," he replied.

"I believe you are aware that during her autopsy, the pathologist performed a paternity test as part of the forensic evaluation. The results revealed Dr. Blackwell to be the father, and Ms. Anderson to be the mother. Have you seen those results?" I inquired.

"I have," he replied.

"Based on this revelation, how would you have proceeded with placing the baby with the couple, when he was born?" I questioned.

"Unless someone performed a DNA test before or contemporaneous with the birth, we would not know of this occurrence. However, to answer the question would call for me to speak to an unknown and I can't do that," he said.

"Was there any reason to believe anyone other than the donor family was the parents of the unborn fetus?" I asked.

"No, none whatsoever," he said.

"Dr. Blackwell wouldn't have that knowledge, would he?" I asked.

"I would have no way of knowing what knowledge Dr. Blackwell had or could have had," he replied.

"But Ms. Blake came away from your office that day knowing Ms. Anderson was pregnant. Correct?"

"Yes."

The questions continued for another hour and then concluded. I got what I came for, the physical medical records. Plus, a bonus that Sandra Blake knew Marsha was pregnant.

K. J. MCGILLICK

Had she made the leap that Gabriel might be the father? We will never know.

◎

The ride back to the office was not a pleasant one; traffic was stop and go. This gave Poppy and Dalia time to review the records and tag a few areas that were noteworthy.

"He is correct that she marked a negative for mental illness and drug use. However, on the day she was drug tested, she popped a positive screen test. When questioned about it, she explained she was taking over-the-counter cold preparations with pseudoephedrine in them. They rescheduled her for the week after for another drug analysis, and that next one was clean. They marked it as a false positive because of the OTC cold preparation drugs," Poppy said.

"Well, that is complete bullshit. That was a red flag. We commonly use drugs such as pseudoephedrine, ephedrine, and phenylephrine as decongestants in OTC cold and flu medicines. However, they will not produce a confirmed, positive drug screen. Some of these may cause a specimen to initially screen as non-negative, but in the second step of the two-tiered testing process, OTC drugs will not result in a confirmed positive drug test. They didn't want to either go to the expense of the second step to prove the person a liar. Or they wanted to give the candidate a chance to get the drugs out of her system. They can detect amphetamines in the urine for two to five days after ingested and in the blood up to twelve hours. What they should demand instead is a hair test, that goes back three months for drug use," Dalia said.

"Anything else?" I asked.

"Yes. She terminated two pregnancies in college, but the

judge won't let that in. Also, it states she had a sexually transmitted disease in the last six months treated with no residual problems, again inadmissible," Poppy said.

"I don't know. Maybe we could get it in to show she had a pattern of making poor decisions and didn't think about consequences?" I asked. I knew it was a stretch, but worth some time checking the case law.

"No, I don't think you can show how that has any bearing on whether someone can hold Gabriel liable for her death. Can the family prove he did something negligently or intentionally to cause her death? All you'd be trying to do is assassinate her character, and that would be received poorly by a jury," Dalia said.

"If we could only lock something down to prove he wasn't anywhere near there. Do you think I could dare ask Mary to get her friend Tyler to hack into the city's camera system and find him somewhere on CCTV?" I asked.

"Absolutely not. Besides, Gabriel already said he was at home when it occurred. Sandra wasn't there as an alibi, and now she's dead anyway," Dalia said with a firmness in her voice we knew to go no further.

"Okay. Let's have everyone read the depositions and meet to discuss where we can go with this," I said. "You might disagree with me, but I think we should start looking at Sandra Blake as the person who killed her. I'm not clear on the means or opportunity, but she had a motive all day and all night long."

"I haven't discounted that," Dalia replied.

"Have you heard if the judge will allow you to take the donor family deposition?" Poppy asked.

"Not yet. The judge is probably balancing their privacy, and what we can accomplish," I said.

As we turned into the parking area, I could see Vanessa pacing outside of the building on the pavement. Her phone was pressed to her ear and she was waving her arm as if she was arguing with the person on the other end.

"Shit," Dalia said.

"I got this," I assured her.

CHAPTER TWENTY-SIX

Tallulah

"LET ME HANDLE THIS, AND I'LL SEE WHAT SHE WANTS. YOU bring Mary up to speed on what took place at the deposition. You know, something tells me, well, it's my gut speaking, but there may be plenty of surrogate children out there that might not be the child of the donor parents. I could start a whole practice suing doctors for the very thing that happened with Marsha. There seems to be a carelessness about this whole operation," I said.

"Do not go there. I'm just going to check in, and then I want to go out to the jail and talk to Gabriel. Judge Greely took us seriously, and her clerk placed the case on her rocket docket, and we are on her calendar for the jury trial next up. She's slated Sandra's case first, and directly after that Marsha's. James Bradshaw looked as if he would have a nervous breakdown. He gave all kinds of excuses why the state couldn't be ready; they had experts to line up, more witnesses to track down, blah blah blah. However, Judge Greely was having none of it. She told him that they shouldn't have brought the case forward and indicted Dr. Blackwell if they weren't ready to try it," Dalia said.

"It is rather unprecedented, isn't it? I mean having a case

show up so fast. Most jury trials can take up to two years to conclude," I observed.

"Who knows what goes through Greely's mind. Any day she's not snoozing on the bench is a good day. So, yeah, I'll take it. Come on, Poppy, let's get inside, bring Mary some good news and then beat it out of here for the jail," she said.

I didn't have to wait long to find out what Vanessa wanted. She cut off the person she was speaking to and charged at me. Before I knew what hit me, her face was millimeters away from mine. She was so close I could smell her minty breath as she spoke.

"What the fuck is wrong with all you people?" she yelled. For emphasis, she flapped her arms around as if ready for takeoff.

"Step back, Vanessa, and lower your voice. Walk with me inside, and we can talk," I said, turning so she should follow.

"Why? So that robot of a man can tell me there is no way you can help me get at my money?" Her hands fisted on her hips and her legs spread for balance.

"Do you mean Mr. Martin?" I asked. As if I even had to verify who she meant.

"How the hell should I know his name? That mean old bitch at the desk, who, by the way, is too old to be working, shoved me off on some free body. Does the man have any social skills whatsoever?" she asked.

"Look, I insist you calm down and take a step back. We can go inside and discuss this in my office," I reiterated.

She quickly turned on her heel and power walked her way to the entrance. Dalia and Poppy followed. The ride up in the elevator was awkward, but blissfully silent.

The chilly reception Vanessa received from Mary spoke

volumes. Things would probably only deteriorate from here.

"Mary, please have Mr. Martin meet us in the conference room," I said.

"Your lucky day, Mr. Martin's still in there. He's probably deciding whether to quit after Mrs. Abernathy unleashed her colorful vocabulary on him," Mary said, looking straight at Vanessa.

"Well, if he can't take a little straight talk, then he doesn't belong in this profession. Also, might I remind you my money funds his salary," Vanessa informed us. With that statement, she crossed her arms across her chest in a defiant position.

That was it; this had to stop. This woman was totally out of control.

"Vanessa, we are going to go into that conference room and attempt to solve whatever problem you are having. Also, you will treat Mr. Martin with the respect he deserves. If you can't do that, then you need to think about finding another firm to represent you. He, as well as I, represents your interests, but we are not about to take any type of abusive behavior," I said in a tone I didn't even know I could muster. "And, Mary, can you ask Jackson if he can take a conference call with us?"

"No need, he's in there already," she said, with a raised eyebrow.

"Well then, let's go," I ordered.

Stepping into the room, Jackson appeared ready to leave. When he eyed Vanessa behind me, he stopped what he was doing. Mr. Martin continued to input data into his computer, oblivious to us.

"Gentlemen, I met Vanessa outside the building, and it seems we have a problem that erupted while I was out of the office," I stated.

Jackson put his file back on the table, and Mr. Martin stopped his typing.

"Problem is a mild term to reference what is going on here. You people are supposed to be working on my behalf, and no one is lifting a finger to help me. I am now in charge of an empire, and it appears no one is taking my position seriously. The partners have barred me from attending any meetings, and banks won't give me access to safe-deposit boxes. Yet that other woman Richard was carrying on with still has access to funds she shared with Richard. She's most likely wiping them out as we speak. He's dead, cremated, and they issued his death certificate. Now I want to access all the funds I am entitled to." She issued her demand, and she tossed her enormous bag on the table.

I suppose she had expected us to follow her from bank to bank and help her clear out all the safe-deposit boxes.

"Can someone tell me what is going on?" I removed my coat and sat.

"I explained to Mrs. Abernathy that the death certificate had been released. However, Mrs. Evans is still in the process of probating the will and having Mrs. Abernathy appointed the executrix. We have not received an order from the court appointing her as such, and thus, cannot move forward. Without that court order, the people who oversee Mr. Abernathy's property cannot release anything to her," Mr. Martin stated. Short, sweet, and to the point.

"Vanessa, Richard had a substantial estate, and we've spoken about this before. His estate is composed of questionable assets. By that, I mean they are likely illegal. Sometimes when there are problems with ownership of assets, the process takes longer to move along. Even when everything goes smoothly, and there aren't many assets to distribute, it can take up to a year to close out the matter. I'm certain that Eloise has explained the process to you. This could easily take several years to conclude. Richard not only had domestic corporations but also incorporated some internationally. And those international ones have a separate set of laws from ours. So, you must be patient."

"Tallulah, can I speak to you in the hall for a second?" Jackson interjected.

"Wait. Before you go out there and start conspiring and covering each other's asses, I want to know about the insurance check. The life insurance," she clarified.

"I have to refer you to Eloise for an answer to that. However, if you are the direct beneficiary, then it comes directly to you. If it's made to the estate as the beneficiary it remains part of the probate," I said.

"What about all those corporations I am listed on, I should be able to access all of them," she said.

"Yes, you should as an equal partner. However, once again, I must advise you that we believe they were part of a money-laundering scheme. It is my opinion, if you do not disavow ownership, you might be liable for a criminal act. Now give me a minute to speak to Jackson," I said, stood, and turned to leave.

I stepped outside, leaving Mr. Martin to return to his typing and Vanessa to cool her heels.

"I made some informal inquiries, and the Department of Justice is planning on interceding in the will probate. They appear to have enough evidence to seize some of those corporations. Now, what I am telling you is what I have read between the lines, so take it for what it's worth. You know they can't give me a heads-up. However, from working in the division long enough, what is glaringly evident is they aren't convinced Mrs.

Abernathy isn't a co-conspirator. If you can't get her to sign off on the assets we discussed, she is more than likely facing an arrest the moment she lays her hands on any of the property. I know for a fact they have already seized the bank footage showing us going into the bank where she removed the property," he said.

"God. Also, I got something from Richard's attorney this morning, indicating the company released the funds on the stolen art and books. They released the check to him, and he wants that off his desk. He said the check was made out to Mr. Richard Abernathy or Mrs. Vanessa Abernathy so she can cash it without him. His attorney wanted to know what to do with it. I told him to hang onto it, and I would get back to him."

"Could be a trap. Maybe it's the domino that will send the rest of them crashing down and be the one to bury her," he said.

"Let's go back inside," I told him. "Give me a second. I want to get something I had Mary draw up to cover this very thing."

After taking a seat, I thought about recording the conversation. This was the conundrum we had discussed that could come back and force us to be witnesses against Vanessa. If future crimes were discussed, we were not protected under the attorney-client privilege.

"Vanessa, we are here to give you advice and legal counsel. What you do with that is up to you. We spoke about the fact that Mr. Evans and Mr. Martin did some deep and intense research regarding your husband's corporations. We've told you it's clear that some of them are just vehicles to launder money. How exactly each performs we can't know, but it gives that appearance. If you take possession of these corporations, you are opening yourself up to potential criminal consequences," I said, but was quickly interrupted.

"But you don't know that for certain, so don't try to scare me. No one, not even the big brain over there, can know what those corporations are really all about until I take possession. Right now, you're just guessing. Nothing ventured, nothing gained," Vanessa said. Her position was defiant and her face hard as stone.

"In addition to the criminal penalties, you also have to consider Richard may have been dealing with unsavory people. Maybe a cartel or foreign mafia. For all we know, someone killed him over his business dealings. The truck that hit him is registered to a corporation that exists on paper and has no physical facility. Also, they never found the driver," I said.

"Now you're just trying to alarm me," she said with irritation in her tone.

"No, madam, she's trying to save your life," Mr. Martin interjected.

"No, she's being dramatic, so I will do what she wants and walk away from a pot of money. I haven't gotten to where I am today without taking a few risks," she said.

"And where would that be?" Jackson asked with an amused smirk on his face.

"The wife of one of the wealthiest men in Colorado. And now I'll be one of the wealthiest women," she told us.

"Okay, I see that your mind is made up. It's clear that talking any further is wasting our breath and your time. I have prepared a document indicating you release the firm from any actions you take outside the scope of our advice. I'm asking you to sign that document. Then you and Eloise can determine how to proceed with the estate portion as a separate matter. As of now with this document I am released as your attorney," I said.

I handed her the paper and watched her read through it.

"Richard's attorney called me this morning, and he has the insurance check releasing the funds to you for the stolen property. I suggest that you place the funds in an escrow account until the probate matter is concluded. I'm afraid that this may be a trap. Once you cash it, it may trip several mechanisms to start in motion," I said.

"Again, you're overdramatizing the situation. I'm certain the insurance company would not release the check unless their internal investigation was concluded, and they found everything was on the up-and-up," Vanessa lectured me.

"What if law enforcement is working with the insurance company to see if you'll take the check? If they think you are a co-conspirator with Mr. Abernathy, this could come back to bite you hard. You'd be talking about federal charges here, Mrs. Abernathy," Jackson said.

"Then that would be entrapment," she threw back.

"I'm not here to offer you legal advice, that's what you have lawyers for. What I will tell you is there is a vast difference between entrapment and giving the person the opportunity to commit a crime. You have to ask yourself, is law enforcement inducing you to commit a crime? That would be a no. The authorities may be watching to see if you cash that check. Now that's all I will say. As part of your legal team, I encourage you to place it in an escrow account in addition to everything else that is questionable. Once the probate shakes out, then determine what you should do," he said.

Jackson was between a rock and a hard place. He did the best he could to warn her, we all did.

"Anything else?" she asked.

"No," I said.

"Please tell his lawyer I am on my way over to get that check. Whether you people know it or not, I'm not just some dumb trophy wife. I know exactly what I'm doing," she said with a smile the devil would approve of.

She signed the paper and left.

We sat for a moment in silence. Jackson was the first to speak.

"Anyone else thinks that last statement was more than just bravado? I mean, did she have us all fooled thinking she was just a selfish airhead when maybe she was in it with him all along?" Jackson asked.

"I believe if she were completely innocent, she would want to wash her hands of any criminal activity. Even a whiff would send someone innocent running," Mr. Martin replied.

"What's your thought, Jackson?" I asked.

"I think the feds are having the papers prepared right now to land a RICO charge at her door. It's my guess they will freeze any assets she has in his name and hers. It would not surprise me if she's arrested when she goes to cash that check," he said.

"Uh, I am just done with this whole drama. I've got to finish up the Blackwell stuff. I've washed my hands of the divorce, and I have a feeling the DOJ is going to land in the middle of the probate matter," I said.

"Of that, I have no doubt," Mr. Martin agreed.

CHAPTER
TWENTY-SEVEN

Poppy

I MUST BE CULTIVATING A DUAL PERSONALITY. A DRAMA AND CHAOS-driven one. Truth be told, I didn't want to be dragged away from the spectacle about to ensue at the office. I wanted to have a front-row seat to Tallulah lose her mind with that crazy-ass Vanessa Abernathy. I'd pay good money to watch her wrestle her to the ground and beat some sense into her. Oh my God, I had to get ahold of myself.

"Poppy!" I heard Dalia say, and she snapped her fingers in front of my face.

"Where were you?" she asked, putting her hand back on the wheel.

"Sorry. I was thinking about Vanessa Abernathy," I replied sheepishly.

If she could only read my mind, she would undoubtedly fire my ass.

"My email chimed. Open it up and see if that's Mary sending us information about Liza McCarthy," she stated.

"Oh, sorry. What's your passcode to open the phone?" I asked.

"Here, give it to me," she declared, reaching for it.

Not good to be breaking the law on the way to a place hundreds of lawbreakers now resided.

"So, what does it say?" she asked.

"You want everything? All her stats?" I asked, skimming the email.

"Yes, I got a vibe off her I didn't like," she added.

"Oh, what a shocker. I wonder why. Maybe because she enjoys being spanked and punished by that freak Gabriel Blackwell. Not that I'm judging the whole BDSM thing, mind you. Just saying, with him admitting to having sex with a person in a coma-like state made me think about that saying, monsters hide in plain sight," I said not sure if she'd appreciate my candor.

She laughed, but just a small laugh to acknowledge my statement.

"No. I can't put my finger on it, but Liza seems like… what do I want to say? Not an outwardly troubled person, that's not what I'm going for. I feel she has trust issues and is a lone wolf. Maybe clingy and needy," she said.

"You got all that from the deposition?"

It stunned me. We hadn't even delved into her social life. It would have been irrelevant and objected to as it had nothing to do with Marsha's murder. Or did it?

"No. I don't know; I must be having a free stream of consciousness going on. I'm trying to connect things that make little sense. Just read me what Mary dug up," she said, tapping the wheel with her index finger.

"Okay. Liza McCarthy was born in Manhattan, New York, on February 10, 1989. She grew up in Scarsdale, which is in Westchester County right outside of Manhattan. Oh, that's where that Scarsdale Diet Doctor Herman Tarnower lived and was murdered by his lover. You know his lover was a headmistress of that posh girls' school in Virginia," I told Dalia.

"Is that editorial jibber-jabber or relevant to what I need to know?" she asked, giving me the side eye.

"Jibber-jabber I suppose. I store all these weird facts in my mind. Anyway, she attended an all-girl private school, make that an all-girl private Catholic school, from kindergarten through high school. Upon graduation from high school, she attended Columbia University, School of Nursing as an undergraduate, and then entered Columbia University, Graduate School of Nursing. That's where her anesthesia degree comes in. Wow, she must have a big brain and wealthy parents. She graduated both places summa cum laude and did not incur any student loans.

"She worked at Mount Sinai Hospital, in Manhattan on their neuro intensive care unit. Liza started there immediately after graduating from nursing school and worked there during grad school. When she left, she had a position of evening charge nurse of the unit. This is interesting. She left there to take a job in clinical research for a pharmaceutical company. Oh, get this, she was with a company in Nuremberg, Germany. Mary wrote a note that that company manufactures succinylcholine and Pavulon, both neuromuscular blocking agents. Mary also noted Pavulon is like curare, which differs from succinylcholine. Anyway, Mary said 'the girl seems to love the neuro system, and manipulation of it,'" I repeated.

"Wait, stop. Liza never told us she was employed by a pharmaceutical company. She left the impression her experience was only with clinical nursing. Can you open my text app and ask Mary to find out if she carried out testing on Phase 1, 2 or 3 of the clinical trials for the company," she added.

"Why would that be important?" I asked as my thumbs

tapped out her request.

"I want to see if she had more experience in the research and development aspect which would be more Phase 1. Or the actual administration, which would be along the lines of Phase 3. It's just a curiosity and might mean nothing," she said.

"Okay, continuing. Yes, she stayed there for a year, no eighteen months, and then returned to the US and took the job she now has here in Denver," I explained.

"Any arrests?" she asked.

"Nada," I replied.

"Marriages," she followed up.

"None, and no children," I told her.

"So, all we know is she's a thirty-year-old woman who went to an all-girl Catholic school, then Ivy League and is un-doubtedly operating at a genius level. She has a thing for the neurological system and might have issues involving control and likes being controlled," she said.

"Au contraire," I replied.

"What?" she asked, turning toward me with raised eyebrows.

"In the dominant-submissive world the submissive has all the power and control," I told her.

"How so?" she asked.

"The submissive is the one that can stop the game, or a scene as they call it, by saying the safe word. If someone in-vokes the safe word, then the dominant must honor that re-quest," I told Dalia.

"But it's all about humiliation," she stated.

"Oh no, not at all. It's about an exchange of power. Maybe in the world of sadism and masochism, it is all about humiliation or shame, but not in a truly dominant and submissive world. In fact, the dominant is in charge of the submissive's well-being. Don't make the mistake of confusing either with a sado-masochist relationship, which is all kinds of messed up," I told her.

"Poppy, I'm scared to ask how you know all this," she said with hesitation.

"Advanced constitutional law in law school and the study of the first amendment. Frankly, I find it fascinating. It's actually a real study of the human mind. I read nearly a hundred articles and psychological studies about it when I was preparing to write my paper. Some people equate it with orgies, swingers, and ménage à trois, but nothing could be farther from the truth. It's a very personal relationship between two people. Which, depending on the people involved can also involve exhibitionism or voyeurism," I told her.

"Well, more than I needed to know. However, it gives me a glimpse into Ms. Liza McCarthy. As she indicated, it is a casual thing for her," Dalia reminded me.

"Don't you for one minute believe that. There is no doubt in my mind, she is highly invested in this relationship. In fact, I believe she would go to great lengths to protect it," I said.

"Enough to murder someone?" she asked.

"Absolutely," I insisted.

The remaining fifteen minutes to the adult detention center was spent in silence, each with our thoughts.

The lobby in the detention center was pleasant enough. This must be visiting day considering the large number of visitors. But not the overcrowding you would expect from people missing their loved ones. It was orderly and the children well behaved.

Dalia and I showed our state bar card to the person staffing the desk. We informed the deputy we were there for an attorney conference with Dr. Blackwell and would need a conference room to meet. The attendant clicked a few keys, scrolled through to the screen he needed, studied it for a moment, and advised us Dr. Blackwell had a visitor with him.

"I'm sending a message to the guard to let him know you are waiting. He'll check to determine if Dr. Blackwell wants to cut the visit with his visitor short. Have a seat right here to the left. I'll be right back to you as soon as I have an answer," he told us.

It seemed almost immediately that he notified us the inmate was ready to meet us. He asked us to walk through the metal detector, and then to wait for someone who would escort us to an attorney conference room. I happened to look up from my phone, and what I saw stunned me. I jabbed Dalia, who also had been studying her phone messages, and we both stood ramrod straight at attention.

We watched as a guard accompanied Liza McCarthy exiting an area to our right. She had changed her clothes since the deposition a few days earlier. Looking at her now, Liza could pass for a subdued small-town librarian, a real chameleon. Her hair pulled back in a tight bun, she wore barely any makeup and had exchanged black-framed glasses for her green contacts. Her skirt fell gracefully below her knees, almost to her calf and her blouse was white, high-collared, and cotton. The only thing out of place was her shoes. Not the drab shoes of a prissy librarian, but stiletto "fuck me" shoes.

She didn't make eye contact with us as she passed. Her

gaze remained straight ahead and revealed no emotion.

"Aren't you going to go after her and ask her what she's doing here?" I asked, grabbing Dalia's arm.

"Why? Isn't it obvious she's here to report back to Gabriel? Why waste my time?" she replied.

"Well, I'd want to confront her about her statement indicating she wasn't attached to him emotionally. Also, why she had forgotten she worked in Germany for a pharmaceutical company for over a year," I told her.

"Like you implied, Poppy, it's a complex relationship. What we are doing is peeling back the layers to see if the core has anything to do with our case," she said.

"Ladies, follow me," the guard told us.

We followed him down a long tiled hall that had three colored stripes, directing the visitor to different parts of the building. We followed the blue one to a metal door which opened by swiping a card. Dr. Blackwell was already seated at the metal table waiting for us. We made ourselves as comfortable as you could on brown chairs filled with hard foam and a metal back.

Dalia did not remove her pad for notes. She planned to conduct this as more a conversation; I was the note taker.

"Good afternoon, Gabriel. You look well. How are things going?" she asked, folding her hands in front of her and placing them on the table.

"Seriously?" he responded with a raised brow.

"I have a few things to talk about so let's get to it. We have a court date," she said.

That caused him to sit up and take notice.

"We are slated for Sandra's trial first. I've filed numerous motions that the judge has to rule on, and once that's completed, we will move to the actual trial. We've been very busy getting everything to our experts. They've been working at a double-time pace so they are prepared to testify at trial on such short notice if we need them. I have a pharmacologist, pathologist, and neurologist ready to testify. Our technical experts have what appears to be your car, a half hour away from the scene of the crime at the time of death. What I don't have is a clear picture of who's driving the car," she told him.

"And?" he prompted.

"And I also have an expert legal witness. She will testify that she believes you could have moved to void the reconciliation agreement and won. That will take the motive of the reconciliation agreement out of play. What I also have is an alternate suspect for the crime," she said.

His eyebrows almost hit his scalp. "Why haven't I heard about this before?"

"Because the pieces just fell into place," she replied with an evenness to her voice that was scary.

Whom was she going to name?

"Well then, care to share?" he asked.

He leaned back against his chair and crossed his arms over his chest.

"Why don't you tell me? You're the one with all the secrets. I just can't figure if the two of you were working together," she responded.

"Obviously I have no idea whom you are talking about," he told with a sneer.

An expression that suggested he knew exactly where she was going with this theory.

"Liza McCarthy," Dalia said.

"What about her?" He shrugged now leaning forward, almost in an aggressive posture.

"Her deposition was quite revealing," she told him.

Silence.

"If you would have given me a heads-up about how deeply you were involved with her, I could have moved it in another direction. You left me and her exposed. Once she put the breadcrumbs out there, that she overheard Marsha telling someone about the OB-GYN visit, I could have cut it off. I would have left that information dangling. However, I went full throttle. Now, everyone knows you and she have, shall I say, an unusual relationship. Would she kill for you? Hell, I don't know. However, now I can throw her under the bus. Should I? Should I, Gabriel? Because I can make a great case against her." Anger apparent in her voice.

He remained silent. He was staring at Dalia and taunting her with his eyes.

"Was that your plan all along? Get her to do it. Or go to trial and raise a reasonable doubt. There isn't enough to convict her right now, and there may never be. Once we point to her, and if only one person buys it, you walk. Double jeopardy attaches, and the both of you may get away with murder," Dalia said.

He did not break his silence.

"Were you hoping that someone would think Sandra was depressed and killed herself? Was that the purpose of those pills on the table? Pills she didn't have a prescription for I might add. Nor did they find any residue of those pills in her stomach. I suppose you didn't count on the death being ruled anything but a suicide. You or maybe Liza hadn't figured on a second pathologist finding the injection site nor looking at brain slices. What I want to know was where's the syringe?" she said with an angry challenge to her voice.

Nothing. No denial. No answer. But his silence was his answer.

"I'm going to ask the judge to allow me to withdraw from representing you," she informed him as she stood.

"No, you won't," he told her. "And sit down, we're not finished."

She remained standing.

"No judge will allow you to withdraw so close to trial. If you did, it would prejudice my case. So now that you've exhausted all my funds, well until the probate money and life insurance shakes loose, I am unable to hire anyone else. So, Dalia, you are in this fight to the bitter end," he sneered.

"I am not your indentured servant, Gabriel."

"No, you're not, but you owe me a duty of care. What's the term Sandy always used? Yes, you have to be a zealous advocate. I won't tell you how to run your case; however, actions have consequences."

He had her boxed in between a rock and a hard place. No way a judge would let her out now, he's right. Also, if she didn't give her all for defending him, that could land her an ineffective assistance of counsel charge on appeal if he lost.

"Poppy, let the guard know we are done," she said, not losing eye contact with him.

I tapped the button to alert the guard and waited to hear the door lock disengage. We left Dr. Blackwell sitting at the table without a readable expression on his face.

Once we cleared the building, she stopped and leaned on a stone structure outside the front. Her breaths came hard and fast. I was afraid she might pass out or throw up. Which would be worse? For me, helping her clean vomit off her shoes would be worse. Because there was a chance if she puked, I would soon follow suit.

"I'm sorry that this is your first big case, Poppy. This is the time I've dreaded since leaving the D.A.'s office. I might be defending a murderer and afraid I am obligated to help him evade justice," she said.

My stomach sank hearing her say those words. Because in the back of my mind, I was thinking of how we could plant evidence to make Dr. Blackwell face his punishment.

"Dalia, I really have no idea who committed the murder. They are both equal suspects, and I think one or both may have perpetrated the perfect crime," I suggested.

"And the sad part, Poppy, is, all you need is one woman on that jury to fall under his spell, and there's your acquittal," she said.

CHAPTER
TWENTY-EIGHT

Poppy

THE DAY OF SANDRA BLAKE'S TRIAL HAD ARRIVED. DALIA AND THE prosecutor spent arguing pretrial motions in front of Judge Greely for the better part of the morning. Some we won, and most we lost. The one thing was clear. Everyone had lost the will to fight for him, but fight we must.

Although the fate of Dr. Gabriel Blackwell was not in my hands, I felt as if the entire world was sitting on my shoulders. Pushing down on them and making every muscle in my body ache. My primary role was to make certain that all the documents were marked and ready to be tendered into the court record. My focus was to observe the jury for any reflection of disdain or anger toward Dr. Blackwell. More important, I was to keep Mary appraised if it looked like the floor would open suddenly and swallow us wholly into the bowels of hell.

After hours of arguing amongst ourselves, we had decided to go with what we called the Mr. Martin defense. A defense predicated on the supposition that Sandra Blake had killed herself. We accepted this would be an uphill battle, arguing against an autopsy report signed off by two pathologists indicating a homicide had occurred.

Yes, we got lucky. Weeks after the death of Sandra Blake occurred, a syringe had surfaced. During the process of the pool being winterized, the pool guy found a lone hypodermic syringe lodged in the pool's grate. One would think a syringe submerged in water would have no forensic value. Not so. A new one on me. But that's possible that July 2018 from the forensic journal backs it up. However, the fact that the lab could lift Sandra Blake's prints from a syringe lodged in the grate so long made the evidence suspect.

The argument our expert proposed, was that the body of the syringe, the barrel, was not totally immersed. It had found an air pocket where it lodged. The prosecution insisted someone had recently planted it. However, Dr. Blackwell, the only person that would benefit from that, had remained in jail with no ability to plant this piece of evidence. Thus, the judge allowed the syringe to be admitted into evidence. The judge would charge the jury that it was up to them to determine if it was the murder weapon or an instrument of suicide.

The jury was picked and sworn in to serve and uphold justice. Double jeopardy had now attached. Eight women and four men comprised our panel. The members of the jury's race were not a consideration; we wanted it packed with women. Unlike a popular television show, we didn't have a jury consultant nor a mirror jury to rely upon. All we had was our gut feelings. My gut feeling said two women were eyeing Dr. Blackwell over as if they wanted to rip his clothes off. *If I was honest, if you didn't know his real character, who wouldn't.*

His time in detention hadn't caused him to lose his good looks. His body was enhanced by the fact he was more involved in physical activity. He was careful not to dress in a manner which would make the men feel their egos were threatened, and yet, projected a sexual allure for the ladies. Black designer glasses replaced his contacts, and he looked more like a sexy software engineer than a physician. Or a murderer.

"All rise. The Court is now in session, the Honorable Judge Karen Greely presiding."

"Everyone remain standing until the judge enters and she is seated," the bailiff announced.

"Bailiff, please call the day's calendar," Judge Greely requested.

"Your Honor, today's case is the State of Colorado versus Gabriel Blackwell. You may now be seated," the bailiff instructed the crowd who had come to watch the spectacle.

"Ladies and gentlemen, the rule of sequestration has been invoked. If there are any witnesses for either side in the gallery, you are now to leave until called to testify," the judge said.

She waited to see if anyone stood. No one did, so she continued.

"Is the state ready?" she inquired.

"James Bradshaw for the state and yes, Your Honor, we are ready," the prosecutor responded.

"Is the defendant ready to proceed?" she asked.

"Dalia Grey for the defendant and we are ready, Judge," Dalia told her.

The testimony of witnesses develops the actual trial. Some lawyers preferred to call witnesses in a chronological order to advance a story. Others preferred to call expert witnesses first to lay the groundwork and state the facts they would rely upon. It was a skilled balancing act mixing dry, boring facts and keeping the jury excited to learn more about the victim and the defendant.

It was no surprise that the prosecution had planned for Liza

McCarthy being their star witness after they found out what she had testified to in the wrongful death deposition. However, the prosecution had failed to serve her in a timely fashion with a subpoena demanding she appears in court, and thus she had slipped through their fingers. It seemed after we had seen Liza visiting Dr. Blackwell that day in jail, she disappeared. She quit her job, vanished as if she had never been a resident of Denver, and left no forwarding address. Liza had not transferred her nursing license to another state nor applied for a new driver's license. Despite a valiant effort they could not find her and drag her back to court to testify. No one would hear from her lips she and Dr. Blackwell had an unusual, well, deviant-type relationship to some people's minds, because she would not be there to tell them. No one would be told she had intimate knowledge about the drug that killed Sandra Blake. Nor would the jury be allowed to conclude that Dr. Blackwell and Liza McCarthy had conspired to kill his wife. The prosecution's case was rather thin, and without Liza, it had lost a lot of steam.

Opening statements are one of the most critical components of a trial. It is the first opportunity to present the case to the jury and to shape the jury's perspective of the entire trial. This is where the prosecutor missed his mark right out of the gate.

An opening statement should be like turning over a book and reading the back cover. A back cover does the reader no favor if it provides an overly detailed chronology of events. Or bores the reader with a recitation of the characters' names in the order they will appear in the book. A good opening statement, like a back cover, captures the essence of the book in a way that gives the reader a general sense of the book's theme, entices the reader to proceed further, and leaves the reader to make his own judgment regarding the final meaning of the story.

What the jury really wants to know is, what happened here. The prosecutor could not deliver that answer in his opening statement. And he knew it.

Mr. Bradshaw stood up quickly, spoke with confidence, gave the impression he was prepared and sure of what he was saying.

"May it please the court, and ladies and gentlemen of the jury. My name is James Bradshaw, and I am the state's attorney. I am here to present evidence to you, which at the end of my case you will be convinced that Gabriel Blackwell, sitting at the defense table, killed his wife. Murdered her in a premeditated, cold-blooded manner using a drug that caused her to suffocate to death. And, as her lungs could not take in air, and her heart slowly refused to beat, her mind remained alert to what was occurring to her body. She remained a prisoner of her mind as each part of her body shut down and died. Alone, in a pool, she spent her last minutes of life.

"This is a man who calls himself a sex addict, I call him an adulterer. A serial adulterer who humiliated and shamed his wife. So, when she had had enough and demanded he leave, he killed her," Bradshaw told them. "And why? Greed. She would wipe him out in a divorce, and he would not allow that to happen."

He moved around the podium toward our table and landed what he thought was a final blow as he pointed at Gabriel. Dr. Gabriel Blackwell now stood accused.

The jury swung their eyes toward Dr. Blackwell, and he remained calm and did not lose eye contact with the prosecutor. Almost as if he dared him to go further. Dared him to bring up Marsha Anderson and his unborn child. But, instead, James Bradshaw let that pass, knowing the hammer of the judge would come down upon him if he did. Instead, he returned to the more mundane tasks of telling the jury what evidence the prosecution would provide to prove their case. He went over a witness-by-witness catalog of testimony and a litany of what documents he would present that would convince them of Dr. Blackwell's guilt.

What you wanted from your narration during the opening statement was for the jury to remember and recognize each character of your story as he or she would appear in the trial. Your goal was to have the jury look forward to hearing the story unfold as the trial progressed. However, the facts he presented seemed confusing and unrelated. His story was disjointed. The result of Mr. Bradshaw's opening statement was the jury's eyes glazing over. He had lost their interest. A disaster, he probably would not recover from.

When he concluded his two-hour diatribe with, "That is why we are here today, ladies and gentlemen. To hold this defendant accountable." The Judge immediately thanked him and declared a two-hour lunch recess.

Now it was our turn. Your first impression on the jury should always be compelling. Maybe even a bit dramatic. A less seasoned lawyer than Dalia might have wasted time explaining the purpose of the opening statement and thanked the jury for their time and service to the community. Or even have gone through lengthy introductions of co-counsel. But not Dalia, she was ready to begin the moment her opportunity arose. She set the theme of the case, Gabriel did not murder his wife, and the state cannot prove it. She set the scene, Dr. Blackwell was an innocent man not even close to the house Why? Because his car could be tracked through the city, miles away from the house where the death occurred. And she precisely narrated the story of how we came to be here today as she introduced the people and documents as they would fit into the case.

Dalia explained what she expected the evidence to prove. That being that Sandra Blake was likely depressed. And because of that, took her own life using drugs she purchased on the Darknet. Dalia avoided expressing any opinions; did not make direct statements why a particular piece of evidence was not believable; and with much restraint did not vigorously attack her opponent's case. In other words, she stayed in her own lane, which can be challenging to do.

A problem the prosecutor had, was his excessive use of, "The evidence will show..." This quickly became boring for the jury to hear. Instead, Dalia told the jury she would describe what the evidence would establish, and then never said again. She told the jury with confidence that the facts would argue our case.

The most challenging part of her opening statement was to mitigate the smear that the prosecution had put on Gabriel as a philandering sex addict. A man with no moral compass who could murder his wife. Her job was to personalize Gabriel, bad character and all. She had to win the jury's trust by acknowledging he had some character flaws, but the good outweighed the bad.

She used this time to point out evidentiary gaps, and what was missing from their case. Proof. Dalia concluded her opening statement with an explicit denial of the accusation of murder and pointed out how the evidence contradicted the theory of their case. Whereas the prosecutor's opening statement was filled with emotion and promises, he could not likely keep,

Dalia's was measured and deliberate with planned stops.

At the conclusion, the jury made eye contact with Gabriel, and some women nodded as Dalia made her point. Some lawyers say the outcome of a case is determined by who presents the most compelling opening statement. Although she had yet to present any evidence, I, for one, believe Dalia had swayed the jury our way.

Evidence comes in four basic forms: demonstrative, documentary, real, and testimonial. Over the next few days, the prosecution would use all four forms to try to convince the jury Dr. Blackwell had murdered his wife. We would do our best to challenge that evidence and dismantle their case as each of their witnesses took the stand.

The first to take the stand was the pool guy who found Sandra's body. The prosecutor just used him to start the story of his theory that Gabriel murdered his wife. Dalia had him admitting he may have moved the body with the pole he used to clean the pool. Thus tainting forensic evidence and possibly even the time of death.

The next to take the stand was the first police officer on the scene. He used his notes to answer the questions about the scene and refreshed his recollection how he cataloged the evidence that was gathered. The prosecution asked how the body appeared when he found it. When the officer offered opinions and editorial responses about facts not in evidence, Dalia was on her feet with an objection that the judge agreed with and sustained. There were several objections to the prosecutor leading the witness, all ruled in our favor, and by the time the prosecutor finished his direct questioning, Dalia had broken his flow, and the jury looked bored and confused.

The purpose of cross-examination is usually to undermine

or discredit an adverse witness's testimony or to cast doubt on the witness's credibility. Cross is also used to develop the facts of consequence omitted in the direct examination, and to clarify potential misimpressions from the witness's testimony. Dalia started right out of the gate attacking his credibility.

"You were first on the scene, Officer Write, is that correct?" she asked, walking toward him with a document in her hand.

"That's right," he answered.

"Judge, I'd like to approach the witness so I may hand him his official police report," she said.

She was granted permission, and she handed him a document marked P-5 for prosecutors exhibit 5.

"Can you identify that document?" she asked.

"It's the incident report I completed," he replied.

"Please point out anywhere in there where you have written that the pool man stated he moved the body," she said, returning to the podium.

"There is nothing in the report," he replied with a look of confusion.

"Would it surprise you if I told you that before you took the stand the pool man testified he moved the body?" she asked.

He sat there almost dumbfounded and looked to the prosecutor for some help. Mr. Bradshaw did not offer him a life preserver.

Officer Write, upon further questioning, admitted he did not think to check the pool grate nor the pool filter. He testified he had no idea if a syringe could have been lodged in the grate and missed. Because at that point, death from an injection wasn't even a thought. Once it was, it still was not followed up with further inspection and investigation. From there she continued to chip away at police procedure, and when she was finished, his credibility was tarnished. Two of the women jurors shook their heads in a disapproving manner.

Her premier moment was when he admitted that he and everyone investigating the case treated it as a suicide, which added points to our side.

Considering it was almost six o'clock when she finished, and the prosecutor waived any re-direct questions, the judge ended the day and sent the jury home.

After the jury had left the jury box, the deputies took Dr. Gabriel back to the holding area.

"Poppy, I'm sure you're fried. I think we're ready for the pathologist tomorrow, so take the night off," she said. Her body looked wired with energy, but her eyes looked tired.

That was fine with me. Mr. Martin was sitting in tomorrow behind us in the first row to monitor the pathologist's testimony. He had a better handle on the drug succinylcholine than we did, and if we missed something, he would pick it up.

So far, we had made the investigation look shoddy, and we were building the bridge to reasonable doubt.

CHAPTER TWENTY-NINE

Poppy

"I'M GLAD YOU ASKED ME OUT FOR BREAKFAST BEFORE THE COURT reconvened," I told Mark.

He was now a detective, albeit a rookie, and worked side by side with Declan. I was afraid that since Dalia had made mincemeat of Officer Write on the stand, that our meal might be awkward. I, for one, would not bring it up, and was grateful he avoided the topic as well.

"Hold on a minute," he said as he looked at his phone. "Let me take this."

He stepped away from the table, and I used the opportunity to make sure I had everything I needed for the case that would start in an hour. Today it should be relatively easy for me. Mr. Martin would track the expert testimony, and I felt like nothing more than window dressing.

When Mark returned, his face looked tight, almost drawn like a mask.

"What's up?"

"You represent Pretty Boy Pete?" he asked with a touch of caution to his voice.

"If you mean Peter Laters then yes, we do. Why?"

I had met Peter to go over his case as it was ready for trial and found him delightful. Well, charming. But then how many con men could make a living being grumpy and mean spirited? It would sort of defeat the purpose.

"I have to meet the ME at his house. It appears he was the victim of a murder-suicide," he said as he pulled his wallet out to pay for the bill.

"Oh my God. What? What happened?" I stammered.

"I don't have very many facts; it just developed an hour ago. The neighbor heard shots and called it in. The first officers on the scene found a man and a woman dead in the living room. It appears the woman shot the man and then herself. The address tracked back to Peter Laters. I'll text you additional details when I have something more. Got to go," he said and gave me a quick kiss on the lips.

As soon as he was out of range, I called Mary to make sure she was all over it. My next call was to Dalia, who took it hard. She too, liked Peter, although he had probably been indeed a charismatic swindler who duped some woman out of her entire fortune.

"Oh no. I feel it's my fault. Peter said she had been acting crazy and because he was on a bond, he wasn't able to have a firearm. Could I have done more? Did you tell Mary?" she asked.

"My first call."

"Okay, we'll talk about it later when she has more details. How did you find out? Was it on the news?" she inquired.

"No, I was having breakfast with Mark," I said.

There was a long silence.

"I wonder why Declan didn't call and tell me. That little punk ass is probably still holding a grudge for what I did to Write yesterday. Why can't these people understand it's the prosecution they should be mad at? He was their witness as well as the pool guy. Just because no police investigator asked the pool guy the right questions from their end, doesn't mean we should be punished for doing our job. Whatever. I'll see you in a few," she said and disconnected.

I wonder if she would call and rip Declan a new one.

Fifteen minutes later I walked into the courtroom, and Mr. Martin was already in the front seat behind Dalia. He had his tablet open, and I could see the autopsy report highlighted and notes written on the side. Although he was the person who had the best grasp of the findings, to let him cross-examine the pathologist would put every one of the jurors to sleep. I wasn't mean, just realistic.

Dalia was talking to the prosecutor about the witnesses for the day when the bailiff called the court to order.

"All rise. The Court is now in session, the Honorable Judge Karen Greely presiding.

"Everyone remain standing until the judge enters and is seated," the bailiff announced.

"Bailiff, please call the day's calendar," Judge Greely requested.

"Your Honor, today's case is the State of Colorado versus Gabriel Blackwell. You may now be seated."

"Before I begin, it has come to my attention that parts of yesterday's court session made it onto YouTube. I want everyone's phone off and placed in either your pocket or pocketbooks. If the bailiff finds any phones or tablets out, I will confiscate them. And not only will you lose your phone or tablet, but I will hold you in contempt of court which can carry a sentence of ten days in jail and a thousand-dollar fine. Now, I'll give you a minute to do that. However, that does not apply to the attorneys trying the case," she added.

When everyone had settled down, she began.

"Mr. Bradshaw, call your first witness," she instructed.

The prosecutor called the medical examiner who had performed the autopsy. Before he delved into the specifics of the report, he had to qualify him as an expert witness. A witness who had the knowledge, skill, experience, training, or education to testify and render an opinion.

The routine questions started with please state your name; where do you work; what is your title there; how long have you been at that job and what are some of your duties at that place of employment? Twenty-five questions later ended with: do you believe your testimony will help assist the judge or jury understand the facts of this case?

"Your Honor, at this time I tender this witness as an expert in pathology," Mr. Bradshaw said.

"No objection," Dalia replied.

Dalia could have waived the voir dire of declaring him an expert and just stated she accepted him as an authority in the area of pathology. However, she wanted the jury lost in the world of boredom and on the verge of a long snooze. If voir dire didn't flip the off switch in their brains, then the mechanics of the autopsy report would.

The state's attorney conducted a two-hour direct examination of the medical examiner, to establish two points. First, that the cause of death of the murder victim was by lethal injection of succinylcholine. Second, that the shot was injected intramuscularly. He also gave his opinion about the time of death and how he came to that conclusion. Along with the autopsy report, he identified a toxicology report performed by the division of forensic science for Colorado.

Mr. Bradshaw had him identify the injection site on the photos marked as Prosecution Exhibit P-8. He then asked the pathologist to explain what led him to believe the drug killed Ms. Sandra Blake. To answer the question, the pathologist asked for the photos of the brain slices marked Prosecution Exhibit P-9 be placed on the overhead projector. The pictures were flashed on a large screen, and using a laser pointer, the pathologist referred to some markers. The jury had not been forewarned of this, and the shock of seeing brain matter up close and personal, almost had a few toss their breakfast on their shoes. From there it was a downhill slide of people tuning out and some staring off into space.

Before the judge could offer the jury a break, Dalia stood.

"Sir, I have two questions for you," she said.

He nodded his acknowledgment.

"You have been shown the syringe that has been marked Defendant Exhibit 1 which was found in the pool. Could that syringe have been the one to inject the drug into Ms. Sandra Blake?" she suggested.

"Yes, that syringe is consistent with what would have made the type of injection at the site," he agreed.

"Hypothetically. If Ms. Sandra Blake had injected herself with the drug, would she have had time to throw it in the pool before the drug took effect?" she inquired.

"Your Honor, I object, those are facts not in evidence, speculation, no foundation laid, and calls for a conclusion," Mr. Bradshaw said, practically bouncing from his seat.

"She has him on cross-examination and not asking for a conclusion. Overruled. The witness can answer," the judge replied.

"Yes, it takes several minutes to act. The fact it was administered intramuscularly gave it a little more time to be absorbed," he said.

Where the prosecutor had lost them in the minutia of the details, Dalia only required their attention for ten minutes. As a bonus, the prosecutor was overruled, making it appear as if he was trying to hide something. As our trial strategy, we had decided not to question other reasons succinct acid could be present in her brain as that might be objected to and sustained.

At the half hour mid-morning break, Dalia was able to get information about Peter from Mary. Mary had sent Lee Stone to the crime scene, hoping, as a former homicide detective, they would open up to him as a representative of the victim. After getting what information he could from law enforcement, he would report back to her. For now, there was no further information.

The next witness was the divorce attorney who had drawn up the reconciliation agreement. His main reason for being there was to identify the document which in the prosecution's eyes would establish a motive for murder. However, our expert ripped the document to shreds poking all kinds of holes in its construction. In the end, our expert concluded that it would not uphold a motion for summary judgment in a divorce trial. And, if the agreement were determined null and void, then there would not be a motive.

After that last witness, the state rested. The only witness slated to testify on our behalf was a technician who could place Dr. Blackwell's car fifteen miles away from the house at the stated time of death and had been parked there for at least a half hour. He showed the jury the route the vehicle traveled and at what time. Through time manipulation techniques he

TRUST ME

followed the car through the streets as it passed businesses and banks. The only conclusion that could be reached was that when the vehicle left the house, it did not return. So, therefore, he could not be in two places at once.

The prosecutor made the same mistake in his closing argument as he did in his opening statement. He went over every aspect of the case again, which earned him yawns and fidgets. Dalia concluded her portion in a half hour as she pointed out the inconsistencies in the state's case. All she sought of the jury was one thing. That was to hold the state accountable to prove every element of the crime.

At 4:30 p.m. the judge read the jury charges to them. As it was late in the day, she inquired if they wanted to start deliberation now or in the morning. The unanimous answer was that they wanted to deliberate that night until they reached a verdict.

While the jury deliberated, we drove back to the office. We didn't want to jinx ourselves, but we were reasonably sure we would obtain an acquittal for Gabriel Blackwell. However, we had to remind ourselves not to get too excited. This was an easy trial. The murder case of Marsha Anderson still lay ahead, and that was far more complex. Although Mr. Martin had always made an excellent case why Dr. Blackwell had not committed the murder; something still niggled at me I couldn't shake.

However, if we could cross this bridge, and get a not guilty, that verdict would be splashed across the papers and the internet. The same pool of people who would read the account would be part of our jury pool for the Anderson trial. The odds would be significantly in our favor that people would remember the state made a mistake once and could this be another. It was all about psychology and the optics.

By the time we had arrived at the office, Lee and Mary were waiting for us with the details about Peter. The sad fact was that Lilian Mathers decided that the justice system would not be a friend to her. And while off her medication for severe depression and anxiety, she decided to take justice into her own hands. It all was detailed in a three-page letter she wrote and left on the table where her body fell, after putting a bullet in her head. An autopsy would be performed, and then the bodies laid to rest. The estate? If the administrator could not find any relatives of Peter Laters, everything would escheat to the state. In other words, the state would own everything.

At 7:30 p.m. we had ordered some Chinese dinner. It was time to discuss the next step in Dr. Blackwell's case if the jury found him not guilty. Indeed, at that point, the judge should grant a bond modification. Mary had just placed the order with the restaurant, and Dalia's phone rang. The jury had reached a verdict.

We arrived back at the courthouse and settled in. The judge had the jury file into the courtroom and waited for them to be seated in the jury box. The deputy returned Dr. Blackwell from the detention center in a different suit with a sexy stubble on his face. One of the two female jurors who had snuck glances at him throughout the last two days turned a wide grin his way. He returned a half smile.

When everyone settled down, the judge began.

"Has the jury reached a verdict?" she inquired.

"We have," the foreperson answered.

"In the case of the State of Colorado versus Gabriel Blackwell on the charge of first-degree murder, how do you find?" the judge asked.

"We find the defendant not guilty," the foreperson responded.

"The clerk shall record the verdict," the judge ordered.

"Your Honor, if it pleases the court, we would like to move for a bail modification," Dalia said.

"Tomorrow afternoon at one p.m. I will hear arguments," the judge replied.

With that, we were dismissed. As we left the courthouse, Declan and Mark were waiting for us. The Chinese meal Mary ordered now long forgotten.

I should feel elated that I had been part of a big win. But I didn't, I just felt empty.

CHAPTER THIRTY

Poppy

APPREHENSION MOUNTED INSIDE ME AS WE WAITED FOR THE guard to bring Dr. Blackwell in to see us. For Dalia's sake, I wanted him to gush his thanks over and over. I wanted him to tell her what a talented attorney she was, and a brilliant woman. She had worked so hard to put this case together, and against all the odds, she won.

The door opened, and he walked in, arrogant and with an obvious swagger. Oh, this was not good. I would have thought he would be more humble and grateful that Dalia had helped him avoid a life sentence in prison. The guard removed the handcuffs and left.

"Good morning, Gabriel. How are you feeling?" she asked.

"Ready to get down to business," he replied, leaning back in his chair.

"I see. So, you know today is the new bond hearing. I believe the judge will be more agreeable to a modification, now that this case has been disposed of in your favor," Dalia said with a weak smile.

"Now I've been acquitted of the murder, will that start the process, allowing the money to flow to me from Sandra's estate?" he asked.

Bastard.

"Yes. Eloise was working on that when we left. I have an authenticated copy of the verdict, so she can send that off. Now, about the hearing," she started.

"Wait, before we jump into that. When do you think the life insurance proceeds will be released? The house is getting ready to go into foreclosure from nonpayment of both mortgages, and I don't want that stain on my credit," he told her.

What a bizarre thing to say. Dr. Blackwell's been accused of a double murder, and he's a self-professed philandering piece of shit and a sexual deviant. Maybe he should get his priorities straight.

"Eloise is well aware of that problem. She was in touch with both banks, and they agreed to put a stay on that proceeding until the money shakes loose. The bank put a lien against the life insurance for the arrears, and everyone's working together on that to protect the property," Dalia said.

"Okay. Now I want to have this whole mess behind me, and I want to have the D.A. drop the charges in Marsha's case," he told us.

For some reason he was holding such intense eye contact with me, I felt like his prey. Like he was sizing me up to determine how big a fight I would put up if cornered.

"That would be the optimum outcome," Dalia said almost with a smirk.

"I have the murder weapon that killed Marsha Anderson," he announced, just like that.

All the oxygen was sucked out of the room. I felt as if I couldn't breathe. Had we just heard him admit to murdering her?

He was the first to break the silence.

"Shall I tell you a story?" he asked, arms dangling from each side of the chair. He appeared not to have a care in the world.

We both nodded. He smiled. *Demon spawn, the son of Satan himself.*

"Sandra had serendipitously crossed paths with Marsha on a routine visit at her GYN office. Who knew what the chances would be, of all the gynecologists in Denver, they shared the same doctor? It appears she heard a nurse congratulate Marsha on her pregnancy. Sandra knew Marsha and I had been involved. What she didn't realize was that we had cooled things off significantly; a byproduct of my commitment to Liza. So, she leaped to the conclusion that the baby must be mine. Hell, and of all things, who knew it actually was. Mind you I had no idea that Marsha was involved in this whole surrogacy thing. She kept that tightly under wraps.

"Sandra confronted me about it. I told her if I was the father, I would distance myself from the child and the situation. However, I would enter into a contract with Marsha to give her a lump sum payment of half a million dollars, which should take care of my end of the child support. She could invest it, she'd be set, and I shouldn't hear from her again. Ever. In exchange, the birth record would not reflect I was the father, and she would never reveal that information. Sandra seemed pleased with that arrangement. However, there was one sticking point," he told us.

"Which was?" Dalia asked with a raised brow. Because she, like me, could think of ten problems right off the bat.

"Sandra would have to invade the corpus of her family trust to get that much cash. The only way she could do that is if she could convince the trustee she needed it for some reason that could harm her life. I suggested Sandra tell the trustee she was a gambling addict, and she needed it for gambling debts. That if she didn't pay them, they had threatened her life. For a little dramatic flair, I suggested she say the people who bought her debt were Brighton Beach Russians. The Russian Mafia always strikes fear in people's minds. I haven't had any personal contact with them. However, I'm certain some missing body parts would be involved if one crossed them," he said and nodded with some bizarre type of satisfaction.

"What were her thoughts on that?" Dalia asked with a straight face. Me? I felt my mouth involuntarily gape open.

"Well, she didn't find the plan a good one. In fact, her anger rose to such a pitch it involved the destruction of some precious porcelain in a fit of violence. I told her to take a few days to reconsider," Dr. Blackwell said.

"So that was the night of their paths crossing. What happened in the next two days that led up to Marsha's death?" Dalia asked.

"Marsha didn't seek me out to tell me about the baby. She didn't demand anything from me. In hindsight, she probably thought the baby was the surrogate couple's baby and the thought it might be mine never entered into the picture.

"I was as stunned as everyone else that Marsha was murdered in such a brutal manner. It was shortly later, after I was arrested, that Sandra started making demands about the way things would go from that point on. She wanted a new start for us in a new city. No more sex clubs and I had to remain faithful. In exchange she assured me she held the key to opening my prison door," he said.

"What the hell does that mean?" Dalia asked, her body almost shaking with anger.

"She had used my phone to call Marsha and arrange a meeting with her. She told Marsha that I was going to divorce her so that Marsha and I could be together. Why in the hell Marsha would buy such a load of crap is beyond me. We weren't about love and romance. We were about moments of risky pleasure, nothing more. Marsha apparently liked the sound of that and met with Sandra. Sandra had a plan, and that did not include Marsha walking away alive." His voice was nonchalant as if he had just told us the bill for breakfast was on him.

It took us both a few minutes to comprehend the enormity of the statement. Was he complicit in her murder? Not really.

"Sandra wanted to teach me a lesson and bring me to heel. She had set the whole thing up to look as if I had reason to kill Marsha and then set the wheels in motion to box me in. She told me once I agreed to her terms, that she would make sure the murder weapon fell into the hands of the police, and I would be exonerated," he said.

"How?"

"She bludgeoned Marsha to death with your garden variety hammer. However, once she killed her, wearing gloves naturally, the head of the hammer had blood and pieces of Marsha's skull attached. The hammer handle was then coated in Marsha's blood as she lay dying. She said she had rolled the handle in it, taking the time to make sure it was wet and sticky. With a quart of whiskey and a hundred dollars cash, she headed for the homeless area in town. Somehow, she found some mentally challenged person who needed a drink and cash and didn't mind grabbing the bloody end of a hammer for the booze and money. Now his prints were on the murder weapon. His prints and Marsha's blood," he said.

"And you know this how?" Dalia asked.

"I have the murder weapon," he said leaning forward.

"You do not," was all I could say, leaning to meet him across the table.

"Oh, Poppy, I do," he assured me.

"How did you get it?" I asked.

"I have to say I was skeptical that Sandra would ever let me out from under her thumb. I wasn't sure that her plan all along wasn't to see me in jail so I could think about my misdeeds every day, for the rest of my life. She could play the aggrieved wife, divorce me, and be a star in the press. Her business would flourish.

"So that night of the bond hearing, when she said I had to leave, it was just a ploy to get me to sign the agreement she had prepared. She wanted me to agree to take a drug that was basically a chemical castration. She assured me that, if she saw I was serious, she would make sure the hammer was found by the authorities the next day. Chemical castration. Can you imagine it? Like I was some sexual deviant or pervert..."

Yeah, go figure.

"I agreed to her terms, but only if we would both plant the hammer together, so I know she wouldn't double cross me. She was giddy with glee. She had the document ready to sign, and I signed it. The bottle of medroxyprogesterone acetate sat there, ready for her to administer my first dose of many. I took it like a champ and then insisted that she produce the hammer. After all, the agreement was we were to plant it that night. Surprisingly, she complied. She went into the house and had it stashed in the safe and returned with it in a plastic bag.

"What she hadn't been prepared for was I had a plan of my own. Once she gave me the bag, I hit her with the succinyl-choline and waited for her to die. Once she started to twitch a bit, I placed a new syringe between her fingers, and voila, her prints were on the syringe. Her eyes begged me to save her, but she couldn't speak. The paralysis had set in. Once I was sure she was dead, I threw her and the syringe in the pool. What I didn't account for was the syringe being sucked into the grate. I thought it would be found once the investigators got there. It almost was my undoing," he said, shaking his head.

"So why wait until now to bring the murder weapon forward?" I asked.

"Double jeopardy, Poppy," Dalia said, taking in a deep breath and turned her head from him. She refused to meet his eyes.

Gabriel smiled a satisfied acknowledgment.

"If he had brought it forth before, the prosecutor would have possibly been able to put a variation of the truth together," she said. "Now even if he does, there's no retrying him for murder."

"So, what, we call the D.A. and say, 'oh, by the way, we just came into possession of the murder weapon and our client has this amazing story'?" I asked.

"Poppy, don't be dense. Tell her, Dalia," he said, placing his right ankle over his left knee.

"He had an accomplice," she said.

"What? How? Who?" I asked.

"If I had to hazard a guess, it was Liza. She drove you there and then drove away so the car could be tracked by cameras. Since the police couldn't find the hard drive for the cameras when they searched the place, I will bet Gabriel has Sandra on film from the house cameras retrieving the murder weapon from the safe. Now Gabriel's problem is he's an accessory after the fact. So, I'll bet what he wants is immunity from any crimes associated with Marsha Anderson," she said.

"Yes, they get the hard drive and the hammer and get to solve the crime," he agreed.

"How will you convince them you and Sandra weren't in on it together?" I asked.

"That's the part of the immunity that Dalia has to work out. Once a jury sees the tape and the hammer, I believe that reasonable doubt would have them swayed to acquit me. I still have the agreement she wanted me to sign and the bottle of medroxyprogesterone acetate. Medroxyprogesterone acetate is every man's nightmare. Also, only her prints are on the bottle," he said. "He'll want to close this out. Trust me."

"Where's Liza?" Dalia asked.

Probably dead just like Sandra and Marsha.

"Safe, and in hiding," he said.

How safe would she be once he was out?

Dalia removed her phone and placed a call to Mr. Bradshaw. We had a meeting in three hours.

"What kind of scam is this?" Bradshaw demanded.

"Look, all I can tell you is that if you agree to immunity, you can have the weapon that killed Marsha Anderson and pretty much a taped video confession," Dalia assured him.

"I don't believe it," he said, standing to pace.

"If you sit, I can run the video from the cameras where she confesses to it and gets the hammer from the safe," I assured him.

"How do I know it's authentic?" he rebuffed.

"Gabriel has the actual hard drive. I don't. However, my techs have told me what you are about to see has not been altered. We can construct the deal based upon the fact that if the evidence has been tampered with, then you have the right to terminate the deal," she said.

"He's had this all along?" he asked again.

"Yes."

"He could have saved everyone hundreds of thousands of dollars," he said, yet it came out more like a question.

Dalia remained silent to the statement. "Do you want to see it?"

He nodded and sat in his cracked red leather chair. Dalia hit a button, and the video footage rolled. He watched with intent, asked it to be rewound in a few spots and made notes. After it finished, we waited for his reply.

"How do I know he's not an accomplice or co-conspirator? How do I know after he had his wife kill his girlfriend that he didn't kill his wife to shut her up?" he asked, looking out the window.

Exactly my thought, bucko.

"I don't have the answers you want or need. I can't give you the assurances you require to ease your mind. What I can say without a doubt is the jury found Gabriel not guilty, and that's never going to change. The question is that once I introduce this at trial after you've invested at least a million dollars in the trial, I believe there will be a reasonable doubt. If you want to do this because you are being stubborn or want to save face, be my guest," she said crossing her leg and appeared far more relaxed than I knew she felt.

He stood, walked to the windows, turned his back on us, placed his hands in his pockets, and then spoke.

"I want a polygraph," he told us.

"Not going to happen. The tape speaks for itself."

There was silence again save for the jingling of coins in his pocket.

"He's got a deal. My office will draw up the papers and have them to you," he said.

"No need, I have something prepared for your review. I'd like to get this done today so you can agree to a consent bond while we work out the final details and you dismiss the charges."

Dalia reached in her bag, produced a document, and handed it to him.

"Here's what it boils down to. In essence, you have offered, and Gabriel Blackwell has accepted, a grant of immunity from state prosecution in connection with the homicide of Marsha Anderson and her unborn child before we speak to you any further about the case. The draft agreement is intended to cover explicitly all possible state criminal exposure he might have for his past conduct related to the homicide itself. Or anything associated with that, specifically his discussions with his wife about the murder and the termination of the fetus which said conversations are covered under spousal immunity. This affords him the opportunity to speak candidly about the events in the past and future. It states that you are more interested in obtaining the complete truth from him on this critical public issue than prosecuting him.

"If he took evidence related to a state criminal investigation, concealed and retained it, such conduct could violate the state laws of Colorado. If he knowingly and willfully made materially false statements to law enforcement, such conduct could violate the state laws of Colorado. Accordingly, the draft agreement makes specific references to those potential violations. However, it is intended to also cover any past conduct in connection with the homicide and concealing of the murder weapon that could violate some other state statute. Any and all potential crimes associated with what happened during and after the homicide is covered by a grant of immunity."

After he read the document, he signed it. She then handed him a consent order he also signed whereby he offered no objection to Gabriel being released on his own recognizance as the state intended to dismiss the charges with prejudice.

By two o'clock today Gabriel would be released from jail, and by tomorrow afternoon he would be a free man. Something still niggled at me that Liza had played more a part in Sandra's death. Could she have killed Sandra, and he's protecting her? The only person to put her at the scene was Gabriel. So, did Liza kill Sandra, and he lied to save her? I'm always disappointed when a liar's pants didn't catch on fire.

CHAPTER THIRTY-ONE

Poppy

"**A**LL RISE. THE COURT IS NOW IN SESSION, THE HONORABLE Judge Karen Greely presiding.

"Everyone remain standing until the judge enters and is seated,," the bailiff announced.

"Good morning, ladies and gentlemen. We are here today on the state's motion to dismiss all charges. What say you, Mr. Bradshaw?" Judge Greely asked.

"Good morning, Your Honor, and may it please the Court, the state has come into evidence which sheds light on the murder of Marsha Anderson. The proof is in the form of a digital recording, captured by the home security system of Dr. Blackwell the defendant, and his wife, Ms. Sandra Blake, deceased.

"Your Honor has reviewed the video *In Camera*, and it is my understanding you have determined the footage should remain under seal.

"For the record, the footage reveals the defendant's wife, Ms. Sandra Blake, make an admission against her interest and admit to the crime of murder. In essence a confession of the murder of Marsha Anderson and her unborn child. The state has authenticated the unaltered footage. We have the murder weapon, a hammer, and the blood on the handle is consistent with the victim. The prints on the hammer are in the system and associated with Daryl Keening, a homeless man, with a history of petty larceny, public drunk charges but no violent crimes. The police have attempted to interview him, but his mental health is such they could not elicit information from him about the event. The state is satisfied that Dr. Blackwell did not commit this murder," he told the judge.

"I have reviewed the tape and am satisfied that Ms. Blake had made a statement against her interest and I am treating such as a confession to the murders. What I viewed on that tape was a deeply disturbed woman. And to your speeches to the press how the jury got it wrong in the case of Sandra Blake's murder, I hope we see a retraction based on these new events. I therefore enter a dismissal with prejudice in the State of Colorado versus Gabriel Blackwell. This matter is permanently dismissed and the case is closed. Dr. Blackwell, you are free to go about your business. A motion has been made to seal the contents of this matter in the clerk's office and the D.A.'s office so the public cannot gain access to it. That motion is granted with the stipulation the attorneys in the civil matter of wrongful death may have access to it.

"Now we have one other matter before the court, and that involves the wrongful death case. Will the attorneys please step forward. It is my understanding that Dr. Blackwell has been dismissed in that action and that the plaintiffs have now added the estate of Sandra Blake as a defendant in that case. That civil lawsuit shall proceed. Are there any other matters before this court?" Judge Greely inquired.

"Yes, Judge, you have before you my motion to withdraw as counsel for Dr. Blackwell in the wrongful death action.

However, as plaintiffs have now dismissed Dr. Blackwell as a defendant, I would ask the court to instruct the clerk to remove my name from the records," Tallulah said standing next to Dalia.

"The clerk shall make a note that the plaintiffs have dismissed with prejudice the defendant Dr. Blackwell from the wrongful death action. Additionally, an order shall follow that Ms. West is released from the representation of the defendant. Ms. Evans appears to have also filed a withdrawal in the probate matter which I have no jurisdiction over, but I've made a note. Unless anyone has any further business before this court, we are adjourned." And with a slap of the gavel, we were done with Dr. Blackwell.

What the hell happened to goes around comes around? Dr. Blackwell most certainly wasn't karma's bitch. Am I wrong to be outraged that we won in this case? That word won, won what? Not a principle of justice. My clients were guilty, of that I never had a doubt. So when they were sentenced for their transgressions it was no skin off my nose. But here she is not only dismissing the case never to be able to be retried again, but she has no idea that Dr. Blackwell *did* kill his wife. Marsha Anderson was a screwed-up chick, but did she deserve to die for carelessly speeding down the Blackwell Highway to Hell?

CHAPTER THIRTY-TWO

Dalia

I HAD SO MANY THOUGHTS, SO MANY QUESTIONS, AND SO MANY doubts. Doubts about our legal system. Self-doubts. How could I possibly let this man get away with murder? How can I live with myself now? I could say I did my job and held the state to account to prove their case, walk away knowing, but for a shoddy investigation, Gabriel would be behind bars. Would James Bradshaw internalize his failure and live with that taint on his conscience? Or I could bring new information forth that I had reason to believe Liza McCarthy had conspired with Gabriel to kill his wife. But I had learned this during my representation of him and if I did that I could be disbarred. If I didn't reveal Liza's part, then both would get away with murder and be free to commit another. It's really a public safety issue. Isn't it? Didn't I have an obligation to protect the innocent community members?

The papers were ready for him to sign releasing the firm from all his cases. Eloise refused to continue to probate the estate. Adamant she didn't want any contact with him, she left the documents for him to sign terminating our representation with me. He should be happy to receive a healthy refund of his unused funds. He was already discharged from the wrongful death lawsuit, which meant Lulu was free of him as well. With the stroke of a pen, he would be out of our lives. Just never out of our minds.

"I'll be here another hour or so, Ms. Grey, I'm in the conference room just finishing up the answer to the subpoena for our records on Abernathy," Mr. Martin advised.

Lulu would never hear the end of this that Mr. Martin was asked to work two hours overtime. *Not my circus, not my monkey.*

"Thank you, Mr. Martin. Dr. Blackwell has to sign some papers and then I'll be gone," I said.

"Hmm. Do you want me to sit in with you until he's gone?" he asked.

"No, I'm fine. If anything goes wrong, I have that panic button Mary insisted on. I've never had to use it and don't expect I will now," I assured him.

"As you wish," he replied and left.

I heard his footsteps coming down the hall. Expensive shoe leather slapping against polished wood floors. Quick, purposeful steps. Confident, moving forward. A glance to the computer monitor revealed he was feet from my office door. *God, he makes my skin crawl.*

"Good evening, Dalia."

So smug, so arrogant. So deadly.

"Gabriel."

Instead of taking a seat to sign the papers I had tagged for him to sign, he stood behind the chair in front of my desk. Silent. Sizing me up with his eyes and determining my mood.

"Such a beautiful night. Walk with me to the window," he invited me, turning to his right and moved that way.

"I'd rather not. Please have a seat, and we can complete the documents I've marked. I'm sure you have celebratory plans tonight," I told him. I hope he caught my flat, dead tone.

"Come, I think you'll find it worth your while," he insisted and waited for me to join him.

I strolled to the window overlooking the street. He appeared fixated on something.

Liza McCarthy. Just standing there leaning against the car, staring up at us.

Well, at least she was alive.

"Now you see who's standing there?"

Suddenly he pressed up behind me, pushing, pinning me between him and the window. I felt a full-body shiver overtake me. Adrenaline was pulsing through me. Fight or flight was taking over. But I had no way to fight, and no place to flee. I was trapped. My gut said to stay silent. He could have a knife and if I screamed he might panic. I could barely catch my breath.

"I saw how anxious you were today at court—fidgeting, pushing your hair behind your ear, picking at your nail. You so wanted to jump up and fill in the blanks for the judge, tell her my secret. Didn't you? It took such restraint not to.

"I'm here to warn you. If you or Poppy ever gets a twinge of conscience, and even think about doing something that is not in my best interest, I want you to remember this talk. London 1978, a prize-winning Bulgarian author and BBC broadcaster was waiting alongside commuters for a bus on Waterloo Bridge, when he felt a stinging pain in his thigh. A stranger dropped an umbrella, mumbled 'sorry' and fled in a taxi. The man thought little of the seemingly trivial incident and continued his journey home; he was dead in three days. The murder weapon, an umbrella, fired a pellet the size of a pinhead, containing the poison ricin. Liza can be just as resourceful," he whispered in my ear.

His hot breath on my neck.

"Are you threatening me, you piece of shit!" I said, trying to push off the window.

But I couldn't. He had his chest pressed hard against my back trapping me to the glass. His arms uplifted above my head, and his palms against the window pane. The more I struggled, the harder he pushed.

"Get off me! You don't intimidate me, you monster. I'll see you and that little psycho locked up behind bars for good by week's end. They will throw away the key, and you'll really know the full impact of the term sadism where you are going." My voice was strong, but my breathing weak.

Without warning, he grabbed my hair by my ponytail, snapped my head back with his left hand, and then forcefully bashed my face forward against the window. Nausea, blurred vision, stars, concussed. Oh my God, the excruciating pain exploded through my head as he did it again and I felt my nose crash against the window. A dull crunching noise announced my nose was broken. Hot blood poured from my nose and cascaded down and over my lips. A quick but forceful punch to my right ribs knocked the wind from me leaving me gasping for much-needed breath, and I felt myself falling to the ground, and he was on top of me.

I sensed I was fighting back, but how could that be true when he had me locked on the floor unable to escape? Had I blacked out? Had he hit me in the head and knocked me unconscious? Either could have occurred, but would it matter which in the end. Not really. I could only focus on his hands around my neck, squeezing, his thumbs pressing an unyielding force against the dip in my neck where in seconds my hyoid bone would be crushed. As I looked into the soulless eyes of the man above me, my life would be extinguished.

Did I hear someone yelling? I don't know. All I could hear was pulsating waves crashing in my ears. No, someone was yelling stop. Was that me?

BOOM!

I heard the earth-shattering sound at the same time as I saw Gabriel's head explode. Right in front of me. Explode as if it were a watermelon dropped ten stories down. Bits of brain matter flew everywhere, and the feel of his hot blood all over my face caused a visceral reaction, vomit was now mixed with his blood.

"Dalia, Dalia. Look at me. You're okay, just breathe. Slow breath in and a slow breath out. Stay with me," he said.

But I couldn't. The last thing I saw was Mr. Martin holding Mary's gun.

CHAPTER THIRTY-THREE

Poppy

A WEEK HAD PASSED, AND MARY CALLED A MEETING SO WE COULD do a postmortem on the cases.

"I call this meeting to order," Mary said ready to bang the striker block.

"So help me, Mary, if you try to hit that block with the gavel, I will wrestle you to the ground for it. And then I will light that thing on fire in the middle of the table," Eloise told her.

"Although that would be a clear violation of the fire code, I believe none of us would stand in your way," Mr. Martin said, looking directly at Mary.

She laid the gavel down.

"Since this is our first meeting since the close of some very ugly business, I think we all agree, we owe a great debt to Mr. Martin. But for his quick thinking, and my gun..."

"Don't even, Mary," Eloise warned.

"As I was saying, but for Mr. Martin's quick, brave actions, well, I'll leave it there. We are grateful to you. Although Liza McCarthy was detained, they had to release her. There was no physical evidence she was a part of Dr. Blackwell Son of Satan's plan. She vehemently denies any part of Sandra Blake's murder. And for emphasis said if we pursue that avenue, a lawsuit will be at our door. Trust me; we are keeping an eye on her. Now we are here to do a postmortem on several matters. Eloise, do you have any information on the Vanessa Abernathy matter?" she asked.

"Yes, but I would also personally like to thank Mr. Martin for saving my best friend, I am forever in your debt. I just wish I could have been part of blowing that pervert to bits. Now moving on. According to a civil forfeiture order, the majority of the estate has been seized by the Department of Justice. Funny enough the only part of the estate that was legit was the part he set up with Tamara Downing. So she walks away scot-free, with something like twenty million dollars. Vanessa was removed as the executrix and administrator of the estate. The probate court frowns upon an administrator being indicted as a co-conspirator in a RICO action with her dead husband. As Jackson predicted, once she cashed the check, the feds were ready to slap the cuffs on her. So there's a special master assigned to that case now to administer the estate," Eloise told us.

"Pretty Boy Pete?" Mary inquired, looking at Dalia.

She still had a necklace of bruises around her neck but insisted on returning to work.

"Well, it appears Peter had an out-of-wedlock child no one knew about. So the child's mother filed a notice on the child's behalf that he was entitled to the entirety of the estate. That came out of nowhere, and I'd rather see his child inherit the estate than the state take a bite of it," Dalia said.

"Won't there be a fight from the Mathers woman's family if she has any?" Mary asked.

"Slayer rule," Mr. Martin snapped shaking his head.

"Okay, let's not go down that rabbit hole. We're not involved so let's move on," Eloise interjected.

"Now to the part we are all dreading. Dalia has something to say," Mary said and turned to Dalia.

"Not to be dramatic, but I am done with criminal defense. I've spoken to Tyler, and he has offered me a position in his firm. I won't be moving. I can still work here in Denver. However, that moves several pieces around the chessboard of life. Declan and I have set a wedding date, and I am moving in with him next week. Poppy, that means that the house I'm in now is free and if you want to move into it, then it is yours. Mary has graciously offered it to her friends as property without rent, and the keys will be ready to be turned over to you as they had been to me if you want them. Think of it as a perk of the job," she said and smiled. Her nose still looked raw, and her bruises around her raccoon eyes were finally turning brownish yellow. You could tell she was in pain but would never admit it.

"I am stunned. My God, what had I done to earn such good karma? Thank you so much! I accept that kind offer, and if I say more, I'll cry," I said. I felt tears welling that I had to fight back.

"Next, and because of my job offer from Tyler, this involves Poppy. I believe Poppy has enormous potential. Her instincts are on target, and she has a clear mind when it comes to the practice of law. She is stepping into her power to be a great attorney, and with everyone's support here she'll be a master litigator. I've spoken to her, and she's agreed to take on the cases she feels comfortable accepting. The more aggressive ones I've arranged for her to partner with Thomas Blasingame. So we will continue to take criminal defense cases, but be far more selective," Dalia told them, her mood solemn.

No one had addressed what happened that night in full.

Dalia didn't feel able to talk about her feelings yet. All we knew was Mr. Martin had saved Dalia's life with the gun from under the table. What we saw was the bloody aftermath. Liza McCarthy escaped justice for now, but Mary assured us she would never be off her radar. Trust me.

THE END

ABOUT THE AUTHOR

Kathleen McGillick is a practicing attorney who sorts through the pieces of people's lives much like a puzzle master. Each piece carefully placed makes up the whole of this unique person. Who is this person? What drives them? What makes them tick? What are their deepest secrets and unspoken fears? No surprise she ended up writing a legal thriller!

Why and how people commit crimes has always held an interest for her and that is reflected in her latest novel.

Kathleen grew up in New York and has lived in Georgia for thirty-three years. She has enjoyed a career in nursing as well as the law. After obtaining a Bachelor of Science degree in Nursing, and a Master of Science degree in Nursing she set out fifteen years later to obtain her Juris Doctorate. This varied education and experience helped mold the eclectic writer she is today.

She considers herself a global citizen and an avid international traveler. With her son in tow as an early travel companion, she has visited over eighteen countries in the last twenty years. Some cities like Paris, London and Rome deserving multiple returns. A pilgrimage to London at least every two years is a must to keep her batteries charged and give her the history fix she craves. In her spare time, you can find a book in her hand or wandering through an art museum. Kathleen is a mother and grandmother as well as the food lady to her cats and any wild life that wanders to her porch.

CONNECT WITH K. J. MCGILLICK

www.facebook.com/KJMcGillickauthor

kjmcgillick@gmail.com

www.kjmcgillick.com

twitter.com/KJMcGillickAuth

Follow the author on Amazon

Made in the USA
Monee, IL
31 January 2020

21100143R00164